0

# TARGET!

I had been sitting there about five minutes and was just telling myself that I would have to start stirring, to get ready in time to eat, when someone fired two shots in quick succession through the glass of the window behind me. I heard the bullets *hiss* by my ear and *thud* into the wall before me, while I did what every sensible man ought to do. I dropped forward on my hands and knees, so that the bed made a covering behind me. Then I peered over the edge of the bed, gun in hand, and I saw the faintest outline of something beyond the window, and the gleam of a gun poised for another shot.

# MAX BRAND®

# THE GOLDEN CAT

LEISURE BOOKS  NEW YORK CITY

A LEISURE BOOK®

July 2006

Published by special arrangement with Golden West Literary Agency.

Dorchester Publishing Co., Inc.
200 Madison Avenue
New York, NY 10016

Visit us on the web at www.dorchesterpub.com.

# THE GOLDEN CAT

# Chapter 1

Some people attract trouble the way a magnet attracts iron filings; Dennis Rourke says it lies all in the name. Rourke is a name, he says, which naturally causes a punched nose and broken bones; whereas my name of John Jones is sure to give me a peaceful life. Which it would, I have no doubt, if it were not for Dennis. I could live fifty years cheek by jowl with a tribe of wild Comanches and never so much as raise an eyebrow at them, or they at me. The fact is that I hate trouble, although Dennis says it's because of my stupid smile. But no matter how peaceful I may be, Dennis is the power that drags me into trouble; he always has been and he always will be, and he'll always grin at the end.

In the beginning, however, I want to make it clear that my life hasn't been all a piece with the sort of thing I'm describing here. It's necessary to say that, because I've noticed that often people will pick out the half dozen storm centers in their lives and talk about them in detail, so that they give an effect of always living in a high wind. My life has been a dead calm, except where Dennis tugged me into some sort of a whirlpool, and even these usually were shallow affairs out of which I could wade ashore. Only once he drew me in deep and, without meaning it, put the gun to my head.

I thank God that it is ended and that I'm alive to tell what happened. I thank God that Dennis is still alive, too; certainly there is no gratitude owing to Dennis himself.

It is better to begin on the day when the trouble started.

On the morning of that day I got up early because my head was aching too badly to let me sleep. I looked across the hotel room and saw Dennis with the bedclothes huddled in a knot around his head. He squirmed, now and then, and I hoped that he was having a bad dream. The largest nightmare on the books would have been about right for him, I thought.

So I sat down at the window and pretended to enjoy the morning breeze, but I couldn't. There was a breeze, all right, but it was like the wash of hot water against the face. The town was in a narrow valley, you understand, and one could look up to the snow on the mountains any day, but the snow was like a mirage of blue water on the desert—the sight of it merely made you hotter and stickier and more generally miserable. In that valley, the heat of the sun was gathered and focused. There is no hotter sun in the world than that which shines on our Western states. Dennis says that the cows and mustangs are so ornery that they draw the heat. At any rate, that sun baked the earth and cracked it wide all summer, and the heat that the ground soaked up all day, it poured forth all night and the colder currents above refused to come down, and all that happened was a swish now and then, like the stir of a soup pot under the cook's ladle.

However, even if the air was not cool, the sky looked pleasant, being pink and purple—one could imagine that it was a chilly morning, and thinking often helps a lot. So I hung my elbows out the window and looked at the leaves of the big tree, winking and glittering as the wind ruffled them, and down through the gaps among the branches I could look to the back yard itself.

I saw the cook come out and sweep the hard-packed earth with a stable broom. He was Chinese with a bald head, and I watched him with considerable pleasure, because I don't know why it always tickles me a good deal to see a Chinaman working and sweating. They seem almost human, then.

A big mastiff followed the cook around the yard, sniffing at his heels and wagging his tail, so that I put the dog down as a fool to be so interested in that piece of yellow ivory. But at last I saw the reason, for the cook went into the kitchen, the screen door jingled, and after a moment he came out with a wooden chopping bowl filled with tripe.

I ask you to think of putting food for the dog into a chopping bowl! But that's the Chinese for you! I'm a calm and a good-natured man, as I hope to prove before this narrative is over, but there's something about a Chinaman that riles me. He stood by a minute to smile down at the dog that was wolfing the tripe down, then he went into the kitchen again and straightaway somebody else came onto the stage, just like a play.

There was a ladder slanted against the rear fence, and down this ladder, from the top of the wall, came the most miserable-looking dog that you ever saw. It was hardly a dog. It was only half of something; it was like a torn rag, so that you started looking for the other piece. I don't think it weighed eight pounds. It had one ear up, and one ear down, gray fur over its ugly face, and a pair of little black beads shining out at the world. Its tail looked as though it had been bitten off, and altogether you would have said that it had just been blown in by the wind and would soon be blown out again.

This quart measure of ugliness came down the ladder on the run, as easy as though they were stairs, and sashayed up to the feed bowl, and stood there with its head cocked to one side and its nose half an inch from the rim of the bowl.

The mastiff kept his head down, but he stopped eating and the hair of his neck began to lift, and I could see his loose upper lip curling. I thought that the little dog was crazy—because even a puppy knows enough to keep away from the meat dish of another dog—but perhaps in this case it was only hunger, because the ragged pup was as gaunt as a two-year-old in March, after a long freeze. His belly was tucked up flat against his spine and he trembled with starvation.

I was about to shout at him, when the mastiff let out a growl that started from the tip of his tail and ended outside his teeth. He made a lunge, and I looked through the dust to see the mangled remains of the pup, but just then he ran out of the mist with the largest piece of the tripe in his jaws and scooted up the ladder to the top of the wall. There he stretched himself out like a small tiger over a deer. He held the tripe down between his paws and ate it gradually and leisurely. You would have wondered, to see him, because it was plain that this pup was yearning to ravage that tripe and swallow it the way a snake swallows a gopher, but the reason was that the mastiff was putting on a great show down in the yard, and the pup wanted the show to last.

First the big dog tried to climb the ladder, but fell off and landed on his back and knocked out his wind. Then he started trying to claw his way up the side of the wall, while the pup looked over the edge and licked the grease off of his whiskers and smiled—there's no other word for it. He lay there and wagged his tail and ate another bite, and kept watching the mastiff go mad, hollering and howling and frothing, until the Chinaman ran out of the kitchen door with a poker and slammed the big fellow right over the head. A fine place to hit a dog— just what a Chinaman will always do!

The mastiff scooted through the back gate. It was latched after him by John Chinaman, who went back into the house mumbling and shaking his head until his pigtail bobbed.

There was the stage clear, except for the pup off in the wings. Now that his big friend was gone, he showed what he could do by inhaling the rest of that strip of tripe in one breath, and he was about to run down the ladder again when another actor came on, and this was a big Maltese cat. I never saw none no bigger. Suppose that I said fifteen or sixteen pounds? Well, he looked it. He had a great, round head like a lynx, with tufts of fur on the jowls, and he had a forearm like a prize fighter.

He crouched in the middle of the yard and lashed his sides with his tail. Then he went on toward the tripe bowl.

I looked to the dog, feeling sort of sorry for him, but the little fool was coming straight down the ladder! I wondered if he thought that because a mastiff couldn't climb that ladder, a cat wouldn't be able to turn the trick? At any rate, down he came, slinking, his head lowered and stuck out in front and his stub of a tail wagging so fast that it disappeared and looked like no tail at all. As a matter of fact, I saw that Rags felt he was about to put something over on the cat.

Imagine a greyhound trying to play tricks on a full-grown mountain lion—that was about the idea. I held my breath. I rubbed my hands over my ribs, almost feeling those big claws sink into my own flesh and go rip-rip.

The cat got to the tripe bowl, all right, licked the edge of it, and then turned his head and gave a look around with his yellow-agate eyes before he began to feed. Then he saw the dog behind him, and that fool of a dog was jumping up and down and looking nearly pleased to death with himself. Mr. Tomcat arched his back. He stuck out every hair on his tail, flattened his ears, and, with a raised forepaw, he waited for the party to start. But the pup was in no hurry. No, sir, Rags began to trot around that he-lion in gray fur with his tail still wagging, and the cat began to turn around to keep facing the pup. Pretty soon he seemed to be a little dizzy. He changed paws. That instant Rags charged. The cat jumped stiff-legged into the air to come down on the dog's neck, but it was only a feint. Rags was back, a little quicker than a lightning flash, and started on his marathon around the cat again.

It must have been a good deal of a strain on the Tom. He had to stand at attention every instant, while Rags was taking it easy; I got more and more interested. Still, I was surprised when the big cat whirled and bolted for the fence.

He was a good runner, that Maltese, and with his morale all broke down by the antics of that Rags, he fairly sailed for the wall. But Rags dissolved in the air from a standing start, and, when he came into view again, he had that cat by the back of the neck.

They turned into a spinning circle, spitting like a Roman candle, and I couldn't make out whether the dog was shaking the cat or the cat was shaking the dog.

At last, they stood up enough for me to see the finish, which was Mr. Tom lying limp, and Rags gripping him by the throat. When he was sure the cat was dead, Rags licked his wounds—he was bleeding plenty—and trotted over to the tripe bowl. I wanted to stand up and give him a cheer, but just then Rourke touched me on the shoulder.

# Chapter 2

So I turned about and looked at Rourke.

His hair was on end. He was ten percent dressed and the rest of him bare. But still Rourke always looked easy and at home, even in a roughhouse.

He said to me with a sour smile: "Hello, beautiful."

That was a rude remark. I always think it's pretty lowdown to taunt a man with being the way that nature made him. You look at it in the right way, and you'll see that it's sacrilegious, as a matter of fact. The mule that kicked my nose lopsided hadn't helped me much, and the knife cut that crossed one cheek wasn't really a beauty mark, either. But who can help accidents.

I swallowed my anger, though. I usually did, when I talked to Rourke. Otherwise, we would always have been having trouble, because he was like a buzz saw cutting through a post full of nails. Sparks started flying before Rourke had been around very long.

"How's the mornin' with you, darlin'?" says

Rourke to me. "Pretty fine, I guess, after spoiling my party last night."

"Which I saved your face," I told him. "That was what I did for you."

"Thanks," said Rourke. "But I'm one of those funny guys that wants to take care of his own face. Speakin' of map savin'," says Rourke, "you might start at home, like the book says about it."

Maybe you observed the kind of grammar that Rourke used, but I tried never to hold that against him, him not having all the advantages what I had used.

I merely said to him: "Speaking of books, did you ever read one, kid?"

Says Rourke: "The ejjucation I got I never show you, Johnny. I don't want to embarrass you none comin' over you with what I know."

I reached about in my mind for something to say, but nothing came handy to me. It usually was that way, when I was talking with Rourke; he seemed to get me sort of tied up. An hour afterward, or that night in bed, I'd think of what I should have said, and then lie awake and grit my teeth.

He went on in his soothing way: "But if you'd been raised anywhere outside of a stable, you would know that it ain't manners to interfere when some gentlemen are havin' an argument."

He waited, set for a comeback. I just swallowed and moistened my lips. Words were hard to find.

Then he said: "Even if you'd been brought up in a decent stable, where they kept a few fightin' dogs, you would've understood better."

"Matter of fact," I told him, "I couldn't tell which was the men and which was the dogs, last night."

This was a pretty good cut, I thought, and I leaned

back and enjoyed myself, but Rourke had a way of brushing over rough places and going right on. He did that now, and said: "But what could I expect of a man with a name like yours?"

It always made me see red when he touched on my name. He never would listen to reason, but I tried to argue him into some sense. I said: "Denny, you ought to know better, and you *do* know better, if you just stop to think. One of the oldest names in the world is Jones."

"Sure it's old," said Rourke. "My great-great-grandfather had a man by name of Jones workin' for him. He used to hold the stirrup when the old man went out to get on his hoss."

"Horse?" I said. "I gotta say that I don't think the Rourkes ever owned horses in Ireland!"

Rourke went straight on: "The Joneses was always glad of pretty near any job they could get. Account of their name, they always worked for half pay, and they never got any days off. Kitchen work and stable cleanin' was their line, mostly."

I closed my eyes. It's a good way, when you want to hold your temper down. Besides, it keeps your dignity pretty well. I hate to lose my dignity; it leaves you sort of naked before the world when it's gone.

I said: "Rourke, if you knew anything, which you don't, you'd know that the greatest hero that ever sailed a ship was a man by the name of Jones. His first name was John, too," I said.

"That's a lie," said Rourke. "His name was Paul. His name was John Paul, and he only picked up the name of Jones by way of a disguise, a sort of an alias . . . because more than one sheriff was lookin' out after that bright young gent. Besides, he was a Scotsman, and no Scotsman was ever any good!"

That stumped me again, a little. It seemed to me that I had read, somewhere, that the name really was John Paul, but how was I to expect that Rourke would know that? He was always that way, turning up with information that he never should have had.

I only said, quiet and reserved: "Maybe you prefer the Irish, because they're raised in stables where there *are* fighting dogs. Mostly they've got the whip, too."

"They've got the what?" says Rourke, speaking with a purr that I'd heard before.

"The whip!" I said.

He licked his lips, and smiled in a way that wasn't good to see. He said: "The talk of a gentleman ain't what can be expected from a gent by the name of Johnny Jones. But there is certain limits outside of which Johnny Jones had ought to have his face punched! Especially when he comes to interferin' in the differences of gentlemen."

"If I hadn't interfered," says I, "they would've torn you in two. One of them had you around the legs, and another was holding down your arms, and a third gent was about to drop the heel of his Colt into your face."

"I was only playing 'possum," said Rourke. "I was about to kick one of them into the side of the wall, and free one arm and massacre the whole lot."

"You were having a booze dream, kid," I said. "You were flattened, and you know it!"

"I was flattened?" Rourke sneered. "A Jones might be flattened, but not a Rourke. A John Jones, that comes of kitchen stock and stable cleaners."

"Denny," I said to him, "I'm pretty patient, and I hate to use hard words, but if you don't shut up, I'm going to knock your teeth out of your head, so's you'll stop biting people in the back."

"John Alias Jones . . . ," began Rourke.

I got up from my chair at that.

Rourke had a slight advantage of position, being standing, and he tried to ram my head off with a straight left, which I managed to duck, and put my left fist halfway through his stomach. It sent him backward, but still fighting, because he was an India rubber man with a frame of whalebone.

I came after him, and he hit me ten times while I was sifting into him, but then I got a right hook over his shoulder and pasted it onto the end of his chin. It overbalanced him, and he fell on his face. So I picked a basin of water off the stand and chucked it over him.

After a while he began to wriggle, and I was sure that he wasn't badly hurt, so I went back to the window and took note of Rags. He'd finished the tripe to the last scrap, and now I was sure that he was a rare dog, because although he'd put six pounds of tripe inside of an eight-pound dog, he didn't show where it had been stowed away. His belly was gaunted up as badly as ever, and his eyes looked as sad and as starved.

Just then came a rap at the door, and a red-headed gent stuck his head in.

He said: "Partners, I don't mind havin' the plaster knocked down on top of my head, but when water is dripped through after it, and the plaster turns into mud, it sort of spoils a gent's sleep."

Rourke stood up with the blood still on his face. "Come in," he said, "and we'll talk it over. Come in, because it seems like I seen you before, handsome."

But the redhead gave him one look and backed out; there was an effect about Rourke like a lump of ice laid on the stomach, or the chilly muzzle of a Colt tucked under your chin in place of a bib.

I looked him over with a good deal of admiration. I'm a lump, covered with knots; Rourke is a sleek cat. And he can do anything in the world. You could drop Rourke fifty feet, and he'd bounce up on his feet. He can do anything he wants with his hands, from daubing a rope or bulldogging a steer, to Mexican knife work and champion six-shooting. Only with fists and rifles could I stand up to him, and the beautiful part of Rourke was that he always met me where I shone. He never would have stepped into his own field, and nothing could have made him mad enough to draw a gun on any man. He did his fighting with his fists, because he loved fighting for its own sake. He saved his Colts for times when his back was against the wall.

Maybe I have left the thing a little doubtful this far, but now I would like to step in and say that there was nobody like him for a pal, except that he was sort of like having a half-tied panther around.

He went over to the washstand and began to clean up. And he talked through the soap bubbles as he worked away.

"That right of yours is what beats me," said Rourke. "I can see what the left does, but that right hook always is sneaked across. No pickpocket could work slicker than you work that right of yours, Johnny. What crook taught you?"

"My great-grandfather," I said, "and he learned it while he was holding horses for the Rourkes."

"What's happening around here?" he asked me.

"Nothing," I said, "except that you're starting back for the hills with me today."

"What have we got?"

"Eight dollars," I said.

"What you been blowing the stuff on?" asks Rourke.

"Bailing you out of jail and paying your damages," I told him.

"Have we picked up anything?" said Rourke.

"Nothing but a dog," I said, "if he likes our looks."

# Chapter 3

Rourke looked out the window at the dog and didn't think much of it. Because you can take it for granted that an Irishman never will take to a thing that has no looks unless he's seen it proved.

For that matter, I couldn't blame him, but I went down to the back yard to see if I could make friends.

He was as chummy as a six-year-old maverick, and he acted like a smart bird that's drawing you away from her nest. I mean to say that he would let me drift up close to him, but he would never let me lay a hand on him.

I wondered more and more what I could do. So I opened the gate, and the mastiff came in like a high flood. He hadn't stopped foaming and by this time he'd reached speechlessness. He came in blithering and green-eyed and went for the pup so fast that he nearly split himself in two; he bowed his back until the toes of his hind legs stuck out in front of his head, the way they do in cartoons of a dog running fast.

Rags watched his coming with his head on one side, and his eyes just mildly interested. At the critical moment he hopped a little to one side, and the big train went by in smoke. The mastiff came again and Rags trotted up the ladder.

The game was his. He treated that mastiff the way a matador treats a bull—I've seen them in Mexico—not in Juárez where they have tired horses and tired beef to murder, but in Mexico City where they bring over special Andalusian bulls and get their money's worth. I mean the bulls do, and so do the fighters.

They had nothing on Rags, but it isn't always the best rider that wins, because sometimes a foot will stick in the stirrup. The mastiff tried to climb the ladder again, but his shoulder hit one side of it, the ladder spun over and over, and poor Rags was flicked into the air. The mastiff stood underneath with his mouth spread wide enough to have swallowed a lion, so I collared him and dragged him away. The brute was half mad. He tried to take off my arm at the wrist to get at Rags, who was staggering in a corner, dead game, but badly stunned. However, I managed to make him peaceful by nearly staving in his ribs, and I kicked him through the gate and closed it in his face, again.

The Chinaman came to the door, bobbing his cursed pigtail at me.

"You likee?" he said.

That was a fool thing to say, as you'll agree. I only said: "Go back and cook me half a dozen chops and see that they're well done, or I'll skin you, and my partner will tan the hide."

He grinned cheerfully back at me. "All li'," he said, and dived back into the blue puffs of smoke that rolled out from the stove.

I turned around, and there was the little dog sitting down on the ladder—it hadn't fallen, mind you—sitting down on a rung of the ladder halfway to the top. I laughed when I saw him. For him to sit there was like a man sitting on a three-inch plank two hundred feet from nothing, but Rags had as fine a sense of balance as a tight-wire performer, and one would have said that he had the claws of a cat for holding on.

I walked up to him again, as careless as a smart young fellow on Sunday afternoon about to ask a pretty girl on the street corner hasn't he seen her before and didn't they meet at what's-his-name's house?

Rags waited until I was arm's reach distant, and then he turned on thin air, so to speak, and jumped to the top of the ladder. I put my fists on my hips. "You damn' little fool," I said to him.

Well, it was exactly as though he had understood, because he trotted down the ladder like the slack-wire lady coming back to take her bow. He wagged his tail out of sight as I put out my hand.

Still, it was reason against instinct. I had my hand almost on his collar when instinct almost got the best of him and me, because he flashed his head about and planted a double row of needle-pointed teeth in my hand.

I knew how that big Tom had died so quickly. Mind you, he hadn't broken the skin, but for ten seconds I didn't move, and neither did he.

Then he let go of my hand and cowered down with his eyes nearly shut and one foot raised, exactly as though he knew that he deserved a licking and expected to get it. I sat down on the bottom rung of the ladder and said to him: "Now, partner, I've made a good many steps to you. Will you make some to me?"

He understood. He hopped right down and licked my ear, and in no time at all he was sitting on my knee, watching my face exactly as he had watched the face of the mastiff at the bowl of tripe.

Here Rourke came out. "Where's the rest of the dog?" he asked.

Rags hopped onto my shoulder on the side away from Rourke and waited, quivering a little. He was as full of trust of strangers as a coyote.

"You better watch your step," I told Rourke. "He's given you a suspended sentence."

"There's a greaser in the street selling cantaloupe," said Rourke. "I'm going out to hold him up."

He left, and the pup dropped down on my knee again. I played a game with him, trying to shake or buck him off that knee, but he rode my leg as fair as any 'puncher ever rode a pitching mustang. I sunfished, and fence-rowed, and jerked, and stopped all shorter and jerkier than a horse could do, and Rags stuck with me every jump. What was worse, he raked me fore and aft as well as a cowboy, by sticking his claws through my trouser leg. He liked the game and he played it fair. Once or twice he lowered his head as though he were tempted to hold himself in place by fastening his teeth in my trousers, but each time he gave up the idea of pulling leather as soon as it came into his head. Finally with a sunfishing leap mixed in with a crazy cross-weave, I got him off. He stood for a moment shaking the dizziness out of his head, then back he popped onto my knee, ready to have the game start all over again.

"Rags," I told him, "you're all right." And I put out my hand to pat his head. But that was where he parted company with other dogs; he didn't like to be petted. Every time a man's hand touched him, he looked sick, and crouched and shuddered, until at last I understood him and left him alone.

Well, it was like this. A real he-boy don't like to be stroked and petted. No more did Rags. Conversation was his idea of a good time. He would listen to my voice for an hour at a stretch and understand about as much of my words as I did myself. Or pulling on a sack or any rag was another way he liked his exercise. But if you took him out hunting, then he was at home. He could stretch himself out as limber as a string to go down a rabbit's hole; he knew how to fight a snake like a mongoose—as they tell me—by hopping into the air when the snake strikes, and taking the reptile behind the head. He could stalk a bird like a cat, and pick one off a low twig as neatly as ever a cat could do the trick. There were a thousand other things he could manage, which I might introduce you to one by one, except that they would need a book by themselves. Besides, I want Rags to come on the stage in something more than tatters. I want to blow a trumpet before him and show you that he was a prince of dogs—a fairy prince, let's say, since he wasn't big enough to fill any larger boots.

I was in the middle of my first talk with Rags when he whipped about on my knee in that way he had, for he always seemed as well balanced as a top that was spinning at full speed. He pointed like a needle to the north, and I saw a round-faced little man had just come into the yard from the side door of the hotel.

"You're Rourke?" he said to me.

He was a red-faced blond with a smile like a salesman and the nodding sort of manners of a dry-goods clerk, always ducking and swallowing and hardly keeping the "sirs" out of his yes and no.

"I'm not Rourke," I told him.

He said that he was sorry, and I agreed with him.

So he stopped a moment as he was getting through the door again and asked if I was Rourke's friend.

"I'm his only friend," I said.

He stopped short and nodded at me. "His *only* friend?" he asked me.

"A rolling stone don't grow a beard," I said to him.

He came back as though he had been invited. He almost shook hands. He said: "Is this the Rourke of Sunnydale?"

"Are you a deputy sheriff?" I asked him, knowing that he wasn't, just wanting to make sure.

He actually blushed. He said that he wasn't a sheriff and that he understood that Mr. Rourke might be bothered by people of that persuasion, but that, for his part, he had no desire except to serve and assist and soothe Mr. Rourke.

"Who in hell might you be?" I asked him.

"I've come to offer Mister Rourke a good position," he told me.

"I'll thank you for him. What sort of a position?" I asked him.

"One hundred a month and all found," he said, and then he smiled down his nose at me as though he had played a trump. He had, at that. This was in the days when doorkeepers didn't get five dollars a day—nor even a dollar. Thirty dollars looked good to a he-cowboy even if he could ride anything that wore hair, daub his rope on a lightning flash, and cut a coyote out of a pack. These later day 'punchers are handier at cutting aces than at cutting cows, but I don't want to get off on that foot.

To go back to the blond stranger, just as he had played his right bower, Rourke walked into the yard with his hat full of little melons no bigger than your fist, and the color of gold. My heart went out to them at the first glance.

I said: "Kid, this is your new boss."

"Thanks," said Rourke. "I don't wear that size."

"This is a hundred a month and found," I said.

"I'm playing a straight part," said Rourke, "and I never learned the lines for an end man. Where's the catch?"

"Well," said the stranger, making a gesture with the palms of both pink hands turned up, "I'm representing a lady who wants to feel secure out here in the wilderness . . . her nerves are a wreck . . . and she feels that she must have the protection of some well-known and reputable man."

# Chapter 4

The manners of Rourke could be as soft as thistle-down, but usually he preferred to cut corners and save time in conversation, and, instead of answering the stranger, he said to me: "Have I got a better reputation than that dog?"

"This is an educated dog, kid," I told him, "and I got to say it, even if I hurt your feelings."

"You see how it is," said Rourke to the blond gent. "I like your money, but I'm out of style. Come on and eat, Johnny."

We went into the hotel dining room, and Rourke told me to look between my feet. Then I saw that Rags was marching just at my heels. Every time I lifted a foot, one of my spurs, which I wear sharp, warmed up his whiskers, and the little devil appeared to like it. His eyes kept jogging to this side and that—he was like a prize fighter shadow-boxing, and getting ready for real trouble.

John Chinaman tried to kick Rags out of the room, but I changed his mind for him, and we sat down at a corner table. It was early for that town. Nobody else bothered us any. We knifed into the melons, and, as soon as they were spread apart, they turned that dining room into a flower garden. Their insides was as golden as honey and tasted the same; they were so full of juice that it was like spooning the meat out of a grape.

We looked up and found the blond salesman was still with us. He'd sat down at a neighboring table.

"Modesty I can understand," said the stranger, "but, after all, facts are facts."

"Not this far west of the mountains," said Rourke.

"Dollars wear the same face East or West," said the stranger.

"There seems to be some reason on his side," I suggested to Rourke.

"It's an easy job," said the stranger. "The lady has to come out here and live in the mountains. She's very delicate. Naturally she didn't want to step into the wilderness unprotected. For my part, I think that her fears are not justified."

He went on to say that this was the 20th century, after all, and that there was sure to be law and order even in the most remote parts of this wilderness.

"Friend," said Rourke, "I can show you places not twenty mile from this town where there's no more law and order than there is tail on that dog. The lady's here for her health, is she?"

The stranger said that she was. She had employed him as her purveyor, which he said meant the fellow who supplied her with everything that might be needful. He already had arranged the purchase of mules and horses and saddles and buggies and wagons, and everything else, down to flour on the one hand and gunpowder on the other, but, after all, there were some things which couldn't be bought outright, and one of them was such a man as Miss Mornay wanted. Miss Frances Mornay was her name. She and her old uncle, who was an invalid, had had Western mountain air recommended. They were making a tremendous effort to do everything that was right to recover their health. He was a broken-down old skipper of sailing ships, and she was a delicate invalid. We would understand when we saw her.

We understood that there was a female companion in the party, too, and there would be a cook and a couple of other servants, besides people to look after the horses, and the transport to and from town, as added supplies were needed.

Altogether, it looked like quite an expedition, and it was aimed at the heart of the Sierra Negra to a place where there was an old house that once had been a monastery, or some such place. Mission, I believe he said.

It was a pleasure to hear this fellow talk. He went on as easily as water running downhill. It was no more trouble for him to curl his tongue around a hundred dollars' worth of words than it was for me to hook my fingers onto a hundred in real yellow gold—if I had the chance.

While that fellow was taking ten-syllable words out of his vest pocket and making them disappear into thin air, it gradually dawned on us that the pink-faced idiot really intended to chaperone an old man who couldn't use his legs and two young girls into a slice of mountains where there wasn't railroad or telegraph in sight, and where the mountain lions were so unused to the sight of a man that they knew Mexicans chiefly by their taste and *gringos* by the dust they raised getting away.

Some of this Rourke let into the lady's agent, and he rubbed his soft chin with his dimpled knuckles and said that he was surprised and shocked. "Really shocked," he said.

I put in my oar and told him the facts without stretching. Up there in the Sierra Negra the only currents of human life consisted of cattle rustlers, yeggs in hiding, and garlic-sweating greaser bandits who were lying low and digesting their last murders and robberies.

James Cattrin—that was the name of this shorthorn—said that he was very much impressed. He would tell all of these things to Miss Frances Mornay. No doubt she would change her mind.

"If she don't," said Rourke, with a chop on the end of his fork, "tell her that, anyway, I don't work separated from my partner, here . . . who's going by the name of Johnny Jones, just now. He's got a better name somewhere, which he's trying to forget." And he winked at Mr. Cattrin.

James Cattrin, licking his pink, puffy lips, looked me over as though I were a horse and seemed to decide that I might have points. Then an idea hit him. You could see it ripple over his face like dawn on a mountain lake. This was his idea—that, although it might be reasonably dangerous for the party to entrust itself to the guardianship of one seasoned fighter, two men of guns would surely be able to make everything comfortable for even a nervous invalid.

Rourke said: "Cattrin, when a lot of greasers get hungry and start landsliding in any direction, don't you make any mistake about it . . . it takes their weight in white men to stop 'em from sliding."

However, if there was a chance for a hundred apiece, and that was what it looked like—short hours and not much but responsibility to carry—it was a shame to turn down a possibility. Cattrin suggested that we go downtown and talk to Miss Mornay, and I have to admit that I burned the roots of my tongue getting rid of the last of my coffee. As for Rourke, he could have swallowed melted brass without stopping his smile.

We hadn't gotten far downtown when we saw the preparations that were starting. Three big wagons, good for four ton each, were trailed along the side of the street, with eight mules in front of every one. One of those wagons had been bought outright, together with five pair of mules, the best that money could buy; the other outfits looked mangier, but they would get there, all right, because they were hired at a fancy price. There was a buckboard and a neat little buggy with a sassy span of Morgan horses in front of each, and every one of those three big wagons fairly bulged with comfort of all kinds. They were loaded to the roofs of their tarpaulin frames.

This wasn't all, because we saw a dozen or so fine saddle stock, with several saddles up, and the whole town, except the cook at the hotel, was hanging around to see the outfit start. Now and then they looked off at the mountains and shook their heads. Mind you, those were times when the Wild West hadn't been reduced to newspaper talk and silly stories. The very shadows in the gullies made me think of the blue of smoking guns, and, when I saw the size of those wagons and thought of the gaunted-up yeggs and crooks who were drifting through the Sierra Negra at every season of the year, I shook my head, too.

Rourke was an optimist, always, but even Rourke had a sour grin as he sized up the procession.

Cattrin led us to the general merchandise store,

and said that Miss Mornay was now settling accounts in the office of the store owner. If we would come in, one by one, no doubt she would be pleased to talk to us and perhaps she could reach an agreement with us.

Rourke was elected first. He said to me before he went in: "This invalid is going to need a new set of springs after the road that I show her. I'll squelch all of this damn' foolishness."

Then he went in with Cattrin, who came out, after a minute, looking pretty satisfied. I spent five minutes wandering through the aisles of that store. The stock of blue jeans and cowhide boots hadn't been eaten into, much, but, otherwise, I would have been glad to trade the store for Miss Mornay's account. I said so to a young man at the ammunition counter, and he grinned so hard his ears wiggled.

After a while, I began to wonder why Rourke didn't come out. He was a quick worker, as a rule. He knew where to put the right words in the right place. I would rather be punched in the face than have Rourke give me a drubbing with his tongue.

I think it was an hour or so before the clouded glass door of the manager's shop opened and Rourke came out. He was feeling his way down the aisle as though the light from the street windows blinded him, and, when he came to me, I had to chuck him in the ribs with my elbow before he knew me. He didn't even swear.

"Is it finished, kid?" I asked him.

Then he looked at me with a long-distance squint and gradually a smile started on his face. "She wants to talk to you, too," he said. "Go on in and talk for yourself."

I hesitated a minute. "Rourke," I told him, "if you've been fooling around with my name any more, I'm going to come out and punch your head off."

He said: "Aw, shut up. I've just been giving you a reputation. If you keep your face shut and act wise, she'll not know that you've never been in jail. Go on in, John Alias Jones."

I give him a pretty hard look, but it was like telling a drunk the time of night. He sashayed on down the aisle in the same fumbling way, pulling himself from counter to counter with one hand and wearing the same dizzy smile.

"Shall I go in now?" I said to Cattrin.

He looked over his shoulder at Rourke and seemed to swallow a smile. "All right," he said, "but just leave your dog outside. She's got a cat with her."

"She'd better put the cat out the window, then," I told him. "Rags stays with me."

He gave me an ugly look, then he shrugged his shoulders and opened the door for me.

# Chapter 5

I smoothed my face out a few degrees when I went into the room, because it's always a good deal better to treat a lady with a smile, even if you have to smile at her, instead of with her. But when I stepped inside the door, I saw the farthest thing from a nervous invalid that I ever laid my eyes on—and this was a red-headed girl with freckles walking across the bridge of her nose, sitting on the edge of a table, and swinging her feet. She looked at me as straight as a gun barrel. I'd met that kind of a girl before.

Take them, by and large, women split up into several large categories. There's the sad-eyed kind, and there's the jolly good-fellow kind that wears sensible shoes, there's the baby doll, the earnest worker, and the you-be-damned kind. There are shades and shades and a few mixtures of those combinations, but, if you boil them down, you'll find out that they all can be shifted into one or another of those shelves. I leave out the sixteen-year-old brats who don't belong on any shelf because they're too mean to stay put.

But when I took one flash at this red-headed girl

on the table, I knew her like a sister. I'd *had* a sister just her kind; she was a you-be-damned.

This girl was dressed in strong, cheap cloth that looked like the devil but promised to wear. That was before the days when women dressed like men for riding—a fool fashion, because their hips always show up too big for their shoulders—and the red-head had on divided skirts. Even those were looked on as being pretty daring. She had spurs on her heels, and riding gloves that were black and slick inside the forefinger, so that I knew she'd been there before. She had one fist on her hip, and she looked at me like we were going to put on boxing gloves and she wanted to size me up.

She said: "Are you Rourke's friend?"

"I am," I said. "Are you Miss Mornay?"

"Not half," said the girl. "I'm Ruth Derrick."

"You're the companion, are you?" I asked her.

"Yes," she said, "I'm on the pay list, too. Do you want the job?"

"If Rourke is going to take it," I told her.

She smiled a little and said right out: "Oh, he'll take it."

"Will he?" I asked. "Because of the hundred a month? I'm not sure."

"Anyway," she said, "if you want the place, don't go in there with that dog behind you. Miss Mornay doesn't like dogs."

Of course that made me stare, and I said: "This pup fits me like my skin and I'd as soon part with him as my hide."

"All right," said the redhead. "You can take care of your own shins."

She shrugged her shoulders at me, and I tapped on the inner door, because this was only an outer sort of corridor where the books were kept on a set of shelves. I was told to come in, and, when I got inside the door, I opened my mouth and shut it again, like a fish out of water.

The manager of the store wasn't a little man, and he had as loud a face as you'll meet most places, but I have to say that he just faded into the shadows and looked like an old photograph hanging on the wall without a frame. Because yonder, near the window, sat the loveliest woman that ever walked the face of this earth. I have roamed and ranged some, and I could state that a Kanaka half- or quarter-breed is hard to come over, and a Mexican girl with plenty of Castilian blood can be a wonder to look at, and the range has its own kind of girl, as good as they ever are found, so I'd looked here and there and never tried specially hard to keep my eyes to myself, but there never was anything like Frances Mornay.

You walked deeper and deeper into the atmosphere of her, and yet you never reached her. You could feel why nations went to war and why man bought poison and the stuff that lies behind songs— but tie my tongue around the right words, I can't. I didn't hunt for words when I was with her. It was like having your legs knocked out from under you; you sit down and don't know how you got there.

Right away quick I made up my mind to two things—that she was unhappy, and that I was going to help her. I knew that before she had said a word, because she had only put those velvet violet eyes on me one instant, when I was caught like a fly on tanglefoot. She didn't hold you off with her eyes like the redhead and sort of measure you for a straight left, but she looked at me and took me in, in a dizzy sort of a way.

All of this occupied a couple of seconds, maybe—
I was paralyzed.

She spoke to me in just the sort of a voice I expected, low, rather faint, and with a sort of husky
sweetness about it. She asked me if I were Rourke's
friend, which I said I was, and if I would be willing
to go with him in this work? And I said I would. She
had heard that the mountains might be rather dangerous, and I smiled a little because it seemed to me
that I had seen those mountains, and seen the dangers in them, but now the troubles seemed as far
away and long ago as something told to me in a
dream.

She noticed the smile, and smiled a little in return,
pathetically. Strong men, like me, she allowed, cared
very little for dangers. But she had to be very careful, because—and here she leaned forward toward
me a little, and then glanced aside at the manager.
He couldn't fail to take the hint. He got up slowly
from his chair and went out of the office like a man
walking in his sleep. And she smiled a little at me
again, as much as to say that she was glad that we
two were alone. I was digging my nails into the
palms of my hands to keep myself together.

"I have to be sure of protection," she said, "because I know there are people who won't want me
in the house."

I asked her what house she meant, and she said it
was the old Mornay house, back there in the Sierra
Negra. For two generations it had been allowed to
go to pieces and now no doubt it was very little better than a place where they could camp out. But
there were people who would not be glad to have
her come to the place.

I could believe that. Any house in those mountains was sure to be used by the thugs who rode in

those valleys and camped on those hills. But, some-how, all of this didn't seem very important to me. She went on in her talk. She understood that I was a great friend of Rourke's; perhaps I could tell her something about him, because he wouldn't talk about himself.

This question about Rourke waked me up a little, and I asked her how he'd been recommended to her in the first place. She said that Rourke had been named to her as a fearless young man. I added to that: "He's the straightest shot and the best hand with a horse in these parts. Trouble? He eats it."

"And you are a great friend of his?" she asked, with a very inclusive sort of a smile.

I told her that I was no hero, that I liked a sound skin, but that I generally aimed to stay as long as I could where I was needed. She seemed pleased. Straight off she said that she would take me on at the same wages she had offered Rourke, $100 a month.

"But you won't need to take the little dog, of course?" she said.

I saw two new things, then. One was that Rags was lying out on the rail of an armchair, balanced mostly on thin air, and watching a cat that was in the lap of Frances Mornay—the most beautiful cat I ever had seen. It was a Persian, I suppose, with long, tawny hair that was really more than tawny—it was a fluff of gold—and the cat had velvet violet eyes, just like its mistress. Now it had spotted Rags and was trying to climb up on the shoulder of the girl, with all its fur standing out like the fuzz in the head of a thistle. Its whiskers were working and its tail curling with anger and disgust.

"You won't need to take the little dog," said Frances Mornay to me.

She looked away from me at Rags and she didn't

smile, now, but her mouth stiffened a little. It made her beautiful in a different way—it made her like a thing carved out of white stone—it made her like a lovely statue of disgust. But this waked me more out of my dream than anything else, because I never had seen any other person in the world that felt that way about a dog.

However, Rags was hardly like other dogs. He was more of a cartoon than the real thing, as I may have said before, and, lying there on the rail of that chair, where hardly a bird could have perched if it so much as had blunt talons, he looked more queer and out of place than usual.

I walked over to him and snapped my fingers at him to bring him down onto the floor, and I was about to tell her that a matter of a dog or two, one way or another, made no difference at all, but Rags didn't understand my signal, and, instead of jumping down onto the floor, he leaped up to my shoulder and sat up like a monkey, pricking his ears.

"You see," I said, "that he's pretty harmless."

She nodded her head and allowed a bit of her smile to return. "He's not very big," she said.

"He could be drawed through a ring," I said.

"And how is he about cats?" she asked me.

I laughed a little, and shifted my weight to my other foot.

"Matter of fact, ma'am," I said, "he lost his mother when he was a pup. . . ."

"Poor little thing," said the velvet eyes.

"Which we didn't have no other way, there being no milk on the ranch, except to raise him with a cat's litter."

"Ah, really," she said, and she leaned forward, her lips parted a little, and looking a wonderful lot lovelier than ever before. Her eyes shone as she looked at Rags. "Then he's friendly with cats?"

"With practically every cat," I said, "Rags is a chum. It makes him kind of sad that most cats, though, put up their backs at him . . . he's so used to having his foster brothers and sisters play with him."

"He looks intelligent," she said.

I told her that there was never a brighter dog in the world, and, with that, she engaged me on the spot, and said that Rags could come, too, if I had to have him.

The yellow Persian seemed to understand all of this. Because now she opened a pink mouth filled with clean, white needles and spat at Rags—not making a noise, you understand, but a sort of a breathless hiss of hate.

I didn't wait for Frances Mornay to notice. I got out of the room fast.

# Chapter 6

From the way Rags performed in the room with Frances Mornay, I began to take it for granted that he was going to be a lucky and an understanding dog. But I was no sooner outside of the store than he gave me a scare.

I was so busy in my mind that I'd forgotten Rags was perched on my shoulder, but, as we stepped out the door into the street, a gray cat strolled by, and Rags dropped at it like an eagle at a fish hawk. The cat must have seen the brush of the shadow, because it dodged and swarmed up a telephone pole until it could get sidewise onto the top of the store awning. Rags stayed below, looking up very bright and wistful, first at the cat, and then at me, as much as to wonder why I didn't brush that cat off of the awning and down into his reach. I damned him through my teeth and he trotted up to my feet and sat down, raising a dust cloud with the wagging of his tail. I couldn't stay mad with him. He was like Rourke, always in trouble and always happy, but I hoped that nobody had seen except the teamster next at hand, who was grinning in an appreciative sort of way.

Then I saw Rourke himself standing in the gutter and rolling a cigarette; his head was bare; the sun was pouring on him hot enough to melt wax. So I went up to him and said: "Where's your hat? You grinning idiot, you'll get sunstroke."

He looked at me with a dopey smile. "Hello, Johnny," he said as though he hadn't seen me for days.

"I'm still here," I told him, "but you look as if you'd just got back from a trip. Where you been?" I pulled him back into the shadow and told him that he looked like a half-wit.

"Have you got a match?" said Rourke.

"Listen to me," I said. "I'm taken along at the same fancy rate of pay, if that pleases you. Only, she's against dogs, and I had to tell her that Rags loves cats. You understand? It won't matter when once he gets up there in the mountains."

He lighted a match; his eyes were as empty as the eyes of a cow.

"You hear me?" I asked him.

"About what?" he said.

I saw that he was over his head, and so I left off talking except to tell him to go and get his hat in the store where he'd left it, and then come back to me and we'd get our horses. We went over to the hotel, then, and paid our bill, which was plenty, and got out our ponies and came back for the caravan—because that string of rigs was about big enough to pass for one. At the head of the street, my pinto decided to put on a show and he did it proper because he hadn't a saddle on him for all of two days and he was full of beans. He walked on two legs and he stood on one like a Japanese acrobat, and then he turned out four blocks of fancy bucking, never two licks in the same style. When I first got Pinto, he used to pile me about once a week, but there's a good deal in learning the style of a pony, and I knew Pinto clear down to the footnotes, so that I could forget about pulling leather and sit up and scratch him from his ears to the roots of his tail.

That little job warmed up the boys a little, and, when we lined up with the rest of the caravan, the teamsters seemed glad to have us along. My riding had made them look favorable at me, and, of course, Rourke never needed any introduction, because one glance at him showed that he was all wool and a couple of yards wide. You can tell some men by the way they sit the saddle and hold their heads, and one flash at Rourke showed that he was a lightning rod that had been hit a good many times and had saved up the charges to pass along.

A big buck of a muleskinner hailed us as we went by, and asked us if we belonged to the party, and we pulled up and said that we did. He was a bull of a man with a faded blue flannel shirt on, and a red flannel undershirt beneath; he was one of those fellows who are always steaming in their own perspiration with a drop of sweat always running down the bridge of the nose, but he never seemed put out by the heat. His name was Dorgan, he said, and he was the regular teamster who was to be kept at the house in the Sierra Negra for hauling up whatever supplies were needed.

Rourke said he thought there was enough to keep a hundred men in chuck for half a year in those wagons, even if the hundred were buck privates in Uncle Sam's fine army, but Dorgan had a different idea. He told us something about the loads of those wagons that opened our eyes. About half of it was furniture. And not ordinary camp furniture, either, but couches, and rugs, and such things to fix up the house.

"Like the inside lining of a god damn boodwar," said Dorgan.

I took to Dorgan right away. I liked the arch of his neck and he had a busted nose, like me. He told us a good deal about the outfit. Counting him, there were five servants, two house *mozos,* and two more Mexicans for looking after the horses and doing outside jobs around the place. Rourke and I were servants, too, in a way. That made seven of that order. The party we were to take care of were the two girls, Cattrin—who had been introduced—the old man, whose name was Palliser, and another young fellow who Dorgan said was engaged to Frances Mornay.

When Rourke heard this, he pulled leather and got gray around the gills, but he steadied up enough to ask who the man was. He went by the name of Hugh Shirley, according to Dorgan. Rourke got on a thoughtful expression that I had seen before. I guessed that it meant trouble. So I changed the talk by asking who was the cook.

"There he goes," said Dorgan. "I forgot and left him out of the count."

I saw a John Chinaman go trotting by with his head bobbing and a couple of big wicker baskets slung across his shoulders on a pole. Dorgan said that he had been down at the river marketing among the Mexicans there, before the start for the mountains.

It made my gall rise to see that pig-tailed Oriental; it seems as though I can't get shed of Chinamen, no matter where I get, and I said my thought out loud. Dorgan wrinkled up his red face in a grin and agreed, and just then a big voice bellowed from ahead of us.

"God damn your run and counter! If you stumble again, I'll keelhaul you, you damned lubber, you freshwater fool!"

I peeled my eye around the corner of the wagon, and saw an old man, whose legs looked helpless, being lifted into the buckboard by a couple of Mexicans and a tall, slim young fellow.

Dorgan saw, and he said that the old man was Palliser, the skipper, and that the young chap was Hugh Shirley. I took a good look at Hugh, but it was nothing to the way that my partner Rourke put the eye on him. This fellow Shirley was all done up like a real center-fire cowpuncher, with chaps and bandanna, and silver *conchas,* and a big-brimmed sombrero, Mexican-style. He had a gun belted around his waist, and he wore a checked shirt. All his appointments were all right, but his horse looked a little on the side of hot blood, and too tender to work cows. That whole outfit was so new that it seemed to sort of creak, even in the distance.

"He looks kind of pretty, don't he?" Rourke said to me.

I said that he did, and that I hoped that nothing would happen to spoil his looks, and Rourke grinned at me like a starved dog that sees a side of beef straight above his nose—and in jumping distance.

"Does he like the kind of soup that old devil dishes out to him?" asked Rourke.

Dorgan said that Palliser cussed everybody, and that he hardly could talk even to his niece, Frances Mornay, without swearing, but, particularly, he took out his spite on Hugh Shirley. Rourke asked why he would stand for the gaff, and Dorgan said that was simple: Palliser had the money that might go to Frances Mornay.

"He's a hound, then," said Rourke, "that'll take a licking for the sake of the pie and coffee afterward."

Dorgan said nothing, but he scratched the bristles on his chin and looked after Rourke as my partner rode down the street.

"The kid is quick on the think," he said. "He makes up his mind, I'll tell a man."

"His hand is quicker than his head," I said, and I looked straight at Dorgan.

"Hum," said Dorgan.

I knew that no more would have to be said on that subject, but Dorgan would pass the word along to the rest of the boys that Rourke was pepper and not to be upset if they didn't want to get him in their eyes. A good deal of trouble I'd always avoided for Rourke by advertising him a little as we went along. He had free and easy ways that often meant no harm, but he was so fast at the bat that a good many gents thought they were over the plate just as he slammed them for a home run. Rourke was one of the agreeable kind, who are always willing to meet you at your own pet game. If a tightrope walker had challenged him to walk a wire across Niagara Falls, he would have taken up the game without thinking twice. I saw him fight with knives, blindfolded and tied by the wrist on an eight-foot cord to a French-Canadian. It was a pretty game. They struck in turns, and the man who drew blood could strike again, always in the dark. Rourke made that Frenchman howl for help in half a minute, because he had the instinct for fighting with anything and he could see his way in the dark to trouble. By spreading the news about him along the line, I kept him out of prison and kept other people all together.

I asked Dorgan what he thought of this trip, and he said it was just a tenderfoot's freak idea, and that the whole batch would be down out of the hills five days after they landed there, because it would be about that long before the first batch of greaser bandits turned up on the skyline, ready to pick up any crumbs that fell from the table.

Then I rode ahead up the wagon line, and, as I came even with the buckboard where Palliser was sitting, he bellowed at me: "You! Hey!"

I pretended not to hear, because I don't like to be impolite to old men. Straightaway he sent a blast at me and damned my heart and liver and told me to open my ears, so I drew Pinto up and looked at him.

# Chapter 7

Even if I had known the part that this old man was going to take in what was coming, I couldn't have given him a harder look. Most faces rub off your mind like charcoal off a rock, but a few are like photographs that you slip away and keep forever. I can remember Palliser to this minute exactly as he was that day, and everything about him and behind him, just as though a mental camera had clicked and secured that much forever. For instance, I remember that his head was framed against the sign over the carpenter's shop, which said ALFRED BERTRAM, in big letters, and beneath that, WHEELWRIGHT, CARPENTER, CABINET WORKER. As a matter of fact, he was a cheap, rough carpenter, and that let him out, but in the West of those days everybody believed in taking a chance. If a man had a saw and a knife and a bottle of castor oil, he'd set up as a camp doctor, and a hammer and a bag of nails made anyone an expert carpenter.

Under that sign, there was an awning of brown cloth, sun-faded in spots, and the wind flapped and billowed it so that it loomed rather like a sail moving behind the old man's back—a pretty good background for a ship's captain, as you'll admit.

Old Palliser had a snow-white cane in his hand, made out of the bone of a shark's fin, I think, and there was a snaky twist of carving running along the whole length of it. He leaned on that cane while he stared at me. I never saw such an old devil of a man.

Mind you, in spite of all of his years at sea, his face was a dirty white because of the sickness and helplessness that had kept him indoors lately. He'd been shot through the small of the back, injuring the spine so that his legs were useless to him and he was in horrible pain always. He never groaned and he never howled, but he kept striking out at everybody around him and giving them part of the hell he was living in. Nobody could describe the face of Palliser without borrowing a paint brush, but suppose I tell you that his head was covered with gray, shaggy hair, and he could pull down his overgrown eyebrows, so that he looked out through them like a mountain lion through a brush. His lips were smooth shaven, and, as he kept compressing and working his mouth while the hell-fire boiled in him, his square black beard worked and twitched, also.

"Are you one of this outfit?" he roared at me.

I mean to say, that was the central part of his question, which was all purple- and red-trimmed with fancy swearing. I looked up and down the line and saw the teamsters and the greasers, and even John Chinaman the cook, walking out to see me get my first dressing-down from Palliser. I admitted that I belonged to the outfit.

He shouted: "When I speak to you, move . . . and when you move, run! Come here!"

I rode Pinto alongside the wagon, and he looked at me straight in the face like a snake. I looked straight back. At last I said to him: "Up in these parts, we got some of the finest plain and fancy cussers in the world. I dunno anybody that ever could lay over some of the swearing that I've heard out of the muleskinners, unless it's the talk of the 'punchers at a roundup. But I never heard any talk that would cut out a calf and I never seen any tongue hot enough to slap a brand on its hide. Do you think that you can rope and throw me with your chatter?"

His face turned a queer color—crimson patched with purple—that made you sick to see. He broke out in a roar like a sea lion, the words so crowded that they spoiled one another, and up and down that street there were a hundred faces wearing grins so deep and wide that a cow pony would've busted his leg if he stepped in them.

When Palliser paused for a breath, I said to him: "Back up, old horse. You've come into the wrong stall. But if you talk like this to me again, I'll pull your tongue out and nail it to a tree."

He bit at a couple of words with his one yellow tusk, but no sounds came. He was choked and silent, he was so mad, and he turned around on Hugh Shirley who was standing by, looking handsome and sadder than ever. He asked Shirley if he called himself a man, standing by like this and listening while a young puppy insulted a sea captain.

"You a man?" roared Palliser. "By God, I apologize to every man that ever walked a deck for callin' you a man. You ain't a man! You're a putty-faced imitation of a man. You couldn't've worked as ship's boy on the *Tamerlane*!"

Hugh Shirley looked across at me. There wasn't

any enthusiasm in his face, but I must say that there wasn't much fear, either. He said at last: "Do you think that I ought to offer to fight that man?"

"Ought to?" bellowed Palliser. "You ought to rip him in two!"

You could have puffed me out of the saddle with one breath when Hugh Shirley walked straight out on the street toward me. He looked as grave and as dignified as a young deacon walking down the aisle of a church with the collection plate, and I was just sizing up the length of his arm and the weight of his shoulders when Palliser yelled to him to come back.

"I don't send out a tame seal to try to chew up a killer whale," he said. "That man would swaller you, Hugh. Come back here where I can take care of you." The old devil began to laugh. He rocked back and forth in his seat, supporting himself with his cane, and his great shoulders shaking. Even in the half of him that was left, there looked to be strength enough to root up a main mast and throw it overboard.

"Who are you?" he yelled at me.

I told him my name was John Jones, and he laughed again.

"I've sailed with about ten officers by that same name," he said, "and they all found that Jones made a good change for 'em. I've had many a Jones turn into a Smith in Chinese waters, and many a Smith that turned into a Jones entering Sidney Bay. Jones, god damn you, did you ever hear of the *Tamerlane*?"

I never had, before this day, but I guessed that I could please him. I'm ashamed to say that I *wanted* to please him. A mean horse always has the most wear in him. I feel a little bit the same way about men.

I said—"You mean the famous ship?"—because, of course, I could guess that he meant a ship by that name.

Palliser drew down his head a little and his eyes glittered out at me through the brush. "You've heard about her, eh? Famous ship? She never got the fame that was coming to her! Why? Because they cut her down before a real man ever walked her poop. They cut her down. She was a lame duck before I ever got her. But, even that way, I did something. If I'd had her in her prime, the beauty, you would've looked through hell to find a faster ship than her!"

"I've heard that she was hard to beat," I lied to him.

"Whatever beat her? Whatever passed her on the same course, except *The Thermopylae* and the *Cutty Sark* with their picked crews and their fancy rates? They could afford to have clean bottoms and never a scrap of ragged copper. But the *Tamerlane* had to smash her way around the world like a beggar and not like the queen that she was. I'm going to talk to you, Jones, because I like your god damn ugly face . . . it has the sort of a look that I used to put on my men. In them days my knuckles was always raw for the first half of the passage out. Why? Because I kept 'em bleeding, knocking the fool look off my men, and knocking some proper hell into 'em."

I went on not quite knowing what had happened, but mighty interested in that skipper and his ways, and feeling that by accident I'd made a friend in this outfit. The whole thing seemed bad to me—I mean the whole caravan and the purpose of the trip, and all. I never had seen so many interesting and queer-looking people. It was as if a strong light was on the lot of us—and altogether I thought that even the greasers were special men, and that their like wouldn't be found again if you looked up and down the length of Mexico.

You may wonder what I mean by calling the men extraordinary, and that I can't quite answer except by saying that whenever you get in with a bunch of men of half a dozen or more, there are a few who stand out—usually just one. The rest are the sheep around the bellwether. But in this outfit every one looked a man.

I watched them lining out their teams and thought I'd never seen harder-boiled muleskinners, even if muleskinners as a lot are the toughest customers in the world. I looked at the greasers who were to work in the house and with the horses, but they didn't have the round, soft faces of most peons. They looked more like Indians, tall and straight. When one of them took a step, it looked as though he was getting ready to run at full speed—they were so light and easy on their feet. If you've seen first-rate wild Indians, you know what I mean. When you spoke to them, even, these fellows didn't sink their eyes and answer in a weak voice. They looked straight at you.

Even the Chinaman who was to cook for us looked like a handy man for a fight, especially when he wrinkled up his eyes with a smile, because his squinted eyes made me think of the edges of knives traveling at my throat. There were only two people among the whole lot who seemed soft. Of course, I mean Frances Mornay herself, who took a rear seat in the buckboard with the golden cat, Mimi, in her arms; Cattrin, also, I guessed, wasn't too tough to break.

Wherever we were going, I couldn't help feeling that it would take a steep grade to stop us.

The word was given, the blacksnakes cracked, the muleskinners shouted, and I gave an Indian yell to warm up the blood a little and let off steam. I listened to hear that yell echoed by Rourke. But I didn't hear a sound.

I hunted around for him in the front of things, where he was always apt to be, but I finally found him in the rear of the whole procession, where the dust rolled in thick drifts. He was going along with his hands crossed on the pommel of his saddle and a sad, faraway look in his eyes. I pulled him to one side and snarled at him and asked him if he wanted to choke himself. Rourke shook his shoulders like a dog getting out of water, but he didn't even rouse enough to swear at me a little. He went on with a dreamy look in his eyes.

# Chapter 8

We did fifteen miles a day over the worst sort of roads and the worst sort of grades, including a half-mile rise where we had to half unload the wagons and bring up their loads by relays. That one bit took us half a day, with all hands working like mad, and just as we were in the midst of the business, with half the goods at the bottom of the slope and one teamster at the top with me, a drove of mounted men drifted out of a pine wood not far off and came sauntering over toward us.

You can be dignified and indifferent in a time like that, or else you can accept trouble before it's really showed its face. My theory is that a hungry dog will steal raw meat if he can, and that tattered lot of thugs had starvation in their hearts, I'd have wagered. So I dived into the bed of a wagon, behind the front seat, and lay there easy with a sort of natural trench protecting me, because the wagon box was filled with good-size rocks that the teamster had ready for hazing his string over stiff pulls. That bunch of heavy rocks promised to shunt bullets aside from me, so I dumped a .30-30 Winchester bullet into the dust at the feet of the leading rider.

He stopped, and the rest pooled around him, and they all started talking at once. Then a few of them came toward me with their hands outspread and their heads on one side, obviously shouting that they were innocent men who I was abusing. I just sent a bullet skimming over their heads, and that seemed to convince them. They turned around and rode off, shaking their fists at me, and making insulting gestures, as much as to say that, if I wanted trouble, they would see that I got plenty of it later on. The main point was that they hadn't gotten near enough to rush us, although the fool of a teamster, who had been standing by with a double-barreled shotgun in his hands, thought that I had made a lot of fuss about nothing. You have to kill some men in order to teach them what's what.

Of course, there was nothing very important about this moment. A thousand other little caravans have been scared by groups of mounted men who appear and disappear in the Sierra Negra, but from that day forward I was worried and carried a shadow constantly in the back of my mind.

I explained my meaning to old Palliser that day, when he came up in his buggy, driving it himself, for he had a harness arranged to hold him up and brace him in the seat and he used to range that buggy around over the toughest ground you ever saw. He carried a single-shot cannon that he told me he had used on elephants, besides some revolvers and whatnot. He said he didn't want trouble, but I knew better.

"That gun would never be good for elephants," I told him.

"Why, you damn 'fore-and-after," said Palliser, "why wouldn't it be any good?"

"Because," I said, "a cannonball that size could be seen a mile away, and a whole herd of elephants would have time to get into the woods before the slug caught up with them!"

The skipper glowered at me for a minute, with his black beard spreading like a fan and closing again as his mouth worked. Then he bellowed a laugh and sank his one yellow fang into a cut of Star tobacco. He used to carry half a yard of that dynamite around with him, and his idea of a chew was a handful. Pretty soon he stowed that chew in the side of his face where it made a great lump with a white point on the top.

I said to him: "And if you don't mind a little good advice, I wouldn't get that buggy of yours into so much trouble, because there's a point where even iron and hickory is sure to give way. An antelope would break his leg trying to follow you."

Palliser glared at me again. I don't think that in his entire life anybody ever had kidded him before, and he didn't quite know what to make of it. But whenever he could understand what I was about, it tickled him, as a lion would be tickled if a mouse stood up and jawed at him. Because although he was a cripple now, and very old, Palliser really felt that he was to any other man as a lion is to a mouse. He bellowed with pleasure again. "I heard you firin' your bow guns up here," he said, "and I thought maybe I could get up in time for the racket to start. Matter of fact," he went on, eyeing the dust cloud that was dissolving among the trees, "we almost could catch them now."

I had to persuade him out of that and repeat that pretty soon he would take a wheel off his rig and then the ponies would run away and use him for a harrow on a lot of hard rocks.

"I got this here boat's crew in hand, mister," he told me, "and all they know how to do is to spring on the oars when I tell 'em to let fall. The rest of the time they're more steadier than lambs. And as for this here skiff, she's a boat with bad lines but with good stayin' powers, and there ain't anything that she likes better than the surf, even when she's shipping a little white water. Why did you start sniping that craft, yonder?"

I told him that I hadn't liked their appearance very well, and that they looked like a lot of yeggs to me, and that the sight of them convinced me that we were going to have a lot of trouble in these mountains.

He said: "Every skipper that shakes when he sees white water has a good chance of putting his ship on the rocks, mister."

I have to explain that "mister" is what the mate is called at sea by the captain; coming from Palliser, it was a great compliment to me, even if he damned me a good deal.

"We're in white water," I told him, "but we won't drift on the rocks . . . the rocks are more likely to drift on us."

"How's that?" barked Palliser. "Ain't there been a thousand other wagons through here before us?"

"There have," I told him, "but they kept up by going ahead full speed."

"Aye," he said, "and we're going to anchor. There's a difference there. But we're anchoring in harbor."

"Where there's no police," I said.

"*I'll* be the police," he said. "I'll be the lookout, and I'll be the marines, too!"

He was a bulldog; he was fairly aching for a scrap.

Then I explained to him that the Mexicans were apt to be like Indians. They would hang about and take a long time making up their minds, but, if they had a chance to spend a long time thinking up a plan, they might devise a very clever attack on the house where we were living. I gathered that it was a big place, and there were not many of us to garrison it.

Instead of being down-hearted, old Palliser seemed to enjoy the prospect, and he advised me not to speak about it to the others, because he was sure that nothing would come of it, after all.

On that day, the skipper gave me the impression of a man who wants to get into one more fight and sink with his ship. I don't know what impressed me more—his courage or his wickedness. But I enjoyed being with him. For one thing, he had taken a fancy to Rags, and used to get the pup into his buggy whenever he could. Rags would stay there until a rabbit started up, and then he would bound out over the wheel and take after the jack. One of the jack's leaps made twenty of Rag's, but he never stopped trying for them. Only when they got into a burrow, he would slide down and come up pink and happy, with a full belly.

All during that week of slogging away at the grades, I had very few words out of Rourke. He was in the same sad dream that he had walked into when he entered the store and talked to Frances Mornay. He would stand around like a wooden Indian at every camp and stare at her until the whole outfit could see why he forgot to eat. I was disgusted with him and told him so, but he was too sick to take any notice. I was glad of only one thing—that he didn't buttonhole me and start telling me how wonderful she was.

With the rest of the party I got on very well. Dorgan was the best of the teamsters and a pretty good fellow, but mighty rough. He'd done a few turns at sea, and he was one of those men who get themselves covered with tattooing. He had enough on his hide to make it sell for wallpaper. With Cattrin I couldn't get on. He seemed to me a straight-out bad one with a soft, spongy way as though they were always trying to get something out of one. As for Shirley, he talked so little that it was hard to know what he was; he was always gloomy and depressed, except when he had a few minutes with Frances Mornay, and then he looked a changed man. I didn't wonder at his depression, seeing that old Palliser never stopped riding him. The skipper seemed to hate his heart, and was always raking him fore and aft like a bronco, and Shirley never paying a word back.

I wondered that Frances Mornay, who was the only person in the world that Palliser cared about, didn't break in and say a word for her lover, but she only looked down at the ground at times like that and turned sad, like Shirley. The single person in the outfit, outside of myself, who ever exchanged words with Palliser, was the red-headed girl, Ruth Derrick. She hated him like poison, and he hated her. They used to have some hard goes, I can tell you, and they detested each other so thoroughly that I wondered why they would remain in the same place together. The reason was that they both loved Frances Mornay. The skipper was mad about his niece. He seemed to forget his pain when she was beside him in his buggy in the cool of the morning or the evening, but in the middle of the day he insisted upon her going back to the buckboard, which had a big canvas top that kept off the sun. She was kept from the heat of the worst part of the sun, there.

Ruth Derrick was as fond of Frances as the old skipper was. She worshipped that golden-haired beauty in just the same way, and, when they sat at the campfire of an evening, you'd always find that the redhead was watching the beauty with a little smile of perfect satisfaction—the way that a mother watches a child, say.

So we slogged along through the entire week, until we came to the top of the ridge and saw the old Mornay house beneath us.

It made a fine picture. It was almost the close of the day, and the upper ridges were still bright, but the valley was drifted away with thin blue smoke, as you might say. From that high point, we could turn around and look straight south at the desert out of which we had been climbing all this while. It was a streak of dim purple in the distance, and that horizon was a dirty yellowish tinge with the desert dust, also. But under our feet was as neat a valley as you'd ask to find. It had water running down through it. There were patches of trees of a good size, and there were all sorts of ground, from rocky hills to fine green levels near the water.

That water came out of the highlands on the other side of the valley. It went streaking down to a low shoulder. On that shoulder stood the Mornay house, and from its eastern side, facing us at that moment, the water gushed out again and went racing down the valley.

It was as good a place as a man could find for the building of a house. Wood, water, and grass are what you look for when you are camping, and here was everything. It was high enough to catch rain outside of the rainy season, too, for we had been traveling for an entire week over brown, ragged hills, and here we found another spring. When we dipped over the edge of the ridge onto the downgrade, the big wheels, which had been gritting and grinding all of this while, suddenly were silent, for they were rolling over green velvet that had grown up thick and fine on the disused road. There was only the chucking of the wheels and the snorting of the mules as they cleared the desert dust out of their lungs.

When we came down a little lower, a fine cool breeze blew up the valley and all of the teams, and all of the saddle horses, and all the spans at the buggies and buckboards, stopped as though they had heard a signal and put their heads into that cool wind.

We went on lower, dipping into the shadow, and when we forded the stream, it was thick dusk. Looking up, we saw the stars beginning to rise, and in the west a big red planet, I don't know which one.

# Chapter 9

Like a good many things that have a black ending, our stay in the Mornay house began well. The house itself was better than I had imagined it would be, and because of what has to be told, it is better to make a pause right here and attempt to describe it a little. The valley ran almost due north and south; the house faced east, if it could be said to face in any direction, since it really just faced inward on its patio, because it was an old Spanish type. Nearly half of it had fallen down—in earthquakes, I suppose, but what remained looked good for another century or two.

It had been built in the days when peon labor cost only the corn required to feed it, and corn was the cheapest thing in Mexico. The rock was there at hand for building the place. The peons must have been brought up in a drove, and then the house was built. It would have cost them a good deal to bring mortar, and so mortar was very largely dispensed with by using great square blocks of stone that fitted wonderfully together, with just a film between to stick one stone to the next, and very often the stone faces were so exact that no mortar at all could have been squeezed into the space between. I suppose that this did not make the best sort of masonry, and that they should have used no mortar at all, or else plenty of it, but it made a mighty fine series of walls to look at.

There was so much cheap labor that all of the sheds and the outhouses and the barns around the house had been built of the same sort of beautifully worked stone; the very corral fences—and these were almost intact, for some reason—were built up of strong stone walls. I never saw such a waste of labor, when a few strings of barbed wire would have done just as well for cows, or maybe better. There was enough stonework in those corrals to have built a church bigger than the one in the town where I was born.

The southern half of the house had been extended on built-up foundations over quite a steep slope. That was the part that had fallen down and lay in a rubble of great and small stones littered down the slope. Even with all those stones lying there ready for replacing, I've no doubt that the rebuilding of that wing would cost as much, now, or maybe five times as much, as the whole house had cost when it was run up by the poor peons. The same breed that used to carry 150-pound baskets of ore up the long ladders of the mines.

Of all that southern wing, nothing was left except the northern wall. Of course, if that had gone, the whole house would have slumped down. This wall made the southern boundary of the patio; west of the patio was a broken-down wing with only one good room in it, and the skipper insisted that he should have that. When we arrived, he had himself carried all over the house by the *mozos*, and he picked out that solitary room in the western wing for himself. He said that it would make him think he was at sea again, to look out his window, and see the sharp ridges of the hills parting before the prow of his ship. I've often wondered what would have happened if he'd taken a fancy to one of the other rooms in the place.

The remaining two wings of the house—that to the north and that to the east were intact in both stories, and a good spacious building they made of it, after all. As much room as any modern outfit would need. But in the old days they used a regular barracks—partly for armed fighting men to keep off the Indians, and partly because two or three families generally were lodged under one roof.

Of course, there was plenty of room for all of us in this place, especially after the two extra wagons had rested their mules and the teamsters had started back for civilization. But I don't want to waste time telling what the inside of the building was like; I want to give you a clear picture of the house itself as a general scheme. Most important of all, you must remember that Palliser was sleeping and living in his room in the western wing, alone and cut off from the rest of the house and the people living in it. He was separated from the northern wing by the great gateway, the arch of which had fallen down, leaving a thirty-foot gap. He was connected with the eastern wing only by the upper, ragged rim of the wall that framed the patio to the south.

That isolation of the skipper's room, which caused all of the trouble, is the thing to keep fixed in mind so that what happened can be made clear.

It was a foolish thing, because it meant that in case he needed anything, he would have to yell at the top of his lungs for it. But he insisted on having that place even against the best advice. When we were looking the place over, Frances Mornay told her uncle that Shirley had the plans of the house and that he had picked out the rooms for everybody long before. And Shirley told the skipper that almost any room in the upstairs would be good, especially the one in the southwest corner. There was only one bad room that he absolutely must not take, and that was the one off by itself in the wing.

"*You* pick and choose for me!" yelled Palliser in one of his sudden rages. "I'll pick and choose for myself! You freshwater shellback! That room is the one that has the lines for me. It's the poop of the ship. It's where I belong!"

The days went on smooth as running water, at first. I used to live according to a program, taking Pinto out with Rags in the morning to make a tour of the hills, and examine the ground for sign of stray men or horses about, and, in the afternoon, going out for a little hunting. There was every kind of meat that you could want around that house, from rabbit to bear, and I had the fun of getting the chuck nearly all by myself.

Cattrin and Shirley both said that they knew nothing about guns and hunting, and they seemed to care even less. Rourke was in a trance, and Frances Mornay was still too delicate to ride over that rough going. So I had it to myself, me and Ruth Derrick.

The redhead was as keen as mustard; she hit something now and then, and her eyes went wild with joy when she saw it drop. I am a bad hand on a trail, and the girl knew very little about it, although I think she had a better natural sense than I. But Rags was a help to us. That dog had the nose of a bloodhound. When we were riding hard, he would hop up onto my stirrup and so into my lap, and all the time that we swept along, he would be scanning the ground, as though he were reading print at long distance. The minute we lost the sign, we dropped him, and he cut for it like a good bone. When he found it, he didn't make a sound but stood still with his tail nearly wagging out of sight and his head turned in the right direction. He beat any dog I ever saw, in every way. If there had been five more pounds of him, he could have run down and killed a grizzly singlehanded, and, if he'd been the size of an Airedale, he would have eaten a tiger a day and thought nothing of it.

I taught Ruth Derrick how to shoot, how to skin, and how to cut up bear and venison and everything else. There was nothing namby-pamby about her. She would roll up her sleeves and dig in and work like a man at it, only making a face now and then at the blood. There was more boy than woman in her. In addition, she kept her eyes open, and she would see for herself what she should do. She was as quick as a monkey in imitating, and she was strong, too.

We never were very chatty on these trips. Sometimes we'd ride for two or three hours and never speak a word, and sometimes we'd go out and back without speaking twice. Our hands and heads were full of what we were doing and there was no need of a lot of foolish chatter, and that was what surprised me when she opened up a little, on a day.

She said: "Johnny, is Rourke a great friend of yours?"

I looked at her and said: "What you think, Red?"

"Oh, I know," drawled the redhead. "What wings are to the bird and legs to the antelope, and all that. But tell me, on the square, you think a lot of him?"

"He's my bunkie," I told her.

Then she said, quick as a wink: "You better get him out of here . . . he's losing his mind."

"About her?" I said.

"Sure, about her," said Red. "He's getting sick."

"Why don't you tell her?" I suggested. "She could jerk him out of it with a word or two."

"You might as well ask a tame dove to fly at his face!"

"Anyway," I said, "she could do something. She must know how he is."

"She doesn't," said Red. "The point is, everybody around her always has been in love with her. She is used to men acting like idiots . . . moony idiots, you see."

"Doesn't she know it's her fault?" I asked her.

Said the redhead: "Does a mosquito know that it carries yellow fever?"

There was something about that question that hit me. I turned to Ruth Derrick and saw her for the first time, as you might say. All at once she looked pretty and pleasant to me, and my blood warmed up a little.

"You're all right, Red," I told her.

She shook her head. "I'm talking about Rourke," she said. "You'd better get him out of this camp."

"Hold on," I said. "He'll get over this case of calf love. They always do."

"You're wrong," said Red. "Besides, this is dangerous. This is more dangerous by a lot than yellow fever, since we're talking about that."

"Dangerous?" I said. "How do you mean dangerous, Red?"

She seemed angry and flushed a little. "Is a bullet through the head dangerous?" she said.

# Chapter 10

She said that in such a way that you would have thought I must have heard beforehand that Rourke was in a great deal of danger, and that the thing was obvious. I pulled Pinto in a little closer to her.

"Is this a joke that you've framed on me?" I asked her.

I could see that she was more than half sorry that she'd said so much. She bit her lip and looked away, and then she looked back at me. There was doubt in her eyes, as though something lay between what she wanted to say and her saying of it.

"You've got a good deal on your mind," I suggested to her. "What's the inside steer about Rourke?"

"He's making a fool of himself, for one thing," she answered.

"You don't have to tell me that. I could see he was making a jackass of himself. I've told him so five or six times a day since he left the town with this crew."

"If that's not enough," she said, "you ought to

know that there are other good reasons. You know him better than I do. Suppose a fighting man like Rourke got it into his head that somebody was in his way?"

"He'd never take advantage of a fellow like Shirley, who doesn't understand guns," I said.

She started to speak, changed her mind, and then she said outright: "Look here, I'm going to say one thing. Don't be so sure that Shirley doesn't understand all about guns."

That staggered me almost as much as her first remark, and I looked at her for a while trying to pry back to the meanings which seemed to be hidden behind her eyes, and behind her words. Rags, in the meantime, kept in exercise by jumping from the pommel of my saddle to the pommel of hers, and back again. The horses had grown so used to the antics of that midget that they never paid any attention to him. Neither did Ruth Derrick and me, most of the time. He'd jump from the ground up to my stirrup or to hers—because he'd adopted her and taken her into the family—and then he'd pop up to my pommel, or to the cantle. Sometimes he'd spring onto my shoulder, and then ride there for a mile at a time, so light I forgot to know he was there. Then he'd jump down and curl up on the hips of the horse and sleep, or pretend to sleep. I've even seen him stand with his two back legs propped against the front of the fork, and his two forepaws stretched out and dug into the mane of the horse as Pinto jogged uphill and galloped down. I never seen such a sense of balance as that mite of a dog had!

Now I watched Rags popping from one saddle to the other, having a grand game. I watched him and didn't see him, I was so absent-minded. After a while I said to the girl: "Red, I don't know how you figger this. But Rourke is my friend. He's the best friend that I got."

"Is he ahead of Pinto and Rags?" she asked me with her flashing grin.

"Don't get silly," I said to Red. "Rourke is my bunkie. You know something about him that's important. But you're holding back on him, which is holding back on me, and you and me are partners, I suppose?"

"Are you trying to make a Benedict Arnold out of me?" said the redhead. "I don't want to shock you too much. I'm just telling you my opinion."

"Will you tell me besides what you know" I asked her.

She hesitated a long time, fighting with herself. At last she said that she wouldn't, because a great deal of what she thought was simply guesswork, and she couldn't quote her guesses as authority. "But there's something behind what I say," she told me. "You get Rourke out of here, or there'll be grand trouble, and that's a fact."

That was about the most unsatisfactory conversation that I ever had in my life. It worried me, and it made me mad because she wouldn't say any more. Finally I told myself that she was going on woman's instinct and that I wouldn't pay any more attention to what she said, but, ten minutes after we got to the old house, I hunted up Rourke and begged him to go away from there.

He listened to me with his head canted to one side and his eyes on the distance, and, when I got through, he waited for a time. I felt sorry for him. I knew that he was taking what I said seriously. Then he leaned forward and touched my knee.

"Johnny," he said to me, "this afternoon, she smiled at me."

I waited for what else was going to come out after a fool remark like that, but he was silent again, until he finally said: "I watched Mimi"—that was the cat—"stalking a couple of birds in the patio. She couldn't catch them. I shot them and gave them to her. She was sitting in the corner. . . ."

"Mimi?" I asked him.

"Miss Mornay," he said. "And I put the birds down before her. . . ."

"Miss Mornay?" I said.

"The cat," he said. "Then she smiled."

"Mimi?" I asked.

"Damnation! No! She smiled, and put her book down. She put her book down and smiled at me. Then she stretched out her hand a little. The sun fell on it and shone through it and made it white and pink. . . ." He half closed his eyes, remembering.

"After she shook hands," I said, "did she congratulate you on the shooting?"

"You got no sense," said Rourke. "She didn't shake hands. She was only making a gesture. And then she said . . . 'How kind you are to me and to poor, dear Mimi.'"

"Poor, dear Mimi ate the birds, I guess?" I said. "But now look here. This is the point. I've got it from the inside that somebody is going to eat *you*, if you stay around here much longer."

He said to me gravely: "Lemme tell you something, Johnny. It's possible to live more in five minutes sometimes, than it is to live in six months other times. Every day, here . . . I tell you what . . . I'm travelin' into strange countries . . . I see things. . . ."

"You talk like a drunk," I told him, and got up

and turned away just as Palliser sang out from his room with a roar, calling for me.

I went up to him. He had a wheelchair made of cane, light and strong, and with that chair he could get around his room wonderfully fast and easy. He was backing it from the window when I came through the door, and, as he heard me, he gave the chair a spin and faced me. A soldier couldn't make an about-face any more neatly. He wanted to play pinochle, which we often did at the tail end of a day, and so I got out the cards and pulled up a small table in front of him, straddling his legs. We never played for big stakes, but he had the luck of the devil and he won my money about as fast as I was making it. He never picked up less than a pinochle, or a card that filled a sequence. That afternoon he started in by bidding 350 twice in a row, and the second time, after his pick up, he could meld 320.

I said: "What do you do to these cards? I never saw such luck!"

"It's not luck," said Palliser.

"What is it?" I asked. "You can make a dog come when you whistle, and my Pinto horse will do tricks for you, too, and so will Rags"—he was standing on the back of my chair and my shoulder, at that minute—"but can you talk to the cards?"

Palliser grinned until his beard stuck out like a porcupine's tail. "They used to say on the clipper ships that some captains had all the luck. But it's no way possible that a skipper can have luck ten voyages in a row. Only, him that plays the winds like he knew their first names, he gets them in his pocket at the right times. Going down to Anjers from the China coast, they used to cuss the light winds, but I never made a bad passage. And coming east around Cape Stiff, I've heard of ships held up for a month.

Because they was afraid of the teeth of the Horn, I tell you! But I used to press in, carry on, and press in again, and I never was a day off Cape Stiff without logging something. Pinochle isn't a sailing ship, but it's the same idea. You take the right chances . . . and you're bound to go right."

"Sure," I said, "if you know which chances are right. That's the easiest answer in the world."

He only laughed at me, his tobacco-stained lips gaping out of all shape of a mouth, and his yellow fang showing, and his black beard spreading. "I could teach you . . . on a ship," he said. "I could teach you on ship, mister."

There was hell in his eyes, and I could see that hell was what he must have served out aboard his ships, and plenty of belaying pin soup. Thinking of that, I reminded him that he never had told me how he was shot in the back.

He said: "Because I followed a young man's calling when I was too old for it. That was why I was shot in the back. Then I knew that I was finished with the sea. I come to try my luck on land, eh?"

"You've got enough left for pinochle," I told him, and just then something flashed through the window and clinked loudly on the floor. It lay right in the middle of the sun patch on the floor, blinding bright, so that I couldn't make out what it was. Only by straining my eyes, I saw that it was a silver coin about the spread of a dollar.

"What damn' monkeyshines is this?" asked Palliser of his beard.

I got up and made to stoop and pick up the coin when all at once Palliser let out a yell and knocked the table over. "Get out of here!" he shouted at me, and, as I jumped back, he shot his chair across to the sun patch, and scooped the coin off the floor. He held it in his hand and read the face of it for a long moment, and then he looked up at me with his lips twitching and his eyes like the eyes of a mad dog. "Did you do this, mister?" he said to me. "Oh, damn your lights, did you do this?"

He rolled his chair a little toward me, stealing up on me, as you might say, and there was something about that cripple that turned my heart to water and made me back toward the door. I told him that I didn't know how the thing had come there, unless it had been thrown through the window.

"Through the window!" he gasped. "Aye, aye. To the window, mister, and see what craft is in the offing."

I ran to the window, but there was nothing beneath it except a lame mule in the nearest corral.

# Chapter 11

When I told Palliser that there was no one in sight, he damned me in a terrible rage and said that I was a lumphead and a fool, and ordered me to go down and search around the house. But when I went to the door, glad to get away from him, he called me back.

"It's no use," said Palliser. "You'll never find him, because there's bound to be some hole that he'd crawl into. Below or aloft, he'd find some sort of a shelter, I know! Stay here with me. Stay here with me. Oh, God, oh, God!"

I thought he was going to die of a stroke, his face was so swollen and darkened with congested blood that made his eyes thrust out and turned his lips to a swollen, purple-gray.

"I have to lie down," he said. "I ought to be let bleed. Are you man enough to do that for me, mister?"

He stammered this out in a voice turned weak and husky, and I thought again that there was not much life in him. I told him that I was no doctor or surgeon, but I pushed his chair over beside his bed and helped him into it. His great thick arms had lost their strength; they sagged and buckled under his weight and I had to lift with all my might to stretch him on the bed. However, it was managed, and he lay like a cross, with his arms thrown out wide, opening and closing his bulging eyes, and breathing with a groan.

He could only gasp out: "Don't leave me, mister. Mind the helm and keep a lookout . . . squall . . . soon blow over . . . God! God!"

He kept on repeating that word several times, in such an agony that it made me sweat to listen to him. I poured some water from a pitcher on his dressing stand onto a towel. With that I swabbed his face and throat and hairy chest, and then fanned him.

He turned gradually from purple to a bright crimson. His whole big body began to shake and jerk, and every now and then he clutched his big hands into fists. I told him that I wouldn't leave him. I reassured him several times, and he, at last, seemed to comprehend and turned his eyes on me with what he intended for a smile, I have no doubt. It was a terrific grimace.

After a little time he began to recover himself, not suddenly or completely, but enough to speak, and this he did rapidly, keeping his speech almost entirely to a whisper. It gave an unpleasant hissing sound. His lips writhed. His eyes still were bulging horribly.

He wanted a rifle placed in easy grip of him. He had me bring him a double-barreled shotgun, which he loaded almost to the muzzle with big shot and iron scrap. There was a club, too, that was big enough for a giant, a big, curved, Oriental-looking knife, and a pair of new .45 Colts. When he had this little armory around him, he seemed to feel better still. He dragged a fresh pillow under his head with hands that still shook a good deal, and had me pull out the foot of his bed so that he was able to look at all of the doors and windows that opened into his room without much difficulty. The number of these troubled him, however, and he cursed under his breath even while he lay there choking with fear and the shock he'd endured. He swore that he would have one door and one window bricked up, but no sooner had he said this than he threw up his hands toward the ceiling and groaned in a low and rapid voice: "It makes no difference! If they've come here, they'll still come on till they get me. They'd burrow under walls ... they'd fly through the air like birds ... they'd blow poison at me ... but some way they'll come at me!" This excited him still more. He heaved his bulk up on one elbow and took a fresh, hard grip on the shotgun.

"If they come, there's enough juice in this to wash half a dozen of them to hell. You range around outside, mister. Range around and, mind you, if you see a man with a nautical walk ... a sort of a roll in his step, like the ground was bucking a bit beneath him ... don't you fail to up and drop him. I've heard how you can shoot. Mister, I'll pay you by the head."

He seemed to see that didn't please me very much, and, as I stood by the bed, he took my arm with his great, sprawling, trembling hand and half panting and groaning, half whispering and whining, he said to me: "You'll think that I'm a devil, mister, but I've got a place for you in mind. I've got a memory for you in my heart. And besides that, I've got money in my pocket! Whist! Jones!" He winked at me and grinned all on one side of his face. Then he whispered: "Be straight and true to me, and I'll make a rich man of you."

I told him that I'd do my best for him for $100 a month and that he didn't need to bribe me—I was being paid enough already.

Then the old devil fell into another change of mind and bellowed like thunder at me: "Then why don't you get out and search the ground for me? It ain't an angel that threw the . . . the thing in at me! It's a man, and a man wearin' sea boots, most likely. Get out of here, you fool, and show me that you can work for your grub and your pay."

I was very glad to get out of that room. Mind you, I was sorry for him, but it seemed to me that the accumulated badness of years was breaking out through his skin, so to speak. Poison of his own brewing was curdling his blood and turning it black in his face.

I hurried out of the room and ran down the steps into the patio, a long flight with a turn that doubled back and brought you down the two stories to the patio level. As I got down lower, I could hear the voice of the skipper booming out behind me with a melancholy roar, like a foghorn: "Frances! Frances!"

She was there in the patio before me as I stepped from the stairs, and, at the sight of me, she dropped her book and leaned forward in her chair, listening to old Palliser calling and looking too afraid to answer him. Mimi, the golden cat, saw Rags galloping at my heels and sprang up to the back of the chair and stood there with her back arched and her tail sticking straight up. Her violet eyes were green with fear of that little devil dog, and it seemed to me that the eyes of Frances Mornay were green with fear, too. It made one of those beautiful pictures of her that are lodged in my mind, put away like treasures that can be taken out and wondered at.

She laid a hand on her breast to quiet her heart. "Oh, what have you done to him?" she said to me.

"You'd better go up to him," I told her. "He's had a little shock, sort of, but he's better now."

She flashed out of the chair and raced up the stairs with Mimi still in her arms, and a blue kind of a wrap streaming out from her shoulders. I watched her, as I'd watched an antelope while I lay in the tall grass and it didn't dream it was being observed. At the top of the stairs, I remember that the sun flashed on her, so that her head seemed clad in flames as she stepped into the room of Palliser. At the same time, when she had a sight of Palliser, I heard her cry of fright and sympathy. She could not make an ugly gesture or sound; that outcry of hers was like the coo of a dove beating down softly to me, and I waited there in the courtyard for a moment filled with the thought of her beauty and her grace, like the sweetness of a rose garden after a summer rain. By her empty chair lay a handkerchief like a wisp of mist, and a book in Italian face down—something about a Borgia. It was a touch like the prick of a knife, that title. It made me wonder how long a girl as delicate and good as Frances Mornay would have lasted back there in the good old days of Italian murder.

Then I went outside and took a look at the mountains. There was something about their hard lines, and something in the keen mountain air that lifted the thought of Frances Mornay from my mind, and I was very glad of that. Let Rourke stifle in her beauty. I preferred to keep outside of the dream.

All about the western wing, where Palliser's room was, I searched the ground for the slightest sign of man or of beast, but I found nothing. You must understand that part of the western wing, also, had fallen down, as I said before, and there was a scattering of disjointed or broken stones lying about. I went around to the southern slopes, which fell away sharply, littered with the ruins of half of the big old house, and here I found nothing again except a bright, little circle of wire. I picked it up. It was piano wire, thin as hair and strong as the devil, and I wondered a little how it could have come to a place like this, lying among the rocks. However, I knew that it was used a lot for different sorts of things—picture hanging, for one thing. It was so flexible that anything could be done with it, and I stowed it away in my pocket; I might have a use for it personally, one of these days. Well, thank God, that I didn't guess what it was to lead to before so many days. It seems to me that in that time I was wading through a thick fog, not knowing whether the moon or the sun was shining above me, not guessing at the devilishness that was under my feet, walking in my shadow.

I did my work as well as I could, wishing that Rags could tell me whatever information he was picking off the rocks with that keen nose of his. Then I straightened up and stared about me, actually half expecting to see a man in sailor's trousers that fan out at the bottom, and walking with an ambling sort of step.

But there was no one in sight, of course. I wasn't even very sure what a sailor's walk was like. But yonder in the corral, I saw Dorgan, the big teamster, trying to ride a mule without a saddle on it, and it was so funny that I forgot everything about the sailor, and the piece of silver money—if it *was* money—and I went over and sat on the edge of the stone wall that fenced the corral and watched, and bellowed with laughter, while Dorgan cussed and raged and swore that he *would* ride the beast. But a snake is not much slipperier than a bucking mule, and this one went through Dorgan's hands and legs with no trouble at all.

"Ride him yourself, and be damned," said Dorgan.

It wasn't hard. All you needed was to be in practice. A mule is so narrow forward that it don't give you much hold. However, I soon had that gray devil tame and Dorgan got on her in turn.

"Now where are you going to take her?" I asked him.

"Why . . . I dunno," said Dorgan.

"Why did you get on her, then?"

"Why," said Dorgan, scratching his head, "it just come into my mind that it was something to do."

I went off, laughing. Teamsters, by and large, are a funny lot.

# Chapter 12

I wondered a good deal, of course, what wickedness old Palliser had been up to in his days at sea, but, whatever it was, I could guess that the throwing of that bit of silver into his room he had taken as a warning that death was straight ahead of him. I pitied him a little, not that I thought he was innocent of any crime, for he had the devil printed on his face in capital letters too big to be doubted, but because he was only a fraction of what he used to be. When the lower half of him had matched the torso, he must have been a giant and, even at his years, a tough one to tackle; I thought that the right end for him was on the poop of some clipper as old and as famous as himself, fighting through the smoke of the sea off Cape Stiff. But here he was, like a stranded ship, all his strength tied up and useless.

I saw Ruth Derrick cutting for the stable just then, and I went out there with her and saddled Pinto and another horse I fixed for her, a neat little bay that she liked to ride.

We rode straight up the slope through the rocks and brush, with Rags bobbing around us until he spotted a deer trail and took us down it. Not a mile from the house, that deer roused out of a hollow fifty yards from us; there wasn't time to unlimber my rifle, but I stuck a lucky revolver shot through his left shoulder and we had him. We skinned him and worked him up on the spot and loaded him onto Pinto. Ruth rode back, and I walked, leading my mustang, the distance was so short and all downhill.

The redhead was feeling pretty good after the hunt. She'd had her own rifle ready and dusted in a couple of shots when the deer jumped up. She thought it was one of her bullets that dropped the stag, so, when I came to my own slug on the far side of the carcass, smashed and flattened a bit by hitting the bones, I cut it out and gave it to her, and told her to keep it as a memento of her first deer.

She didn't know the difference. She was as proud as you please, and she chattered all the way down the hill. She even started giving me a little advice about always having my rifle ready for a shot.

Girls are like children. They only grow up in spots, and the other spots stay young till they're seventy. That's why there's so much freshness about some old women, but men are more apt to ripen all through and then dry up—or rot!

While she was in this fine good humor, I took her bridle rein, all at once, and stopped her bay. I simply said: "Ruth, tell me the straight of it . . . what do you know that makes things so serious for Rourke?"

She stared at me a little, and then the tears rushed into her eyes, which surprised me a good deal. "I won't talk to you," she said. "You've got no right to ask me. I . . . I wish I'd never spoken to you in my life before!" She jerked the rein out of my hand and spurred her bay past me, and went lickety-split for the stable down the slope, dodging along through the rocks until I thought that she'd fall and break her neck. I almost wished that she would, I was so angry, but the anger didn't last very long with me, because I liked that girl right down to the soles of my boots. She was the right kind.

If she had been any bit less sensible, I wouldn't have paid so much attention to her and to her ideas, but it seemed to me worth a lot of notice when the sort of a person she was got half an inch from hysterics on two days' running, about the same subject.

I wandered on slowly down the hill, with Pinto coming a good distance behind me, picking his steps with a good deal of care, because he was a lazy little devil and would waste a lot of time finding the easiest way over every trail, up or down. Now as I looked off the hillside into the northern hollow, I saw a rider come out from a batch of trees and move off toward another grove of pines. The minute I saw him, I knew that he was a stranger. The reason I knew it was not his clothes, but the fine gray horse that he was riding. One flash at the amount of daylight under that animal, and I knew that it had fine blood, hot blood. None of the ragged Mexicans we had glimpses of from time to time would own such an animal as that. They would rather own a little troop of half-wild mustangs and change saddles three times a day than sink all their money into one speedster. Perhaps they were right.

Well, what seemed to me strange was that this white man—since he had to be one—was now heading toward the house, instead of away from it. I shouted out, and, as my voice went booming down into the hollow, he jerked his head around and looked up at me. All that I made out under the wide sweep of his hat was that his face was all shadowed with unshaven beard. When he saw me, he sank spurs into the flanks of the gray and scooted for the woods ahead of him. That didn't look honest. Either he was a crook or a fool to run for cover before he had to, and so I tried a couple of long-distance shots with my six-shooter, not in any hope of hitting him—but it still pleased me a good deal to take those cracks at him.

The minute he was out of the way, I realized what I had tried to do, and it stunned me. Perhaps I haven't given you a fair picture of me, talking about Rourke and the exciting things that had been happening. Perhaps you may have thought that I'm one of those frontier warriors, which I'm not, but always a law-abiding man, I thank God, and always will be till my death in bed. In fact, I'd never stepped over the boundaries far enough to be noticeable. Yet here I was taking a couple of cracks at a stray man on horseback that I never had seen before and that never had done me any kind of harm at all. It staggered me and made me feel rather sick. I went back to that house with all curiosity about the stranger on the gray wiped out of my mind, and a sick feeling about myself, instead.

I unloaded the venison at the kitchen entrance, and Wong, the cook, came out and looked at the meat, and lifted each piece and nodded, and sniffed at it. He didn't look like a Chinaman; he looked like a prize fighter with a skin turned yellow with dye, except that his face didn't grow much hair. He had had smallpox, too, and that hadn't improved his looks much. He was a fine cook, but to me he was a Chinaman—that's all.

I asked him how Palliser was, and he said—"Velly seek! Velly seek!"—jerking his eyes and his hands up as he spoke.

"He'll get well," I said.

Wong drew in his breath through his teeth with a sucking sound. "Wong 'fraid Misler Palliser go away," he said.

He meant "die," of course, and the way he said it made me understand that his heart wouldn't be broken if Palliser should pass on. I asked him what he had against the old skipper, and Wong got terribly excited, telling me that he had nothing against Palliser at all, that Palliser was a very fine gentleman, and a great man, and that he, Wong, loved him like a father, and a lot more stuff. He chattered and chattered, until his pigtail was bobbing from one side to the other, and he followed me a few steps from the house when I went back toward the barn.

If the yellow-skinned idiot hadn't protested so much, I wouldn't have thought a thing about him, but he talked so hard and fast to make out that Palliser was his father or his grandfather and that he loved and honored the old man, that I couldn't help seeing something was wrong. If I hadn't seen how Palliser was bowled over by sudden shock, I would have thought right away that Wong had poisoned his soup for him.

I jotted Wong and his talk down in my mind, and determined that I would try to draw out of Palliser what grudge the Chinaman could have against him, and then I took Pinto over to the barn. Neither of the Mexicans was around—it was their job to put up the horses and feed and water them—so I looked around the end of the building and saw the pair of them chucking knives at a block of fresh sugar pine, so soft that half the blade sank in when they scored a hit. They were pretty accurate. I've heard that Italians can do these knife tricks, also, but I know that

Mexicans can be wizards with cold steel. If they'd give up guns altogether at close quarters and stick to knives, they'd be the most feared barroom fighters in the world. Of this pair, José, the oldest, was a good deal the best. He laid the knife on the palm of his hand and shied it at the mark with a flick of his wrist, an overhand movement that turned the heavy blade into a gleam of light. That gleam always turned into a knife half buried in the center of the wooden block and humming like a big hornet. I admired that knife work for a while before I gave them Pinto to put up.

I said to José: "You could go on the stage and make money, the way you chuck a knife."

He showed me the white of his teeth and the whites of his eyes. "It is better to have sharp knives in this house, *señor*," he said.

"I suppose it's better to have sharp knives anywhere," I told him. "Why particularly here?"

José kept smiling, but there wasn't any good humor in his eyes. He said: "The *señor* knows that it is the habit of people in this house to die by the knife?"

I told him that I knew nothing about it, and he bowed a little to me—Mexicans always have more manners than they need—and said: "Ah, yes, *señor*, ever since the ghost of the lady began to walk."

Ghosts—knives—that sort of truck struck me as being so Mexican that I didn't talk any more about it, but turned away and went back to the house, because I've noticed that every Mexican can fill you up with wonders if he has half a chance, and, while you may not believe in them, they stick in the corner of your mind and make a chill go up your back after dark when you go through unlighted doorways.

However, I wished afterward that I had gotten the story out of José, because then I shouldn't have made such a purple idiot of myself.

We ate in the patio that evening. I say "we" because from the first, Rourke and me had sat in with the rest of the "family." This night, Frances Mornay insisted on having the table set out in the patio, so that she could be nearer to old Palliser. He was still feeling so down that he didn't want to come to the table. During the dinner it was a fine thing to see how that girl would keep rising and flashing up the stairs and floating down again, bringing him pleasant bits to eat—fruit and such, you understand. After she went into his room, we would hear his voice come out in a booming laughter—he loved her so that she could have made him happy on his deathbed.

It disturbed me a good deal, that thought, and Rourke seemed to have the same idea, because he looked after her in a more moon-calf way than ever before. I was ashamed of him.

There wasn't much talk that evening. Shirley never had much to say. Cattrin was the chatterer, and he seemed glum and blue this evening, although I'm sure that the fellow didn't care about a soul in the world except his own pink, soft, puffy self.

Ruth Derrick was worried and silent because Frances Mornay was worried and silent. It was because I wanted to fill up a gap in the talk and bring up a new subject that I said after a while: "Is it a winter or a summer ghost that you have in this house?"

At that, Cattrin barked out: "Great guns!"

Shirley raised up his fallen head and glowered at

me, and the redhead jumped up and ran around the table to Frances Mornay.

It was as if I had shot that beautiful girl through the heart. She gripped the edge of the table, turned pale, and her eyes were deep shadows looking at me sadly, as though she wondered what reason I had for striking her down.

Then she said in her gentle way that she thought she would go up and see how "Uncle Ned" was—that was what she called Palliser. Ruth Derrick went along with her and helped her slowly up the stairs. The men all stared at me, but no one said a word until Ruth ran back down the steps and came to the table. She looked a hole in me hotter than any burning glass could make, and then she sat down to her coffee, but I knew that she wouldn't keep silent long. She had so many words in her that she would have exploded if she'd kept them back.

# Chapter 13

It was a warm, fine evening, with a quiet breeze puffing at us through the patio gate and stirring up our hair on end. The stars were out and drifting slowly toward the west, and Cattrin suddenly began to make talk about them. He was such a nervous lizard that he couldn't bear even the anger that was turning the girl white. He had to say something to smooth things out, so he began to make some remarks about a bright little star he said was Altair, up in the middle of the blackness.

The redhead broke right into the middle of one of his sentences. She said to me: "If there's no sense in you, there might be a little shame."

"Red," I answered her, "the fact is that I didn't know I was stepping on any corns."

"*Humph!*" said Shirley.

"You might've shut up till you found out where you were stepping!" Rourke said, cold as ice.

I looked at him, and he looked back at me while he stirred sugar into his coffee, lump after lump. I was pretty miserable, but I couldn't help having a sort of absent-minded curiosity about whether he would turn that coffee into a thick syrup or not.

"I never heard anything about it before this evening," I told them.

Shirley rarely said anything, but he sank a knife in me now. He said: "Some people are that way. They have to be talking about the last thing that's come into their heads."

I was too down-hearted to take any mean notice of this. Rourke was back on my shoulders again, saying: "Tact is what he's got! Tact and a fine polite manner. Not even sense enough to apologize after he seen that he'd knocked her down. My God, Jones, when'll you grow up into a man?"

The redhead put the finishing touch. "She was shaking like a leaf," she said. "She was shaking like a leaf, poor child . . . but . . . listen."

Out from Palliser's room came his booming laugh down to us, and that fairly made me sick, I tell you. Because it showed that she'd put down her own nerves, weak as she was, and was pouring out her heart's blood, as you might say, trying to cheer up that old sea pirate. It made a pretty picture of me, like I'd made a Christian martyr of somebody.

I said: "I'm sorry. God knows that I didn't mean to hurt her."

"Of course not! Of course not!" chirped Cattrin.

Rourke jerked around in his chair. "Shut up, you damned . . . canary!" he said.

That silenced everybody, just as though a tray of fine china had been dropped with a crash. When we looked at Rourke, we could see the top of his coffee tossed into little bright waves under the lantern light as he raised the cup to his lips. We knew by that his hand was quivering a little, and that meant a great deal to us, for ordinarily a rattler is more nervous than Rourke. He was nervous with fighting madness, and we all knew it, and there was hardly a breath drawn around that table for a minute. It was the redhead who saw what to do, and who did it. She started by saying that she would tell the whole story about the ghost, since the subject had been brought up—just so that all of us would understand how to avoid the subject, hereafter, when Frances Mornay was around. The story she told went something like this:

The first Mornay was called Carvajal. Here Rourke broke in to say: "Mexican . . . it ain't possible!"

"Mostly Castilian, of course," said Ruth Derrick. But Rourke was so hard hit that his mouth sagged open. I didn't feel very happy, either, to think that kind of blood was even a shadow in Frances Mornay.

This Carvajal came up to this neck of the woods when Mexico, of course, owned the whole Southwest. Here he made a little money out of silver mines, and a good deal more out of ranging cattle and selling their hides, and tallow, and whatnot. (Think of butchering cattle for the sake of their hides alone.) And out of his hosts of cattle, he got pretty rich, so that he would spend only about half of the time up here at his house in the north, and the rest of the time he spent in Mexico City among the swells, spending his coin like a prince.

He had a daughter named Anna, and this girl fell in love with an American. Americans never have been very popular south of the Rio Grande, and old Carvajal forbade his daughter to marry the *gringo*. She was a gentle, soft sort of a child, but that's just the kind that may love the hardest, and she up and ran away with the American. They lived a pretty hard life. Finally Carvajal sent word that he would forgive them and give them this house to live in. They came here, and the old devil Carvajal Mornay finished off the American husband on the very first night.

He sent in one of those Mexican knife artists of his, and the bright lad split the heart of the *gringo* at the first lick. Poor Anna woke up and found a dead man beside her in the bed. She pulled the knife out of the wound and went in her nightgown down the hall and into the room of her father. It was the very room that Palliser now was sleeping in. She walked into that room, and the old man woke up and screamed, when he saw the knife in the girl's hand.

But she didn't intend to do justice on his damned miserable heart. She stabbed herself, instead, and died in his arms, with Carvajal yelling to her that if she would come back to life, he would kill himself in her place, and swearing to build churches and whatnot, if she would lift the curse off the family. For it seems that she had dropped a large and liberal curse on the whole Mornay line.

That was a cheerful little yarn, and I didn't wonder that the poor girl had had a shock, especially when I heard the aftermath. This curse of Anna's didn't work at all, in most places, but whenever the Mornays tried to live in this house, they had a death mighty *pronto*.

The first one to have the bad luck was William Mornay, who was a son of Carvajal. By this time, the States had fought and won the Mexican War, and therefore they owned the land where this house stood. William took an American name, became an American citizen, and that was the end of Mexico as far as the Mornays were concerned. But it was the end of William, too. A month after he moved north to this place, American name and all, he was stabbed in the heart, and it was said that the ghost of Anna walked that night, although, of course, the story hardly said that she did the knife work even though she carried one.

Taken in connection with the story of the curse, this death of William Mornay had a great effect for a number of years, but, after a time, there was a hardier young Mornay who came out to build up the fallen-down house and begin to cultivate this fine valley. This fellow lived in the house without coming to harm for about a month, and, at the end of that time, he died exactly the way William Mornay had died before him. His name was Peter.

Now, as I listened to this yarn, I'm ashamed to say that it thickened up my blood a bit with cold. I haven't a superstition in the world, but Ruth Derrick, talking on in her downright way, with a lot of facts and figures about her story, made it all seem extremely real.

I grew nervous, even sitting there with all of those people about me. I couldn't help looking over my shoulder. Fat-faced Cattrin was having the quakes, shifting in his chair, and shrugging his shoulders hard, now and again. Shirley seemed in a trance, and Rourke sat stiffer and stiffer in his chair.

Rourke said in a crisp, quick voice, after a time: "Where is the ghost supposed to walk?"

Ruth Derrick turned in her chair and she pointed to the ridge of rough-edged wall that ran from the main body of the house past the patio on the south side, and toward the room of old Palliser. It gave me a second shock. My imagination was stirred up to such a point that, on my honor, I half expected to see a form in white come gliding out of the shadows with the glimmer of a knife in her hand and go over rough and smooth along the top of that wall to the captain's door.

Rourke had another idea, and that was more to the point and a good deal more ugly than mine. He said: "Is Palliser a Mornay?"

"No," said Ruth Derrick.

"There's no Mornay here except Frances Mornay," said Rourke. "Do you understand what that means?"

# Chapter 14

There could not have been a more grisly moment than this. It's hard to convey exactly the effect that words may have, but I'd ask you to keep in mind the house, and the time of the night, and the loneliness of those mountains, and the pale stars over us, and above all the terribly moved voice in which Rourke spoke.

Most barking dogs have very little bite, but Rourke was not the barking kind, and even a half-wit could have told, in one glance at his wild and beautiful face, that he was a man, and a damned dangerous one. No professor of philosophy who knows all about ghosts could have heard Rourke speak like this without having his breath snatched away from him. And after Rourke stopped talking, we listened to the hushing of the fountain, the pipe of which had been repaired just that morning, so that now it was throwing up a spray into the starlight.

We all looked at each other and got very little comfort by what we saw. I know what was in my mind—I could wager what was in the mind of the other people at the table. I didn't have long to wait in order to have my guess turn out right, for this fellow Shirley—I'd never liked him very well—stiffened up in his chair and laid his hand on the edge of the table.

He said in a very low, murmuring sort of a voice: "I want to speak out the thing that's in my mind. I don't want to make a scene, and I'm afraid that a good many of you will think that I'm making a fool out of myself, but, nevertheless, I have to speak out. I've known of the story about the ghost for a long time. I'm not a believer in that sort of thing. Not a bit of it. But I want to point out a few things to you.

"Frances Mornay and her uncle came up to this place to be cured by the purity of the mountain air. I know why they came. It was because Captain Palliser insisted. I know and can prove to you that Frances never wanted to come. She knew the legend, and she was afraid of it. But Palliser thought that it was a shame for this property to go to waste, and he declared that he would come here if he had to die on the way. Besides, when he saw that Frances was an invalid, he insisted all the more that the mountain air would do her good. And so she came with him. She was never the one to let her fears or her wishes interfere with other people."

His voice began to shake so much that he had to stop for an instant, and yet I wasn't ashamed to look him in the face, for that moment I was respecting him more than I'd ever respected him before, and I could almost understand, for the first time, how Frances Mornay might have seen in this fellow enough to make her want to marry him.

After a little moment he was able to continue. Then he said: "It seems to me that I have felt a fate hanging over this party from the beginning of the trip. We have found good men and true men to help us. . . ." Here he paused and he looked straight at me, and then at Rourke, in a way that made my heart stir. "But," he said, "God knows that what is fated cannot be avoided. I hope you will not take me for a mystic. I am far from that. But I cannot help seeing that since we came into this house, Captain Palliser has failed rapidly. Tonight he cannot leave his bed." He made another pause here, his breast heaving so that everyone could notice it. Then he went on in a softer voice: "The other thing is still plainer to all of you, I know. God forgive me if I am wrong in saying that from day to day it appears to me that Frances is growing paler and paler."

I would rather that he had shouted it, wrangled it, yelled and argued it. But that quiet, broken, uncertain voice took the heart out of me completely.

Cattrin suddenly broke out with a gasp: "Oh, God, oh, God!"

Rourke shot out his hand and fastened it on Cattrin's shoulder. "Shut up," he said in a whisper.

Cattrin shut up, as though he had heard a gun click. In fact, Rourke was growing terribly excited. I was afraid that night. I was afraid of the grisly atmosphere that was gathering around this place. I was afraid of Rourke, too, and what might come of him. It's an ugly comparison, but I've seen a dog go mad, and Rourke was beginning to roll his eyes in an odd way.

I looked across at Ruth Derrick. She was shaking like a leaf, and all at once she covered her face with her hands—clutched at her face with her hands, as though she wanted to squeeze away into darkness the thoughts that were jumping through her mind.

Shirley finished off as quietly as he had been carrying on. He said: "My solemn feeling is that

Frances Mornay has not long to live in this place. Flowers love the sun. I propose that we suggest to her that we must all leave the house at once."

Rourke said harshly: "She never would go. She thinks it's for the good of Palliser, and she never would go. Never! She's gonna stay here and she's going to fight it out."

"And die," said Shirley softly.

Cattrin leaped up from the table, stammering and gasping. "I can't stand it!" he said. "I can't stand it. Do something, somebody. This . . . this talk is driving me crazy!"

"She never would go," said Ruth Derrick, "unless she were shocked into it."

"What sort of a shock?" asked Shirley almost sharply. "But better any sort of shock," he added, "than that she should stay here and wither away for the sake of . . . a buccaneer." He said it bitterly. It was the only time I ever had heard him lift his voice against Palliser, no matter how the old captain had been damning him.

Cattrin broke in with his usual frightened, fluttering way. "It's all very well to say this. But I suppose that you all know. Frances Mornay has to depend on Palliser for money to live on. His estate goes to her, you know. I don't want to interrupt with practical ideas, but if Palliser is disturbed by any. . . ."

Shirley said with a fine ring in his voice: "I'm not rich . . . I'm not a financial genius . . . but I thank God that I am able to support my wife." He said it almost as though she already were married to him, and Rourke turned green. "We'll think this matter over for a little while," said Shirley. "I know the kindness of everyone here. Afterwards, we'll talk, and see what decision we can come to."

That was very good sense.

That dinner was finished without another spoken word. Ruth Derrick, I remember, sat hunched in her chair, as though it were bitterly cold, and looked very white and thoughtful. She got up with a start, at last, and hurried away. Cattrin and Rourke followed her to bed, and, after a moment, Frances Mornay came down the steps from Palliser's room. She went up to Shirley and me and stopped at my chair.

She said: "Dear Uncle Ned has been telling me of your wonderful goodness and kindness to him. I'm afraid that he isn't the man who finds it easy to speak thanks. But I know you'll find that he feels what he won't speak. Will you let me thank you for him . . . please?"

She shook hands with me. I stood before her like a lump of stone, watching her gentle smile, and more aware of her as a human being than ever before—I mean to say, aware of her nearness—and the sense that she was made of flesh, and breathing the scent that was in her hair, like far-away flowers blown down by the wind.

She went off with Shirley, at once, and I saw her leaning heavily on his arm, and knew that she was pretty far spent.

I stood there staring at the blank, dark arch through which the two of them had gone, until I heard violin music begin. She had brought up a talking machine with nothing but violin records on it, and now a sweet and rather sad music went whistling from her room. I had heard it before on that machine, and the redhead said it was "The Meditation" from *Thaïs*. Which is an opera, said Ruth Derrick.

Now, as I listened to that thin, far-off music, and heard finally the rasp of the needle when it came to the end of the record, it struck me all at once that I was alone in this courtyard, and that the stars were pretty far away and dim—and suppose that the ghost of poor Anna Mornay should walk out from the house and float across on the top of the wall toward Captain Palliser's room? I was glad that no one could see me, then, because I backed out of that patio through the gateway, and I was glad to get clear of the house and find myself out in the open.

I felt better at once, with the sweet scent of the pine air in my nostrils, and the big, blunt outlines of the mountains before me. I had known such things—on the desert flats—all my life, and the sense of familiarity did me a lot of good. Only when I turned now and then, and looked back toward the big, black outline of the Mornay house, the chill came back on me. I went on slowly, stopping fairly often, because I had a guilty feeling all the time that I ought to be back there in the house, and yet, with all my might, I wanted to be free from it and far away from it. What urged me away was the feeling that something full of horror was about to break, back there in those big deep rooms. What urged me back was the thought that perhaps, if I were there, I could prevent its happening.

I don't suppose that I covered half a mile in half an hour of this interrupted strolling, and then I came to a sweep of big pines and walked down through them. They were pleasant to have about. They wouldn't walk by starlight, for one thing. Nor would they carry knives. I was just congratulating myself on this, when I came into a little clearing and saw before me the shadow of a horse. The shadow and the glimmer of a horse, I should say, because it was a light gray. I waited, frozen stiff. There was not a sound, and so I lighted a match and made sure that this was the same fine gray I had seen disappearing that evening. There were not apt to be two horses of that cut in these mountains. Where was the rider? Why, at the house, perhaps.

I only took note that the horse had on an English saddle instead of a range armchair. Then I turned and bolted for the house, and I got up to it in time to see a shadowy form, active as a monkey, swing up the western wall, and into a window of the captain's room!

# Chapter 15

I could give an alarm by shouting or shooting, but there was no use in that; the fellow was already in Palliser's room, and, if he wanted to work mischief, he would be pretty sure to manage it unless Palliser himself could stop him. I had a bit of confidence in that, remembering the clutch he kept on the sawed-off shotgun. With a hose that throws a broad spray, any child can hit a penny, and a sawed-off shotgun is like a hose that throws a spray.

It seemed to me that the best thing for me to attempt was to cut off the retreat of this prowler if I could. So I headed for the west wall of the house as fast as I could sprint. I unbuckled and dropped my gun belt and passed a Colt into my hip pocket, then I jerked off my boots and began to climb. The stranger had managed to get up this way, but, before I was half to the top, I wondered how he ever had managed it, because there were only the smallest crevices in which one could get a finger- or toehold. However, I had my hand on the sill of the window when I lost one foothold, and that gave my body a jerk that made the other hold slip. I swung by my left hand from the sill, and looked down at the scattered big stones that were at the base of the wall. However, my finger grip on that sill was strong, and I was able to bring up my right hand to it. I was beginning to draw myself up to the sill, bodily, when I heard Palliser break out in an excited muttering. That surprised me. I never before had known him even to try to keep his voice down. He ended, and another voice began, rapidly, so that I couldn't understand a word that was said. It kept on, coming up to a sort of climax of rapidity, breathing out whatever it was that he was saying.

Then Palliser cried out: "No, no, no! Oh, God, no!"

That was enough for me. I whipped through the window into that room and saw Palliser bolt upright in his bed with his big arms curled about his head, while the stranger still leaned beside his bed with the look of a man who has just made a great stroke. When they heard me enter, Palliser dropped his arms and the stranger leaped up and made a pass to get at a gun. But he saw that I had him covered, and his hand froze at his hip.

Palliser gasped at me, and then he bellowed to know what in hell I was doing there. I told him that I had seen a man swarm up the side of the wall and go in at his window, and therefore I simply had followed to see that no one harm had been done.

"No harm done? The harm's been done, right enough," said Palliser. "Ah, God . . . the harm's been done. Get out of here and leave me alone. Get out!"

I went to the door, pretty sad, and started to open it, when Palliser said: "You didn't see nobody here. You understand, mister? Not a soul but me."

I nodded and went out, and all the way down the

steps and back to my discarded boots I was so hot with anger that I kept muttering to myself. *After you've climbed a wall that would make even a fly dizzy, it's not so pleasant to be damned and ordered out of a place.* I was so mad that the last bit of fear was knocked out of me. I stamped into my boots and walked in across the patio, only asking for a ghost or anything else to give me a bit of trouble. And in the dark of the entrance arch, something pale moved before me. I didn't stop to give any challenge or to ask any questions. I simply went at that glimmering shape like a bulldog, and instantly had a woman in my arms.

The voice of the redhead gasped at my ear: "Are you trying to strangle me or to hug me?"

I let her drop with a jar and stepped back into the patio. She came after me, furious, and asked me if I thought that this was a cattle corral and if I were practicing bulldogging?

I said: "Red, I'm all tied up in knots. Leave me alone, will you?"

"You're all tied up in knots?" Red said. "But it's easy and plain sailing for the rest of us, isn't it?"

"I don't know," I told her. "But I'm going to bed and have a sleep on it."

"Ah, but I wish that I could," she said.

"You've got to persuade Frances Mornay to get out of here," I suggested. "No one can persuade her, except you."

"Haven't I been trying to, for an hour?" asked Ruth Derrick. "She won't listen to me. Suppose that she has to die, what does that matter if she dies doing her duty? She's about seven centuries behind times. She ought to have lived in the days when there was a good market for saints."

"Won't she listen to reason?" I asked.

"She sits and folds her hands and says . . . 'Ruth, darling, I don't want to keep you here while you feel like this. I'll send you back to town tomorrow, and you'll be free from this worry.' That's the way she talks to me. Listen!"

It was that same tune, but not on the talking machine, this time. Frances Mornay was playing it on her own violin, and a bang-up good job she made of it, too.

"What's wrong with that?" I asked.

"You listen. Hear the sobbing she's putting into it. She's getting herself all sad and ripe for dying. It makes me sick," said the redhead. "Why don't you do something? You're a man."

"If I could put my hands on something to do," I told her, "I'd do it. But everybody dodges around the corner and only tells some hint, here and there. What sort of progress can I make that way? *You* tell me what to do."

"I'll tell you," she said. "Go and ask the captain to finish his job and die while he's about it. That would end the waiting and let poor Frances go home."

"Shall I go up and murder him while he's lying in bed?" I asked her.

"Ah . . . well," she said, "that's the way to put it, I suppose. It keeps a man from going to prison . . . looking at things that way." She walked off into the dark beneath the arch and called back a good night over her shoulder, as though she hardly cared whether she ever saw me again, or not.

It made a mighty ugly impression on me. I don't mean to say that I seriously thought she was advising me to slaughter Palliser, but there was something ugly on her mind, and I felt it there.

I went on to the room that I shared with Rourke. He was lying on his face, and so I turned out the light I had made and slipped around soft and easy until I was in bed myself, with Rags lying on top of my knees. I don't know why he preferred to lie there where the bones were the hardest—maybe he hated to be too comfortable, but, anyway, there he was all night, hot or cold, and, if I shifted and turned, he shifted and turned, too. I couldn't shake him off. He rode those restless knees of mine the whole night long.

I barely was settled, and barely had told myself that I wouldn't waste my sleeping hours thinking things over, when the bed of Rourke creaked. Between me and the window, I saw him sit bolt upright.

He said: "Johnny!"

"Well?" I asked him.

"What do you think?" he asked.

"About what?"

"Hell!" said Rourke. "What's there to think about except one thing?"

"What thing is that? You mean the ghost?"

"Oh, damn the ghost. There ain't such things as ghosts. I mean . . . Palliser."

"I think Palliser's pretty sick," I told him.

"You know how sick he is better than the rest of us. How long will he last?"

"Why, I don't know."

"There's another thing."

"Go on, Denny."

"How long will Frances Mornay last?"

"Her? Why, a good many years, I suppose. She's young."

"Johnny, you know what I mean. She's up against murder, in this house."

I lay still, sweating, because I could see how his mind was drifting, and I didn't like what I saw. I didn't like it at all. But I thought it would be a good thing to draw him out. I asked: "Don't you figger that you're taking a lot for granted, old fellow? We've heard a ghost story, that's all."

"You know I don't believe in those things," he said. "But the point is that the Mornays in this house live short lives. That means that there's somebody around that gets rid of them. Well, there you are."

I waited again until he broke out: "What's to be done about it?"

"Why," I said, "what *can* we do, except to keep a close lookout?"

"A close lookout has been kept before," insisted Rourke, "and it didn't save any lives."

Then I said outright: "What's your solution?"

"Well . . . what keeps her here? The poor girl."

"You mean Palliser?"

"Of course!"

"I suppose that he does."

"Suppose that Palliser would hurry up and shuffle off?"

I was silent. It made me sick to hear him. "Rourke," I said at last, "for God's sake, don't keep thinking along that line."

He slipped out of his bed and touched my shoulder. "What do you think I mean?" he asked in a low, hard voice.

"You know what I think," I told him. "Now you go back to bed and forget this."

"Forget," said Rourke. "Forget." He laughed in a whisper.

I listened for him to begin to breathe regularly in sleep, but that time didn't come, and it flashed through me suddenly that he *wouldn't* sleep. He'd lie there awake all of the night and, for a nervous fellow like Rourke, that was worse than poison.

In spite of all my worries, however, in ten more seconds I was unconscious.

# Chapter 16

I woke up the next morning very late. Some people are lucky enough to sleep themselves out of trouble. They can put a fever or a toothache into a dream and leave it there; I'm one of those lucky men. When I got up that morning I felt a little empty-headed. The sun that was usually just turning the sky gray when I got up, was now sending a broad, yellow-white shaft of light through the window, and I hurried to dress and went out feeling guilty, I didn't know why.

Rags was twice himself, bounding around me like a ball and yipping a little. A pair of big, white butterflies was fluttering down low around the fountain in the patio, which glittered like cascades of broken diamonds, and Rags tried to catch them on the wing, and came back to me, shaking his head, but still ready for a lark.

I went around to the kitchen and got me a hand-out from Wong, the cook. Over in a corner of the kitchen, in the dark so that his eyes and teeth seemed brighter than ever, was José, and I thought it was a little strange that a Mexican and a Chinaman should be getting on so well together.

Wong gave me coffee and cold hotcakes, but he gave them with a glowering gloom, and wouldn't meet my eye. He looked more a prize fighter than ever, this morning. I asked him why he was such a sorehead on such a bright morning, but he only nodded at me as if he could tell me plenty of reasons, but they would be past my understanding. I watched him go across the room with the coffeepot, moving with an odd waddle, as though the floor were rising to meet his feet, and suddenly I remembered what Palliser had said about a sailor's walk.

"Wong," I said, "were you ever on a ship?"

He made a start as though he were going to turn sharp around on me. He gave such a start that I heard the coffee slop in the pot, but he checked himself from turning and slowly lifted the pot onto the stove while he told me that he never had been on the ocean; it was too wet and too gray to please him, he said.

When I heard that, I barked at him: "Then how'd you get over to this country, you damned, old, yellow-skinned liar, you!"

He slowly turned around from the stove, but only half toward me. Out of the corner of his eye he gave me a mean look and went back to the rolling out of some pan bread.

I'd heard enough from Mr. Wong to make me sure that the flat-faced devil had a past, and that a size-able chunk of that past had been spent at sea, and that the farther inland he could be now, the better he'd be pleased. Then I finished off my coffee and went out the door with a shadowy consciousness that both Wong and José were making faces behind my back. You nearly always can tell if there's something happening behind you, if ever you've keyed up your nerves.

I went around into the patio just as Frances Mornay came down the steps with her violin in her hand, and I asked her if she had cheered up the skipper with it.

"He didn't want to hear it this morning," she said. "I think that he'll be happier to talk to you. He's very fond of you, John Jones." She seemed about to go past me, and then paused and lingered for a moment. "What do you do that makes you so many friends?" she asked me.

"I don't know. Nothing," I said.

I never could find my tongue around her.

"Ruth and Uncle Ned, both," she said. Then she smiled at me as much as to say that she wished that she could be a third in my friendship. With my heart in my mouth, I watched her walking across the patio, graceful as a bird. I had noticed that she was paler, this morning, and her eyes seemed darker and larger, and her walk was very slow. I'd hardly taken seriously the way Shirley and Ruth Derrick had talked, but now I had a cold thrust of fear in my heart—suppose after all that something *did* happen to her here? There were things in old-time books I had read, about young girls going into declines, the beautiful and the best going most of all.

So I went up the stairs with lead in my heels, and came to the top. The door was locked, to my surprise. I knocked and Palliser boomed out: "Who's there?"

I answered, and heard the whisper of the rubber tires of his chair being wheeled over to the door. He opened it for me, and so I walked in and saw the old

Tartar sitting up with his armory of guns littered over his lap.

He backed his chair away from me, always keeping a grim eye on my face, and with a hand ready on the butt of that shotgun of his.

"I'm not going to jump you," I couldn't help saying.

"Take a look down in the courtyard," he said.

I did as he told me.

"Is there anybody there?"

"Only Cattrin," I told him.

"Damn his heart," said Palliser. "I hope he rots an ounce a day for ten thousand years. Come in . . . lock the door, and double-lock it!"

I did exactly as he told me, but I had a feeling that the old man was losing his mind. Certainly there was a wild glitter in his eyes when I looked at him again, and that black beard of his quivered and worked. I thought that I'd put him a little more right by bringing up a pleasant subject, and so I mentioned meeting Frances Mornay on the steps, but even that name, which usually lighted him up and softened him a good deal, now didn't have the slightest effect.

He said to me: "Jones, I'd bet one to five that you're honest . . . that you're a damn' honest man."

"Thanks," I said. "You'd win on that bet. You call that short odds, I suppose?"

"Shorter," said the captain, "than I'd ever have put on any man before I met up with you. Shorter, I mean, since the days when I was a young fool . . . as young as you." He laughed a little, but it wasn't actually more than a grimace.

"Thanks," I said. "You haven't had many to bank on, then, in your cruises."

"Oh, never a one, never a one, except I'd throwed the fear of the devil into 'em," said Palliser. "Not unless they thought that was the old devil himself back there on the poop, wearin' the black beard. But on board of a ship, you play no favorites and you take no chances, for the first chance that you take loses long knots for you, or else it lands you on the rocks. Oh, aye, once I took chances . . . I was a young man, then . . . I was a fool!" Then he changed his tone a little and barked at me to sit down, which I did. All at once he said: "Jones, about this here Cattrin . . . what would you say about him?"

It was like hearing a lion begin to exchange confidences about a mouse. I stared at him, and then I drew up the picture of Cattrin out of my mind again and examined the pink, soft face, and the mean, bright little eyes.

"I don't know," I said. "I never thought very much about him."

"Nothing about him?" he asked.

"Yes," I admitted. "One thing."

"And what was that, son?"

"Why, it ain't my business, so I'll leave it lay."

He roared at me, so angry that I couldn't make out the words, but he actually scared me into saying that I had thought it a little queer that a fellow like Shirley, a gentleman all the way through, should associate with a man like Cattrin.

"Ah!" said the skipper, breathing out long and hard. "You thought that, did you? Then you don't wear dark glasses, after all. Open that door and look around again."

I did as he said. The patio was empty, now, except where one of the *mozos* was watering the plants that had just been installed in the boxes along the walls. I came back and reported that.

"Maybe that's one of 'em," said the skipper beneath his breath.

"One of what?" I asked him.

"Stand by, stand by, you fool, till you're hailed," he said.

That shut me up, but I wasn't as offended as I might have been, because I could see that this old fox was working his way through a dark passage.

After this, old Palliser said to me: "You've used your eyes a little. What would you say, ordinarily, if you seen a pair like that together?"

I told him what I thought—that really it simply showed that Shirley was a simple sort of a fellow, and not very quick-sighted or quick-witted, so that he didn't have the least idea what a small and mean soul this Cattrin had. But, on the other hand, of course, it might be that Shirley himself wasn't all that I thought.

"Ha!" said Palliser. He sat back in his chair and his eyes burned at me.

So I said: "I'm not accusing him, Captain. You wanted to know everything that a man might think about it. Besides, I don't know anything really bad about Cattrin."

"You will before the day's over," said Palliser. "You can rest easy on that. You will before this here day is over, by God, or else the whole damn' top-hamper will be carried away. But there's gonna blow up a wind here, son."

I waited for him to say something more, but he seemed lost in his own thoughts, and so I finally said that he had wanted me to keep my eye out for a man who walked like a sailor, and I thought that I'd spotted him—the cook.

"Wong!" burst out Palliser. "By God, that might be. Wong!" He waved his great arm toward the door.

"Go and get Wong!" he said. "Drag him up here by his damn' pigtail. I'll have a look at him."

I hesitated. When he got excited, since his explosion of the other day, Palliser turned a decided purple that wasn't pleasant to look at. Purple and pink, at first, but now purple and gray, and it made his face look old and flabby. I wondered if I'd better bring Wong up, but Palliser damned me heartily and told me that I was to tell Wong that the captain wanted him to tell him how to make a kind of sea pudding.

# Chapter 17

I decided that the best thing I could do was not to try to think too much, but simply to do what I was ordered to do. So down I went to the kitchen and said: "Wong!"

He didn't look up from his work, and that made me mad, but I swallowed a couple of yards of my tongue and simply said: "Captain Palliser wants to see you. He wants to tell you how to make a seaman's pudding."

Wong raised his head so quickly that his pigtail jumped up behind his head like a snake. He stared at me, and I thought that there was a bright fear in the man's eyes. However, he nodded his head at me and came out of the kitchen, and went alongside of me with that waddling walk, and up the steps to the captain's room.

When he got inside the room, Palliser didn't wait half a second. He roared out: "What do you know about The Wanderer, you sneaking Chinese devil?"

Wong, when he heard that roar, let out a screech and leaped for the door. I was just closing it, but he burst it open with his shoulder and flew down the steps in two leaps, like a running dog.

Palliser was like a madman behind him, yelling out to shoot down the damned Chinaman and that he'd make me rich if I nailed him.

I don't think I could have done it, if I'd wanted to. Wong was down those stairs like a bird on the wing, and he kept on going in a streak across the patio, dodging as he ran. It was wonderful the way that Chinaman split himself, as he flashed through the gateway.

I followed him fairly fast, but I couldn't run in my boots the way that he could run in his slippers. When I turned the outside corner of the house, there was just a gleam of that snaky pigtail as Wong disappeared into the first patch of brush, and there was something about the way he flew that told me he wouldn't stop running until he'd busted the world's distance record clean in two.

I didn't follow on foot, but I saddled Pinto and skinned out after Wong, taking Rags along on the pommel of my saddle. That little devil would follow the trail of a man as soon as he'd follow the trail of a rat. I lost Wong's tracks a couple of times in the brush, and each time when I dropped Rags, he cut for sign and picked up the right way for me very *pronto*.

I came near leading me into a grave, that day. I had broken out of the woods onto a clear hillside with a nest of rocks in the middle of it, and, as I came on, a Colt began to bark. I could see the nose of the gun jumping and bucking beside one of those rocks, and a loose sleeve behind the gun, but the bullets were coming faster and closer than I cared for. I pulled Pinto's head, getting him back into the trees, and then I scurried him up the next gully and so over the hilltop just in time to see Wong breaking across the bottom of the hollow faster than a dog could run, I should say.

When he heard the hoofs of Pinto coming, he turned around with that screech of his and blazed away again, but he was so excited now that his aim was no good at all. He emptied his Colt, and I rode in on him and poked a gun under his yellow chin. He was scared to death, but he was more mad than scared. He cussed me with a fine flow of Pigeon English, but I walked him back across country for the house after I'd fanned him and taken away his guns and a mighty workman-like-looking knife.

When I dismounted at the gate of the patio, I ran into Ruth Derrick, and she stared, of course, to see the naked gun in my hand. You see, I wasn't taking no chances with any of these *jujitsu* fellows from the Far East.

She said: "Is this the way you get your morning exercise, Johnny?"

"Yes," I answered her. "And I learn my dancing steps dodging bullets."

I herded Wong up the steps to the door of the captain's room, and, when I got him there, I could see him wilt down a mite. Then he pulled himself up and together, and went slowly ahead, as though he were about to face a rifle. He stood back against the wall with his head down and his hands shoved into the alternate sleeves, and there he remained sulking.

Palliser stared at him with a devil in his big ugly face. And suddenly he began to chatter at him in a language I couldn't follow. It sounded like the singing of a mighty bad song, and Wong moistened his white lips, blinked at Palliser, and said nothing at all. This kept up for a few minutes. I could see that Palliser was asking one question after another.

He roared louder and louder, and finally he snatched up the shotgun. As sure as sin, he would have blown the Chinaman in two, because he had his fingers wrapped around both triggers of the gun, but he changed his mind just in time. He stared another minute at Wong, and then he waved to the door. Wong went slowly. In the middle of the doorway we saw him quake as though he'd been kicked from behind, and then he went on down the steps.

I closed the door and turned back to Palliser, who was grinning as though he were pretty well pleased with himself.

"He'll stay here, I guess," said the captain. "The yellow dog will stay here, I think. If he runs, he knows now that you can catch him. I never seen an unhappier Chinaman."

He grinned in his horrible way at the thought of it. Then he said: "But it ain't a thing to the unhappiness that lies there in front of him. I'm gonna make an example of him. He's been pryin' into corners . . . he's been pryin' into dark corners, Jones, and now he's gonna pay for it . . . unless he makes me pay first."

I didn't see how Palliser could have learned very much from Wong, since the captain had done all of the talking, but it was very clear that Palliser was fairly contented. He lighted a stinking, black pipe, and, while he smoked it, he looked more contented still. He said: "They've got everything in the pot by way of seasoning. They got the fire lighted and the water boiling, but they ain't yet landed the big fish to put in. They ain't got me yet, mister, and maybe they won't have me."

After this, he was silent for so long that I thought he was finished with me. There were a hundred questions that I wanted to ask. What or who was

The Wanderer, for instance? And who were "they" who had the pot boiling for the captain? In the midst of this guessing, I turned around and started for the door, thinking that he might be through with me, when he shouted to me to sit down again, which I did.

Palliser said: "Jones, it narrows down and narrows down. The rest I can't count on, but I can count on you. I gotta count on you."

I said: "You can count on me, Captain. I never double-crossed a man in my life, and it's late for me to start that kind of a business now."

He took nothing for granted, but looked me over very carefully. After a while he remarked: "Whether I want to or not, you're the best bit in a bad fry. Jones, even if you ain't got much sense, you can shoot quick and straight. Can anybody around here shoot any quicker or straighter?"

"Rourke," I told him. "But he'll be with me, no matter what."

"Bah!" said Palliser. "That shows that you have no brains at all. No more brains than a salmon." He repeated: "Rourke! He's like a mad dog. He'd like to take me by the throat."

"You're wrong," I said. "But let it go."

I couldn't help quitting that part of the argument, remembering how Rourke had talked the night before, and every moment my respect for Palliser was increasing—my respect for his brains, I mean, because it was plain that he was able to look through people pretty easily.

"There's you, and there's me," said Palliser, "and between us we may be able to work the game."

"What game?" I asked.

"The game of getting me out of this hell-hole!" he said.

That was the last thing in the world that I expected to hear. He was the anchor that was keeping poor Frances Mornay there. So I spoke up and said: "Why not broach the idea and get everybody moving, then? Nobody will stay here against your will. You were the one that brought the party up here, I suppose."

He looked at me with his bright, wicked, old eyes, and after a while he said: "You don't understand! You can't understand! And . . . by God, I ain't got it in me to explain. Only . . . Jones, will you help me to get away from here?"

"Are you in danger?" I asked him.

"Danger?" he boomed at me. Then he paused and checked his voice, and made it low, but still there was a rumble in it, like the echoing of a cannon from a distant hill. "Young man," said the captain, "I'm in mortal danger. They'd sell their hearts to carve me up. I tell you, they got the pot ready for me, and all the seasoning, and the water boiling . . . and all that they need is now to cut my throat."

He actually fingered beneath his beard, as though he were not quite sure that the mischief had not been done already. I felt my hair stir; my scalp was prickling with fear of him, and what might happen to him. But, after all, the main thing was that this old man was in danger . . . and he wasn't the sort to be wrong about it.

So I simply said: "If you want me, I'm with you to the finish. I'll help you all that I can."

"Good!" said the captain. "I expected something like that out of you. Well, then, son, we'll make a night march of it." I blinked a little, and he went on: "We'll start tonight, after dinner, and after everybody has turned in. They go to bed fairly early. Then you get that buckboard, as you call it, ready. Get several rifles on deck. Then come for me, and I'll go down with you. I can shift my own weight when I have to . . . as good as a spider." He laughed. "And suppose that they get me before night?" said Palliser thoughtfully. "Suppose that they get me before night. . . ." Without another word, he pushed the chair over to the table, took a pencil and paper, and wrote rapidly—wrote in that way for at least a half hour, his pencil shooting across the paper at a wonderful speed.

"If they get me before night . . . or on the breakaway, read that, my son, and then ride for a sheriff's posse!"

# Chapter 18

After I left the captain, there was one thing that I thought the strangest and that stuck in my mind the most—the fact that he had some sort of law on his side. Even if murder was done on him, somehow it seemed hardly likely he'd be able to complain, because if there wasn't a trail of dead men behind that sea shark, I was willing to eat any man's hat.

But I liked Palliser. I liked him because he was interesting, if you know what I mean. Everything about him was different from other men, and I could have sat and listened to him talking by the hour. Twenty times that day I felt of the big fat envelope that he had given to me, and I wished with all my might that I could be crooked enough to open it. There are ways of opening envelopes, I knew, chiefly by using steam that softens up the mucilage. But I held back. It wasn't exactly a sense of honor that held me up, but when the old man asked for that envelope the next day, if I had tampered with it, he would know just as a fox would know by the scent, if a strange animal had come into its lair.

This affair made me nervous. I was as impatient as

a cat for night to come. I was eager to make the start, and yet I was uneasy, too, for in a sense it would be letting down Rourke and the redhead, and, above all, it might be working some harm to beautiful Frances Mornay.

There was another shock due to us all, this same day. And it didn't come from Palliser, or Wong either.

As for Wong, I expected that he would light out as soon as he could—but he didn't. He stayed on in his kitchen and worked, and cooked up a boss lunch for us that made even Rourke come alive.

After lunch, I went out for a stroll in the woods, and I was picking up a branch of fallen pine to whittle on, and think, when I saw a shadow moving through the trees, and a horseman came out into plain view. This was a lean, hard-looking, weatherstained, sun-dried man from the desert. Nobody but a desert man would be as sun-dried as this. He was like a desert jack rabbit, all full of skin and bones and speed. He had eyes like the eyes of a bird—gray and small and extremely bright. These eyes he put on me, and immediately I wished that this fellow were on my side.

He said to me: "Top of the day to you."

"Hello, stranger," I said.

"Might you belong to the house?" he asked me.

"I been seen there," I told him.

"Been here with the rest of the party?"

This seemed to me like a lot of questions; I told him so. I said: "Are you plannin' a book about the house, stranger?"

"I'm a hunter," said the stranger. "I been drifting up this way, making tracks for my camp in the hills."

"What hills?"

"Yonder."

"I don't see no big pack with you," I told him.

"My partner is up there with the shack and the traps and whatnot."

"You been down for cash?"

"I been down trying to get young." He smiled a little as he said this. He wasn't old, at that. He was not more than thirty-five or forty, perhaps, but he seemed as dry inside as out, and dusty, and gray. He would look about like this when he was seventy; there didn't seem to be any of the juice of life in him.

"Did you pick up a good time?" I asked him.

"Tequila ain't a drink to call good," he said "any time after the drinking."

I agreed with that. The devil invented that watery-looking stuff with the permanent fire built inside of it.

"I came across your trail," he went on.

"Hello! You been reading our trail," I said.

"I have."

"What you make of it?"

"There's a Chinaman with you."

"Well, you might guess that."

"There's the proof."

Out of his pocket he fished an envelope; out of the envelope, he took a little cigarette butt. "No one but a Chinaman would roll his Bull Durham like that," said the dusty stranger.

"No, that's right," I admitted. I always admired to see what a smart gent would make out of the signs that are left along a trail, and I took it from the first flash of this man that he was no fool.

Then he said: "A cook, this gent is, most likely."

"How would you make that out?" I asked.

"By the trace of grease on the paper. But, of course, that might be a wrong guess."

"Sure," I said. "Anybody might have greasy hands . . . after lunch, say."

"That would be cooked grease. Not raw."

I stared at him a little. He was smart enough to make me a little uneasy. You don't want to be too close to a man who knows too much.

"Well," I came back at him, "suppose that a hunter handled that cigarette, after cutting up a kill?"

"That might be, of course," he began, "but have you seen many Chinamen out tracking deer through these hills?"

He had me beaten. I told him so, and offered him a smoke. It warmed my heart a little to see the way the brain of that gent worked. "What else did you find out about this here party?" I asked him. I was surprised to see the way he talked out, because one of these here smart trailers is apt to be pretty silent, but this fellow didn't mind talking at all.

"Sure," he said, "I found out some other things, I think. You got a mighty pretty girl on this trip, I'd say."

I started. "Look here," I said, "you mean to say you never have seen us? Or heard about us?"

"Is that guess right?" he asked.

"Of course, it's right. But how could you tell? What sort of marks would a special pretty girl make on the trees, or what sort of a cigarette would she roll, maybe?"

This fellow from the desert only laughed at me a little. "This far West," he said, "the old women ain't apt to use the finest kind of French powder. And the young woman ain't, either. It costs too much. They save it for the town . . . they use common American stuff in the hills. But you take a real beauty, and she gets to taking special care of herself all of the time.

Oh, you've got a mighty pretty girl along on this trip!"

I squinted at him. It sounded a good deal like a fairy tale, as you'll admit, but at the same time there seemed to be a regular progression from one stop to another in his reasoning.

"Well," I told him, "I'm willing to take off my hat to you. I don't mind saying that you come over any trailing that I've ever heard talk about, lately. Got an Indian streak on your grandfather's side, partner?"

He grinned back at me, not taking no offense where none was meant.

"What else did you pick up besides the lady's fine French powder can?" I asked him.

"Why," he said, "I'd say that you got a fine shot along here . . . a fine shot and a fast man with a gun."

"Hum!" I said. "What little bird come along and told you that?"

"Well, I could guess," said the stranger. "There must be a pretty famous shot in that party."

"Did you ask one of the skeletons of the deer, or a rabbit skin, how far away it was standing when the gun was fired?"

He answered me, still with his quiet little smile: "I could pace the distance from the nearest hoss sign to a blazed tree, with a bullet through the blaze, and two more below it."

"And how come that you could tell that he was fast with his gun?"

"Why," said the stranger, "I'd ask you how does a fast gunman act with his Colt? The minute that the nozzle of the old hose is free from the leather, he begins to squirt lead, don't he?"

"Yes, that's pretty true, I suppose."

"Of course, it's true. Where a real fast gunman

works, there's often splinters raised up off of the floor."

"And what splinters was raised off the rocks?" I asked him.

"There was a bullet hole near the base of the tree, and one higher up, and then one plumb in the center of the blaze."

"They might have been fired the other way around," I suggested.

"Sure they might," he said. "But I take it that they wasn't. They was fired real fast, they was fired fifty yards off with a forty-five caliber kicking Colt, and they was landed into the mark. The first two of those shots would have killed a hoss . . . the third shot would of killed the rider." He nodded at me, still with his smile.

But now, I'd gotten past smiling. I said to him: "Great guns, man. What else did you find out about us? Pretty soon, you'll be reading my mind."

"There's an old sailor with you," he stated.

That about finished me. I shouted at him: "Look here, partner! I don't want to have no trouble with you, but how come you could tell that there was a sailor with us?"

"An old sailor," he repeated, "that has spent a lot of time on the China coast."

"By God," I said to him. "And you picked that information off of the trail?"

"It ain't so hard to figger out," he explained. "I been at sea myself. This here knot"—he picked a piece of string out of the envelope—"was mostly tied by Chinese sailors along the coast. And there you are!"

"Why wasn't it a Chinaman that tied this, then?"

"Because Chinese don't do things absent-minded. They rather sit with their hands in their laps and watch the edge of the sky."

"That's true. But how do you make out that he must be an *old* sailor?"

"Because that's a knot that youngsters nowadays don't tie. They're too damn' smart to learn the old-fashioned ways, or the ways of other countries. Your old sailor was always the one that used to pick up the stray bits of information."

# Chapter 19

Cattrin and Shirley came out from the house at about this time, and sauntered up in our direction, so I called them over and said to them: "I've heard you say that you'd like to meet up with a real Western trailer, and here's one. I don't know your name yet, stranger, but if you'll tell me, I'll introduce you to these gents."

"Thanks," said the man of the desert. "But I wouldn't be saying that I know such a lot about trailing."

"*Humph*," I remarked, "I dunno about that. I'll tell you what he's done," I said to the two of them. "He's happened to be riding up this way, and he's picked out what the party was made up of by a few scratches that we left along the trail. Why, partner, you ought to write a book about how you do it."

The stranger was really modest and he blushed a little at this, and said that he was not one to put words together and make a fuss about nothing. Just the same, he seemed a little pleased.

Cattrin put in: "What's the hardest trail in the world to follow?"

"Man or animal?" asked the trailer.

"Why, animal, say."

"Grizzly," said the stranger without any hesitation.

"Hold on!" said Cattrin. "You take a great, big, whacking animal like that, and he surely will leave a very decided imprint. Eh, Shirley?"

It's strange how a pair of tenderfeet will always turn to each other for support.

Shirley answered: "They've been almost exterminated, haven't they . . . these clever grizzlies that you speak of, my friend?" He smiled a little. Any Easterner likes to put one over on a Westerner's own ground. And, when you come to think about it, there was a good deal in what he said. He went on, following up when he'd scored a good point: "I can never understand why a grizzly should be so respected. Take the rat. We can't drive him out. He lives under our noses. I'd put him down as a much more difficult animal than the grizzly."

"You trap your rats by the dozen," said the man of the desert, "but they breed so fast that they can't be put down. Besides, they don't stir up men so much. They eat the paring off a cheese . . . a grizzly eats a whole heifer. There's a kind of a difference, there. You don't collect a bounty for a rat's scalp."

"We've traveled for a whole week through the mountains," said Shirley, "and never had a glimpse of a single bear."

"*You* could travel for ten years through the mountains and never see them," answered the man of the desert. "But they's three grizzlies in range of my gun, right now."

This made me start.

"I seen fresh-picked bones of a cow five miles back in a hollow among the trees," said the man of the desert, "and there was the marks of the teeth of one old mama and two cubs."

"How could you tell it was a mama?" asked Cattrin, very sharp and suspicious.

"Would a he-bear have two cubs along with him?" asked the other, very patient. "And, speaking about trails, I'd say that a grizzly is the hardest to follow, because he's got brains. I've spent two hours working out a trail problem that a grizzly had made in five minutes. He'd made the problem and then climbed up and laid out on a rock not fifty yards from me, and laughed himself sick, watching me work."

"But," said Cattrin, "why did you want to waste two hours on a fool of a bear?"

"Because I needed the food," said the man from the desert, as gentle as ever.

"Hello, that's right," said Shirley. "Bear meat can be eaten, after all, I've heard."

"It can," said the man of the desert. "Particular when you ain't had a bite except a few roots for a matter of eighteen days."

"Ha!" said Shirley. "Roots, did you say?"

"Yes, sir."

"Roots, roots," said Shirley. "Well, well!" And he laughed a little. "Have you lived on roots?" he asked.

"I've tried to," said the man of the desert, "but I haven't an Indian's wits for finding the right kind, and I haven't an Indian's stomach for digesting them, either, so I was glad to get that bear finally."

"How long did it take you?" asked Cattrin, grinning with curiosity.

"Eleven days," said the stranger.

"Eleven days of starvation!"

"And it was pretty tough meat when I got to it, but it seemed to me the finest thing that I'd ever tasted."

"Well," said Shirley, "if a bear is the hardest thing to trail among animals, what is the hardest thing among men? An Indian, I suppose?"

"No," answered the stranger. "An Indian don't take to the ground."

"What do you mean? Is there any sort of human that takes to a hole in the ground? We're learning something about humanity," Cattrin announced, and laughed his foolish laughter.

I could feel my upper lip beginning to curl a bit. This fellow Cattrin, I never had liked; I liked him less than usual, today, and the man of the desert looked better and better to me. I understood him better. He looked like a dusty bit of nothing to Cattrin and Shirley, I suppose. But to me he looked pretty real.

"They don't dive into holes out here in the West," said the stranger. "Most usually a Westerner will get onto his hoss and ride away, and you can follow him. Sometimes it would mean a long ride, but a long ride would bring you up with him. But it's different with gents from the East."

"In what way? Do they get down and wriggle into a hole?" asked Cattrin.

"They do," said the man from the desert. "They get onto a train and slide back to their cities . . . their big cities with millions of people in them . . . and they disappear into the crowds, there, and we don't hear any more about them. We gotta follow 'em slow, careful, sort of smellin' the way along."

Cattrin looked at him suddenly with a shrug of the shoulders. "Do you call that taking to the ground?"

"It's crawlin' into a hole, ain't it?" said the man from the desert.

"Well, did you ever follow up a trail like that?"

"Oh, aye."

"From where, then?"

"From a little town in the Big Bend."

"Yeah? And where away did it run to?"

"Why, pretty far East. Through Houston, first, from San Antone."

"And then?"

"Saint Louis, Louisville, Pittsburgh, Cleveland, Buffalo, Boston, New York, Philadelphia, Washington, Philadelphia, New York, Philadelphia. . . ."

"Hold on!" said Cattrin. "Were you running on such a trail as that?"

"Yes. It sure was a long one!"

"How long did you work on it?"

"Eight months and more," said the stranger.

"You get your man?"

"No."

"And who might you be?" Cattrin asked, getting more and more sober. "Who are you, to be chasing men around?"

"I'm a sheriff," said the stranger, "and my name is Shevlin. Jack is the front name, sir."

Cattrin turned gray and backed up with a jump, as though he'd heard a snake rattle. I can't say that I was much surprised, though. What the stranger had said before had half prepared me for this.

He looked at Cattrin and went on: "Eight confounded months I had to give up to that trail, sir."

"And then where did it go?" asked Cattrin.

"It went across the water," said the sheriff, "and I was mighty sick followin' it."

Cattrin fumbled at his chin. He had turned from gray to white. Shirley was staring at Cattrin, and then at the sheriff, looking very puzzled.

I began to smell a rat.

"And then?" Cattrin said huskily.

"Then I had to turn back from England to New York again."

"And then?"

"Why, it was the beginning of a long trip to the West again, and mighty glad I was when I found the sign pointin' back to my own back yard, as you might say."

"And it led you?"

"Up here through the hills, partner," said the sheriff, "until I find my man out here under the trees, callin' himself by the name of Cattrin." And he smiled and nodded gently at Cattrin.

The pink little man quivered all over, like jelly in a shaken glass. "You want me?" he said.

"I want you," said the sheriff. "Will it take you long to get ready to come with me?"

"On what charge?" said Cattrin.

"Why," said the sheriff, "I dunno that it's time to talk too much before too many people. Might say that I want you on a charge of burglary, Cattrin. And then there's a charge of confidence work, too."

"I'll smash those charges to smithereens," said Cattrin. He pounded his hands together. "I'll have out a charge for false arrest against you, Sheriff . . . if you *are* a sheriff!"

"Would you be as hard as that on me?" said the sheriff.

"I'll ruin you," Cattrin assured him with a shivering voice of hate and spite and fear.

"Well," said Shevlin, "if those charges are smashed so dead easy, maybe I'll have to fall back on another. I want you for murder, too, James Cattrin Dole!"

# Chapter 20

Conscience is the sort of a thing that most of us turn up our noses at. It don't matter, until it takes you by the throat. You can turn your back on it and sneer at it, and laugh at the poor fools that let less than a ghost get hold of them. But, all the same, I've stood by and seen it work, savage as a knife thrust in the small of the back, and never did I see it plainer than I did on this day, when Sheriff Jack Shevlin accused Cattrin.

You might say that Cattrin was a very nervous and high-strung sort of a man, and that he would be naturally upset and unbalanced, hearing such a charge made against him, and you could say that this would make him even yell out, and turn green.

But still there would be something left over. He yelled out, you can be sure, and then he reached out both hands on either side of him, exactly as he would have done if he were staggering on a high ledge, without anything to hold him up on either side except the thin air. And he looked at Shevlin as he would have looked at the devil, raising up in hoofs and horn and hair.

I admired the way that Cattrin took on, and I admired the way that the sheriff sat back in his saddle—because all of this time he never had dismounted from his mousy old cow pony—without ever touching a gun. Only, I also noticed that both of his hands were free from the touch of the reins, so that at any minute he could snake out his guns and start working with them.

For my share, I didn't want any part of his game. All at once, he looked terribly like poison to me. I backed up a bit, as Cattrin yelled out: "Hugh, Hugh, for God's sake, stand by me!"

"I shall stand by you," said Shirley, very much calmer and steadier than his companion. "I shall stand by you, and, of course, we'll pull you out of this little scrape in no time. The sheriff has come for the wrong man."

"He has! He has!" croaked Cattrin. "You'll find that he's come for the wrong man, in coming for me. My God, what murder can you accuse me of?"

"I'll tell you in short," said the sheriff, "not that I care a bit what the pair of you think"—and this seemed to include Shirley with Cattrin—"but because I want to convince my friend John Jones, here. I don't want him interfering in the course of the law."

"You won't listen to him, John!" begged Cattrin. "A low bounder . . . a disgusting brute like this . . . you wouldn't listen to him, John!"

Of course, I always had been plain Jones to him, before that minute, but apparently he now thought that he could bring me over to his side with an appeal. I felt it was my duty to say to the sheriff: "All right, Shevlin. If you've got something against this man, you won't mind telling me, to put me right. We can't let you take away a man while we're three to one . . . unless you give us a pretty good reason."

"Three to one?" said the sheriff, and smiled at me a little. It was as much as to say that he didn't mind the odds of the other two. When he had said this, he opened up and said his say, which wasn't any too pretty to listen to.

It was about how there had been a small-time banker down in that neck of the world where the sheriff was working, and this gent had a young wife with less sense than she needed. And along comes Cattrin, so said the sheriff, and turned the head of this woman. He first got the wife to work on her fool of a husband until he had transferred everything to her name. Then he went into the garden with a key to the back gate that the wife had given to him, and stabbed the banker in the throat, and watched him die, kicking in the gloom of the evening and spattering blood around over the rose bushes. After that, Cattrin pulled into the background, while the wife hurried her husband into a grave, and huddled into some black clothes, and drew out her funds from the bank—all the coin that her husband had signed over to her name—and then set off for a change of air that a convenient doctor had ordered up for her, because there is always doctors that is willing to prescribe exactly what a man is apt to want.

Away she went, and nothing was thought, except that Sheriff Shevlin—he really was a deputy, not having been elected to the job, the last time out—noticed that the money had been signed over to his wife just a few days before the murder. It looked funny to him, and he barged off on the trail of the wife to find out the answers to a few questions that he had to ask.

He ran her down in the East, and found her a sadder woman than she had been before, and she confessed, or pretended to confess, how Cattrin had put her up to the business, struck the blow that she helped him to, and then met her in the East and disappeared after relieving her of most of the money.

The sheriff didn't throw her into jail. In a way, she had turned state's evidence. What he wanted was the skunk of a man, and now he said that he had him, and he was going to bring Cattrin back by the nape of his neck to justice.

Shevlin told this story briefly and briskly, hardly longer than I've taken to tell it here, and every time he put in a point, Cattrin's eyes went sidewise, like he'd been knocked on the head.

Finally Shevlin said: "Jones, do you believe what I've told you?"

Cattrin wailed like a cat: "No, John, for God's sake, say no! You don't believe it! It's murder that he's accusing me of!"

"Black an' cowardly murder with a knife," said the sheriff. "That is exactly what I'm accusin' you of!"

I couldn't help looking at Cattrin and seeing the guilt in his soul, because his soul was in his eyes. I said to him: "God help you, because I sure believe that you're a guilty man."

Cattrin tossed up his hands before his face and backed up as though he'd been hit in the stomach.

Shirley stepped a little closer to me and said with a cold, steady face: "Will you help me to stand by poor Cattrin?"

I was a good deal surprised by that. I hadn't thought that there was that much gumption in Shirley, to stand by his friend in spite of a sheriff and the sheriff's guns. I was surprised, and I ad-

mired him for the second time since I'd known him.
I was almost sorry to say that I wouldn't stand by
Cattrin in anything.

Now a long blue barrel shone out of the sheriff's
hand, and he said to Cattrin: "Come back here,
friend, and don't work at your pockets. I'll kill you
like a gopher, if I see you make a wrong move."

"There's no danger of that, Sheriff," I said, "seeing that this gent hardly knows one end of a revolver from the other."

"Is that so?" said Shevlin. "Then I'll ask you to fan
this party for me."

I stepped up to do this trick, while the sheriff said
briskly to Hugh: "Your name is Shirley, I believe.
Now, I want you to stand around in line and not
start sashayin' over to the side where I'll have to
turn my head to watch you. I don't want you . . . this
time."

Men of the law have a pretty rough way of talking; I was a little ashamed to hear him speak like
this to a fellow like Shirley, because, even if Shirley
looked a little like a tenderfoot, he never had
showed a wrong hand around us.

Shirley had a good deal of dignity. He simply
said: "Very well, we'll have to let the law take its
course. After all, there is a way of reprimanding the
brutality of policemen. And by heaven, I'll spend
the last penny I have to make justice take its way
with the sheriff, as he calls himself."

I started operating on Cattrin, and what I found
surprised me. He had on, tucked away into surpris-
ing corners, short-nosed revolvers that would have
fitted easy into the hand of a child. I took two of
these away from him, and, besides that, I lifted a
good long knife from him. A workman-like-looking
knife which, when I saw it, removed all the doubts

from my mind. Cattrin didn't know one end of a pelt from another, so what would he be doing with a tool big enough for the skinning of an elephant? At least, I could answer that question to suit myself, and, when I pulled that long knife out of his clothes, I couldn't help taking Cattrin by the shoulder and shaking him like a rat.

"What in hell are you doing with this?" I snarled at him.

He withered up in my hand, I tell you, and gave me a horrible look of vengefulness and of terror.

I passed the things over to the sheriff, saying to him: "I don't know what sort of a jury you'll have, but, if I was on it, I'd hang this skunk on the evidence that I've pulled out of his clothes, right now."

Shevlin smiled down at me. He said: "I never had much doubt where you'd stand on the job, Jones. Otherwise, you can be sure that I wouldn't have asked you to sort of stand by and introduce me to these folks. But now that you're here, you'll cover my back when I make my retreat, in case friend Shirley, there, decides that a bullet from behind might make me look a lot prettier."

He shook hands with me. It was a clean-feeling hand, with a clean man behind it. I gave it a grip and told him that I'd see him safe away, if he insisted, but it seemed to me right that even a fellow like Cattrin should be allowed to take his things with him.

Shevlin looked down at me with an odd, twisted smile. "Jones," he said, "don't you suppose that I'd give a good deal to take a look at the things of this hound? But although I take a pride that I ain't a coward, I wouldn't risk going into that house and rousing the whole snake's den. I'm glad to be started the way that it is."

He turned his horse around, and herded Cattrin before him with a wave of his gun, and Cattrin went with a sidewise slink, like a scared dog. Suddenly little Rags made a jump at him, barking, and Cattrin stopped and kicked at the dog with a curse. Then Cattrin went on as I called Rags back, and the sheriff hollered to me: "Take care of yourself, Jones!"

# Chapter 21

I had the second surprise in the next couple of minutes when I saw Shirley turn on me with a jump and say: "Jones, if you haven't the courage to stand by a friend and an honest man, for God's sake, turn your head while I borrow one of your guns."

I caught the hand that he stretched out to me. "You poor fool! You poor fool!" I stammered at him. "Would you take a shot at the sheriff?"

"How do you know that he's the sheriff?" he asked.

"I'll stake my last drop of blood that he's what he says he is," I told Shirley. "Keep off. Don't reach for that gun again."

I jumped back. There was a fine fighting light in the eyes of Shirley. Yes, for one instant, I thought that he would be at me with a punch, and the thickness of his shoulders told me that the punch would be worth something.

But then he caught hold of himself. "Very well," said Shirley. "This helps one to form a proper estimate of you, Jones." And he turned and went off toward the house.

I stayed behind. In the first place, I was in no necessary hurry; in the second place, there were a few words ringing in my brain. "Take care of yourself, Jones," the sheriff had said as he went off, and he had said it in such a way that I couldn't forget his intonation. He had said something else, too, about wanting to get into that house in order to examine the possessions of Cattrin, but being afraid of rousing the whole nest of snakes. It was a staggerer, that. I might have said that he was simply too hard-boiled, and jumping in the dark at a lot of conclusions that were not justified, but I had seen beforehand how the mind of the sheriff worked, and a man who worked up a trail the way he did, and made big ideas grow out of small signs, was not apt to be making a mistake when he compared people to snakes.

As a matter of fact, would he, made up of steel springs and copper-wired with nerves, have backed up in his duty unless he thought that there was a terrible danger inside the house—even when he was backed up by me, as I had shown him that I was willing to stand behind him in everything?

Now that I thought it over, rolling a cigarette and smoking faster than was good for the nerves, it appeared to me that I could compare some of those people to snakes myself, beginning particularly with José, and going on to Wong. Perhaps there were more of the Mexicans that shouldn't be trusted any further than their shadows fell at noon.

But if ever a man swore that he would keep his eyes and his ears open, I was the one that minute. Right then and there I took out my pair of Colts from their holsters, and I looked them over fonder than ever a father was of a pair of sons, because I told myself that maybe I would be needing them badly in each hand before the day was over. Then, when I had smoked the cigarette down to a stub, I started back for the house, and, when I arrived there, hell was popping with a vengeance.

My respect for Shirley, which had mounted pretty high since I'd noticed the sober way he talked about his lady the night before, and since I'd seen him willing to fight for Cattrin, his friend, now sank down as low as mud in my estimation. Who would you guess that he had taken his story to in all of that house? Why, to the one person that never should have been bothered about it—to no less than to beautiful Frances Mornay.

I couldn't believe my eyes when I got into the patio and saw her wringing her hands and calling out what should she do. You see how it is. A good woman always figures that every horse and dog and man she's used to must be all right. And there was Frances Mornay crying, and carrying on, and saying that they must do something, and what should it be?

Just then, in comes Rourke, hurrying, like he had been sent for, and she ran up to him and said: "Oh, Mister Rourke . . . Denny, I mean," she said, "because distress makes us all old friends, doesn't it? Oh, Denny, do you know the dreadful thing that's happened? Poor little Cattrin has been arrested by a terrible brute!"

"Hold on," said Rourke. "What under the sky would they arrest Cattrin for? Picking pockets?"

I had to grin a little when I heard that, but Frances Mornay and the rest didn't seem to see any humor in the thing.

"Murder!" she said. "Murder!"

Rourke backed up, the way a fighting dog does just before it charges. "Murder?" he said, and I could see that he was interested. "Who did he kill?"

"No one, no one!" cried Frances Mornay. "Oh, you know poor little Cattrin, he wouldn't harm a child!"

"A child would be about the only thing he could harm," said Rourke, "or an old man."

You will remember that the sheriff had said that the banker was an old man? I can tell you that Rourke was nobody's fool, especially when his brain wasn't paralyzed with the sort of hypnosis that he was in just then.

Frances Mornay couldn't go on talking, just then, but she sank down into a chair with her head back, half fainting, and Rourke dropped on a knee beside her and told her in a voice that was worth remembering that he would do anything up to lifting the house on his shoulders to make her happy.

I was a bit afraid that Shirley, seeing the sort of spirit he had been showing lately, would be angry when he saw Rourke talking like that to his fiancée, but Shirley didn't seem to notice.

I heard Frances Mornay say to Rourke: "Oh, Denny, save poor little Cattrin from that dreadful man!"

What did Rourke say? That he would? That he would be damned if Cattrin should be jailed? No, sir, he simply kissed her hand and stood up, and started out of the patio as I started in. I muzzled one of his arms right away and stopped him.

He said to me with a lot of dignity: "What's the matter with you, Johnny? Do you know better than Miss Mornay what should be done?"

"You blockhead!" I told him. "This gent that took off Cattrin is a hard-boiled one, and, if he's wrong, a pair like you and me never could put him right in a thousand years."

Rourke reached out with his free hand and tapped me on the vest, saying: "Maybe you're correct, Johnny, but this is where I stand . . . just now I'm tired of thinking, and I'm going to let somebody else tell me what to do."

"I'm the man for that, Denny," I said. "Listen to me, son, and I'll put you on the right track."

"You always point away from trouble, John," he said in a sad sort of a way.

It gave me a shock to have him call me John. He hadn't called me that since our acquaintance was three days old, and I walked along beside him out of the patio just as Ruth Derrick came in with a rush. I heard her sing out to Frances Mornay and ask her what under heaven she was trying to do, starting Rourke after a sheriff who had made an arrest in due form?

It soothed me a lot to hear the redhead talk like that, and it warmed my heart to her a lot. I looked back to the pair of them, and they made a pretty picture. I remember that Ruth was trying to draw the hands of Frances down from her face, because, by this time, Frances Mornay was crying in a helpless, childish sort of way, and I saw the blue of Ruth's sapphire ring glint in the sun. Then I passed on out of the patio with Rourke.

I followed him all the way to the barn, arguing, arguing, arguing. He would listen and nod. I pointed out that the sheriff was no four-flusher out to make a sensational arrest, but a real man, doing his work. I told him that I would back the straightness and the good sense of Shevlin against any fellow I'd ever seen, that I was willing to take off my hat and take orders from a man like Shevlin.

But Rourke only went ahead with his business, slowly, methodically, as though he was tired. He took his rifle out of its long holster, and then I went sort of crazy.

I said: "Denny, are you going out to do a murder? Is that what you got in mind?"

Rourke put his hands to his head. He said to me: "God knows, Johnny, I'm a little in a whirl. I don't know. I've been told I've got to march ahead."

I begged him to wait there for five minutes. He swore to me that he would, and I turned and sprinted back to the patio, where I found that Ruth was helping Frances Mornay away to her room. As I came plunging in, Shirley started up before me and said: "What's the matter? Don't startle Frances now."

I jerked him away from me. I would have killed a man that really tried to stop me, and I sprang on before Frances Mornay. I yelled to her: "Do you know what you've done? You've sent Rourke on the trail of the sheriff . . . and he's going with his gun. It means murder, murder! Will you come out here and try to stop him?"

She clung to Ruth Derrick with one hand. The other hand she pushed out before her as though she were trying to shove away a bad dream that wouldn't leave. Then she breathed—"Murder."— and keeled straight over.

I could have torn the world in two! One word from her would have stopped Rourke; nothing else would. The best that I could do was to go along with him, no matter where he tried to go. I thanked God that Pinto was a fast horse. With that, I turned around and ran for the barn again, but, when I got there, Rourke was gone.

I yelled for him, and listened. The hammering of

my heart was so loud that I hardly would have heard him even if he had answered from ten feet away, but suddenly I knew that he wouldn't answer—that he had broken his word and gone off, glad to be shut of me, and that, if he managed to find the sheriff, either the sheriff would die and Rourke become an outlawed man, or else Shevlin would drop my partner dead.

# Chapter 22

What I knew then was that Rourke was dearer than a brother to me, and the thought of what he was heading toward made me sick. I tried to fumble through the dark of my mind, and come out at the door that would show me what was the right thing to do, but I was bewildered.

Automatically I saddled Pinto, and foamed out down the valley. I took the trail on which the sheriff had gone, with Rags on the pommel of my saddle, sticking like a good one. All the while Pinto was dipping up and down over the rough going, I was scanning every break in the woods, every opening, in hope of sighting the sheriff or Rourke. If I could get to Rourke, I would stop him, and, if he saw me with the sheriff, he would come to his senses, of course.

I picked up the trail where I had parted from the sheriff and seen him disappear into the woods, marching that hound of a Cattrin before him. I gave Rags a good scent of the double trail, so that he could help me out if I lost it again, and we went right down to the bank of the little river. I lost the trail there. It went into the water, and didn't come out on the farther side. I cast up the bank in both directions—north and south—and I worked it on both sides, but still I didn't come to the solution until about a half hour before sunset. And the reason was this.

That fox of a Shevlin had gone across the river—not absolutely straight, but bending downstream a little to a point where his horse could climb out on hard shale. The sun had dried up the water his horse dripped in no time, and the wind had blown the scent away, I suppose. Because when I finally stopped my wide cutting for sign and came back to the point where I had lost it in the first place, Rags for all the sharpness of his nose made out only the ghost of a scent. Perhaps the reason was that the sheriff, at this point, had taken up Cattrin before him on his mustang, because a horse leaves a lot less scent on rocks or soil than a man in shoes. I don't know why that should be.

When I had located the trail, I shook my head, because I knew right there that I was beaten. I'd lost hours, and those hours the sheriff would use, not only to put valuable miles between him and me, but, also, to make all kinds of trail problems. If he could read sign the way he was able to, I knew for a fact that he would be able to make a fool out of me.

I gave up his track and went straight back to the barn with Rags to pick up the trail of Rourke. Rags found it and followed it fine for a half mile, and then on a flat gravel stretch he lost it completely. I don't know what the matter with that ground was. Perhaps it might have been a kind of sour grass that grew all around and that Rags started to chew as soon as he landed amongst it. At any rate, he went cold on that trail, and, although I went on cutting for sign until it was pitch dark, Rags never got a smell of it again. He put his heart into his work, I must say, but in that stretch of gravel he lost his way every time.

It was plain enough that Rourke must have known beforehand the property of that grass, and that he had guessed that I would trail him with Rags's nose at my disposal, and that he had deliberately planned the trick to throw me off. Well, it worked. When it was so dark that I couldn't distinguish one tree from another in the pine woods, I gave up the job, and I went back to the house, feeling reasonably sick.

When I went into the patio, I found Shirley sitting about and smoking a cigarette. The sight of him, looking so cool and unconcerned, made me half insane. But I didn't speak to him until he opened up on me by saying: "You've given Frances a frightful shock, Jones. You've confined her to her bed, in fact."

Then I said to him: "You damned shorthorn, you damned pup, you've stood by and let a better man than you'll ever grow into start off on the road to hell. Another yap out of you, and I'll send you there before him." I said this with red before my eyes, in a mist. The words sounded strange to me—they came out of a distance. I listened to them as though another man were speaking them. That is why I can remember them to this day so very well.

I have to say that Shirley handled himself extremely well on this occasion. He looked me straight in the eye, and then he said: "I understand what you mean, Jones. You refer to Rourke on the way behind the sheriff. I'm really sorry that was done. But what could I do to stop it, when you couldn't hold back your friend yourself?"

There was a good deal of sense in this. I finally told Shirley that I had said a good deal more than I should have said, and he was pretty good about it, marking that he didn't want to remember what a man said when he was grieving about a friend. He said this, or words to this effect, and I went off to my room and sat down with my head in my hands.

Before I tell what happened next, it's necessary to say something about the location of that room of mine. I should have said it before, when I first spoke of the place, but that was shuffled away out of my mind at the time.

It was a small room with two single beds, or cots, in it. It stood in almost the extreme northeastern corner of the house. On that northern side, there had been a rose garden—tough roses that would last out the cold of the winter and that climbed up the side of the house for a little distance. They were in bloom, now, making a streaking of little pink blossoms up the wall of the old house, and more than half covering the window of the room, so that the place was pretty shadowy, even in the daytime.

It was not pitch dark, as I've said before. It was about time for dinner, and I'd gone into my room to wash up and comb my hair, but I sat down for a minute on the edge of my bed with my back to the window. I'd lit the lamp. The wick was lopsided and had smoked a good deal the night before, and therefore, when I turned it up, it simply streaked soot up the side of the blackened chimney and made a stroke of crimson in the room—that was all. This light was hardly enough for me to see to part my hair, and I thank God that it was no brighter, because, otherwise, I would not be writing this account of what happened in the Mornay house.

I had been sitting there about five minutes and was just telling myself that I would have to start stirring, to get ready in time to eat, when someone fired two shots in quick succession through the glass of

the window behind me. I heard the bullets *hiss* by
my ear and *thud* into the wall before me, while I did
what every sensible man ought to do. I dropped forward on my hands and knees, so that the bed made
a covering behind me. Then I peered over the edge
of the bed, gun in hand, and I saw the faintest outline of something beyond the window, and the
gleam of a gun poised for another shot.

I would not have been able to see anything at all,
because of the reflection of the dim lamplight in the
pane, but the glass of that window was extra thin
and brittle, so that a big chunk of it had been broken
out. It was through this gap that I saw the shadowy
form standing out there and the faint gleam of the
gun. I couldn't say whether it was the sick light of
my own lamp that showed me this, or the light of
the stars from the sky. At any rate, it was light
enough for me to make a try with my own Colt. I
sent in a shot and followed it with another; the form
jerked out of sight, and I went across that room like a
bullet and jerked the frame up.

The rose vines tangled me for an instant, climbing
through, and then I crawled out onto the path and
looked up and down. I couldn't see a thing. I couldn't
hear a thing, either, because just at that moment a fool
of a mule began to bray from the corrals, and that
noise would have drowned the sound of a marching
army. There was just one thing to do, and I did it. That
is to say, I picked out one direction, and I sprinted as
hard as I could, around the northeastern corner of the
house, and then along the base of the eastern wall. In
that way, I actually rounded the house and came out
on the northern, steep slope, where the big blocks of
the ruins tumbled down the hillside.

I paused there. I'd seen nothing. If my man were
out there, it was pretty likely that he would have

dropped down among the rocks and hidden. If I charged in, he could punch me full of holes. So I turned back to the house, and came around into the patio.

There was a good deal of excitement. A couple of the Mexicans were running about. Dorgan had come down from the corrals with his jaw set and his eye looking like a man who wouldn't run from trouble. Shirley was there, too, giving orders and taking charge in fine style, because he was telling everyone to be quiet, because Miss Mornay was not to be upset again. Just then, sure enough, Frances Mornay appeared at a window of her room, over the patio. She had on a dark-colored dressing gown, as I suppose, and the white of her nightgown showed in front. She called out in her sweet voice, and asked what had happened, and cried out at the end of her own question, asking if Shirley were there to answer her.

He called an answer, and then he ran out of the patio, and I heard him going up the stairs to speak to her. Afterward, I could hear the murmur of his voice in her room, soothing her.

All of this may sound a little trivial, but, in the light of what happened afterward, I want you to remember it. I myself, thinking back to that evening, fit the bits of news together like parts of a jigsaw puzzle, gradually beginning to make it out.

This excitement didn't do me any good. The men all asking me questions was friendly enough, but I was pretty certain that one of these people had held the gun outside my window, and it was from his revolver that the bullet had come that had breathed on the hair of my head. Only Ruth Derrick, as I remembered afterward but didn't notice at the time, kept out of the ruck and didn't speak to me at all.

# Chapter 23

I left the excitement stewing in the patio and went up to the room of Palliser. He had heard the shots, of course, and, when he wanted to know what had happened, I told him. He seemed to take this for granted in the most extraordinary way. He said to me: "You'll have more of that. They get the idea, now, that I'm depending on you a little, and they'll break their hearts trying to snag you. But if the luck is with us, they ain't going to succeed . . . God willing! Tonight is the last night, Johnny. Tonight we break away from this hell on earth."

I said: "It will upset poor Miss Mornay a good deal. Shall I tell her? Shall I give her a hint?"

He looked at me for a moment, and then he closed his eyes. He seemed to be thinking it over, and at last he said in an indecisive way: "No . . . don't breathe a word of it to a soul in the place. Not to her, either."

He wanted to know exactly when I should be ready, and I told him that I would leave the patio to make arrangements for the buckboard and horses and guns at about half past ten, probably. By that time, nearly everyone would have gone to bed. The only thing that might hold me up would be the Mexicans at the stable. Sometimes they didn't turn in until very late.

He shut his eyes again and cursed heavily. But he said that he would resign himself, and not allow himself to think of the escape until eleven o'clock. He seemed so upset that I was afraid that something might have happened during the day to unnerve him, but, when I asked him, he said simply: "This morning we had about three chances out of five of getting away. Now we have one chance in five, but we've got to take that chance, even if it isn't much good."

As long as he didn't care to talk any more openly than this, I didn't press the conversation. I was feeling a little worse than grumpy, as a man is apt to after he has had a pair of slugs whistle about his head, so I went on down to the supper table and there I found a pretty glum lot.

Frances Mornay came down late. She had heard of what had happened, but she held herself in control, pretty well. Only little things showed that she was nearly at the end of her rope. I remember that when José let a plate slip as he was putting it on the table, and it came down with a crash, she half jumped from her chair with a little scream. She apologized afterward, but the rest of us took the hint and started to make cheerful talk to brace her up.

Only Ruth Derrick was no good at it. She sat like a wooden figure all through the meal, looking sick and tired. She looked at me just once, and that was when I tried to make a joke out of the shots that had been fired into my room, saying that I knew it was only a practical joke somebody was trying to play on me—the bullets had missed me so far from such a short range. At this, she gave me a steady glance from the corner of her eye—that was all.

Frances Mornay went up to her room immediately after supper, without waiting to have coffee with us, and Shirley escorted her up. He didn't come down again immediately.

That left me with the redhead, and we didn't make very rapid conversation. She was terribly blue and glum, and finally she got up with a jump.

"I'm going to bed," she said to me.

It was exactly at ten o'clock that she said this, and I remember feeling rather glad, because this pushed the family out of the way before the main job of the night began.

However, she didn't start immediately, but came back where I was standing beside my chair. Some people have a way of walking in right under your eyes—I mean to say, they come in close and look up to you. Ruth Derrick did that now, and, when she was so close, I could see the blue smudge of nervous weariness around her eyes.

She said to me rapidly: "Are you going to be a fool and stay on here? Why don't you get away?"

"Why am I a fool?" I asked her. "I was hired to stay on here."

"You never were hired to be shot at."

"I was, though. That's why the fancy pay."

"Not shot at through windows!"

"Unless I can keep the thugs farther away from the house."

"Who do you think could have done it?" she asked.

"Wong, the cook. Or maybe that devil José. Or maybe some outside man." I was thinking of the rider on the gray horse.

"Still you won't go?" she asked with a great deal

of excitement, pressing my arm a little with her hand, and, in the waver of lamplight on the patio, all at once she looked beautiful to me.

"You better get out of the patio," I warned her. "I'm beginning to feel a little foolish about you."

"What in heaven's name do you mean?" she asked me.

"You," I said.

"Damn such nonsense!" said Ruth Derrick, and left me without another word. By which you'll see that she was pretty much of a modern girl long before the days of short skirts.

It made me laugh a little, after she had gone off and left me alone there, but by this time I felt that I ought to be making myself busy for the getaway. The family was out of sight at least, so I went to my room, got my second rifle, and an extra Colt, two cartridge belts, and returned to the stable.

I was in luck, it seemed, because none of the Mexicans were around, so I got out the pair of Morgan horses and backed them up to the buckboard in the ruins of the wagon shed. I loaded into that buckboard a pair of sacks of crushed barley and some salt that I had brought out, and the guns and ammunition. That was the chief provision. I felt a great deal better when all of this was finished, so I scattered some hay before the horses so that they'd keep fairly quiet in the shed, and then I started back for the house, and ran into the big hulking shadow of Dorgan on the way, and a smaller shadow beside him. That smaller shadow was Wong. I could hardly believe my ears when I heard them talking very confidentially, and talking in Chinese, at that.

I worked up as close as I could to them, and prayed that they might talk English for a spell, but they didn't. All that I could make out was when they came close under the western wall of the house, and there they looked up at the dim flicker of light in the captain's windows. Wong shook his fist at it, and I could see Dorgan nod his big head. Whatever difference there was between them, they agreed on having it in for Palliser. It interested me a lot to know that, and I was gladder than before that I was to get the old man out of the way that night. Not that I was very fond of him—but he *was* old, and I'd grown used to him since the start of this trip.

It was plain that I had better delay a little longer before trying to make a start, because, with Wong and big Dorgan up, an alarm easily could be given if I tried to get away with the buckboard.

So I went back into the patio and put a chair right back against the north wall, between two windows. There I sat down and waited for time to go by. But time is like a pretty girl—minutes turn into hours while you wait for it. However, I didn't so much as smoke a cigarette, but I sat there smelling the chill and the dampness of the mountain trees over the wall, and watching the drift of the stars going West. The violin began in Miss Mornay's room. It stopped and the Victrola started the same piece—"The Meditation," again. It seemed to be getting into her blood, and I didn't like to hear it, because it's bad for any invalid to begin to center on any one thing and shut out the rest.

I was mighty sorry for that girl, and nothing told me how completely upset she was in the mind better than the fact that she hadn't said a word to me about the absence of Cattrin and Rourke. Neither had anybody else. They avoided looking where Cattrin and Rourke used to sit. They took care not to mention the name of either of them.

But it made me feel pretty bitter to think that I was spending my brains and my time taking care of an old man like Palliser, while my partner was out there roaming and searching for a chance to get himself afoul of the law.

I was thinking of that and sitting as still as a stone, the way that you will when your mind is full, when it seemed to me that I heard something breathing above me, and I thought it was the wind, for the wind will form in pools, now and then, and stir with a very human sound. But after a moment, I knew that it was *not* the wind, but a person above me, to the left, at one of those two windows that I've spoken of before.

Now, at the point where I was sitting, a little climbing vine had gone up the wall a distance and thrown its arms out backward toward the court, and these waving arms made a slight screen above me through which I looked as I raised and turned my head. I had very little light to see by—only the glow from the two lanterns that hung in alternate corners of the court—and yet these made enough illumination for me to see the face that was leaning out from the thick blackness of the room.

It was Cattrin, and looking as I never had seen him look before, for although I had seen him jolly, and foolish, and careless, and scared to death, I never had seen this look on him before and I never wanted to see it again on him or any man.

Because it was murder! I knew as I looked up at the puckered face that Cattrin was a killer, and something about the way his eyes went slowly over the patio made me fairly sure that he was looking for me. Perhaps I was wrong, but the unpleasant idea jumped into my mind with a shudder of certainty. I was scared. Of Cattrin? No, I never could be afraid of an insect like him—but afraid of the murder that I saw in his face.

I blinked. When I looked again, he was no longer there, and I had a dreamy feeling that he hadn't been there at all. However, my blood was running cold. I pulled out my watch. It was exactly eighteen minutes to eleven. I told myself that it was time to start up to Palliser's room, but somehow I couldn't make myself get up from my chair.

There was a strange feeling in me that the weight that held me in the chair was the sound of "The Meditation" that the Victrola in Frances Mornay's room still was pouring out.

# Chapter 24

You can imagine why I was weighted down into the chair. If Cattrin was back, how had he managed to escape from the sheriff? Why, by means of the intervention of Rourke, of course, and, if Rourke had intervened, how had he done that except with a revolver?

I saw Shevlin lying somewhere in the woods on his face, dead as a nail, and I saw Rourke riding for his life in another direction. No, he would not even do that. He would come back to the house of Frances Mornay looking for praise, and not realizing that sensitive girl would shun and abhor him after his crime. And what sort of an explosion would that cause in the excited mind of Cattrin?

That was what kept me nerveless in my chair—that and a gathering sense of horror. For suppose that Cattrin had moved to the window on my other side, and that from this he might spot me? Why he should have picked me out for any particular act of malice, I can't say, except that when the sheriff arrested him, I was on the spot and refused to interfere. At any rate, I was in a chill with fear, and I wanted nothing better than to get out of that patio when I saw a crowning horror that knocked Cattrin out of my mind.

Out of the shadows at the end of the wall on the southern side of the patio moved a form in white that turned into a nightmare actually walking over the edge of the wall, with a deadly drop on either side— a nightmare of a woman in white with the glitter of a knife in her right hand, that was turned toward me. She had very long, pale hair that swept from her head to below her waist, and this hair seemed wildly disordered, and did not stir in the air that was fanning the flames of the lanterns so that it made her look like the picture of a ghost painted upon canvas.

Her arms were bare to the elbows. Her feet were bare, also, and over the rough stones, which raggedly made up the top of the wall, she moved without any concern, except that her left hand was raised a little, as though to balance her. This picture walked straight across the top of the wall and I saw nothing that stirred like life about it. But the whole pose and posture were too carelessly unreal for nature. What living creature would walk on such a ridge?

But just before the ghost reached the platform at the top of the stairs, in front of the room of Palliser, the wind struck it, and I distinctly saw the garment blown. I mean to say, the wind that hummed through the ruined gateway of the patio now caught her and I could see the white cloth stir. It ripped a hundred-weight of terror from my brain, I can tell you, and at the same moment I heard the light *clink* of a stone that had stirred under her foot. Even if ghosts have clothes that blow in the wind, they have a weight, I believe.

At this moment, I heard the needle of the Victrola scratch at the end of the record, and immediately begin again at the beginning.

I jumped up with a yell: "Palliser, Palliser! Take care!"

At the same time the figure stepped onto the platform before his door and fumbled at the handle of it, as it seemed to me. I pulled out two guns.

"Stop!" I yelled.

But the door yielded to it that moment, although I could have sworn that Palliser had locked the door safely—I had heard the key grate in the lock when I left his room earlier that same evening.

Then I was able to act. I put two shots straight into that ghost. But there wasn't a yell or a groan or a fall. It merely went straight on into the dark of the room.

There was the roar of Palliser's shotgun. He had given that walking vision both barrels as I could tell by the sound, and I promised myself that the ghost would be in two halves, by this time. But just behind that, I heard a wild yell, and the yell came out of the throat of the old captain. There was fear and horror and rage in it. It was a blast of sound that ripped into my ears and made me dizzy, and sick, and, straight on the heels of this, I heard a scuffling begin and a groaning.

I got to the stairs, at last. Even as I went up them, I threw a look over my shoulder at the two blank windows out of which Cattrin had looked. But they were empty and dark now. I gained the landing, then.

The door was closed. I tried it. Of course, the lock had been turned. I pulled my gun and blew that lock to smithereens, but still there were two bolts that held the door together, and, just then, I heard a frightful, maniacal laughter that belonged not to any human throat, as I thought, but to a horrible beast. It rose and it pealed as I stood in the most leisurely fashion. Through the laughter, as I stood frozen at the door, I thought that I heard another scuffling sound, as though something of a good deal of weight was being moved across the floor. That sound and the laughter stopped—that hideously pealing laughter that made my hair lift and made me feel as though I were all alone in hell!

Then I pumped two more bullets through the door. One of them broke the first bolt. My shoulder tore away the second, and I pitched into the room onto my hands and knees, but with both guns ready for shooting.

There wasn't any need for that. The room was empty except for the body of Palliser.

The pillow was on the floor and his body streamed out of the bed toward the pillow, almost as though a very strong force had caught hold of the sheet and twitched it and the man lying on it out of the bed. His arms were pitched out wide. His feet were still on the bed in the tangle of the bedclothes, and across his throat and his breast there were large smears of blood. He had been stabbed in the hollow of the throat; he had been stabbed in the breast, too, and that second stab had found his heart.

I saw this at my first glance, as I lurched to my feet, and I sprang to the window and looked out, confident that I would nail the murderer before he or she got to the ground. But there was no sign of so much as a rope hanging down the wall, and there was no one in sight.

But this I could have sworn, that no one on God's earth could have gotten out of that window and down to the earth below in the interval that had elapsed since the laughter stopped and I smashed through the door and got to this point of lookout. I thought I was going to faint at that.

This may seem like foolishness, but I swear that the appearance of Cattrin's ugly face, and the sight of the walking ghost, and the horrible mad laughter in the room, and the picture of the captain dead in his blood—none of these things and all of them together had made the effect upon me that was made by lurching into that room as I had done and finding that it was empty except for the dead man.

It made me seem mad. For half an instant, it made me doubt the actuality of anything I had seen or heard here. I gripped the wall and steadied myself. Then I went searching still further. I found nothing beneath the bed—nothing in the heap of bedclothes—nothing in the wardrobe—nothing above or beneath it—no, everything was searched that could have sheltered the bulk of a human being, even a child, and there was no doubt about it that a woman or man or child could not be in this room at the moment.

But how keen I was now, how burning keen to come on some sign of the villain. All the ghostliness was gone from it. It was horrible murder in the middle of the night.

I turned up the flame of the lamp and looked about me, regardless of the shouts that were pouring out into the patio by this time. I felt a sort of contempt for those people who would come upon the scene so late, because I had been there near the heart and kernel of awfulness.

When I looked down to the floor, the first thing that I saw was a glimmer of blue. I picked it up, and the thought that jumped through my mind was a picture of the face of Ruth Derrick. She had a ring like that. I stepped on and looked down at the dead man, his frightful grin and his half-open eyes—as though he were sleeping in this position only for another moment, and presently he would heave himself up and laugh at me and damn me for a fool in his own manner. But in the hand of the captain—in his right hand, the fingers of which were doubled weakly as though to hold something—I saw a glint of red-gold. Half a dozen red hairs were in the hand of Palliser, and the hair of Ruth Derrick's head was exactly that color. I didn't hesitate; I took them away from the fingers that held them, and, as I did so, all my curiosity about the identity of the murderer left me.

Someone has talked about the way proofs pile up. There might have been ten million other sapphires in the world, and the finding of that one on the floor meant not a great deal. But the sapphire and the red hair together were a thousand times more convincing than either of the two alone. People had been hanged for slighter cause than this, as I knew, and in that moment, as I drew the long, silken hairs from the hand of Palliser, I thought of how she would be in the last moments, pale and steady, and giving nothing away, and making no heroics, and never allowing to pass her lips a confession of her motive.

But I knew, in that instant, with a burning of the brain and the heart, I knew why she had done it—for the sake of Frances Mornay, of course. To end the strange charm that kept beautiful Frances Mornay linked to this dangerous place, where so many of her name had died before her, she had keyed herself up, and she had struck Palliser down. That was the wild laughter I had heard—the insane laughter of a woman, say, who looks at her deed for the first time after it is done. Through my mind this leaped in half of a second. Then I looked aside, and I saw that Shirley was standing in the doorway, transfixed, his lips parted.

# Chapter 25

The crowd came piling at the heels of Shirley. The shriek and the gunshots would have been enough to rouse an army, of course, and Mexican ears are quick as hair-triggers. All four of them were swarming up the stairs, and Dorgan, behind them, pulling up the buckle of his gun belt and looking ready for action.

I saw that as I went to the door, telling Shirley that we would have to keep the room clear.

The man seemed paralyzed. He could only nod and gasp. He went slowly inside the room while I stood at the door and checked the rush. Big José looked as though he would charge straight past me, his eyes sparkling. Wong was now bringing up the rear, jabbering to himself, and across the patio I saw Frances Mornay run out, with the golden cat scampering before her, and Ruth Derrick supporting her arm.

It made me pretty sick and cold to see the redhead there, knowing what I knew.

I finally told José in good Spanish that I would knock his head off if he didn't get out of my way, and so José backed up, and the others behind him, while Frances and Ruth ran up the steps. Palliser's niece seemed to know what had happened with that sort of a woman's instinct that will hit close to the truth amazingly often.

She came up to me and took one of my hands in both of her cold ones and begged to come in. I told her that it was no good and that what was in that room I wouldn't let her see. At that, she reeled back a bit, and Ruth put an arm around her and supported her. I was sorry for Frances Mornay. But I was more interested in Ruth. I wanted to see the face of a girl who could do what I was confident she had done and then come straight back to the scene of the murder.

All that I could see, by the shaken lantern light from the patio and that which passed out through the door of Palliser's room, was that she was perfectly white and her eyes looked shadowed with darkness. But she was calm as a rock, and her voice was entirely steady, as she told Frances that I was right and that they had better go back.

"It's Uncle Ned!" moaned the girl. "What has happened? Why don't I hear him? Uncle Ned!"

When she called out like that, it stopped my heart, and for a horrible minute or two I half expected a bubbling, stifled voice to come out of the cut throat of Palliser. He had loved this girl so much, you understand, that I half expected him to rise from the dead when she called to him.

But, of course, there was only silence. Dorgan groaned: "Good God!" And that was all.

"Yes, yes, we'd better go back," Frances said to Ruth in a quick, shivering whisper. "We'd better go back."

I would have gone with them, but I didn't care to

leave that room. I had picked up two things there, and perhaps I might find another, so I told Dorgan to go along with the women and I saw him go down the steps in front of them. I remained in the doorway, while the Mexican chattered and Wong gaped. I saw the two girls get fairly into the dark of the arch on the other side of the patio; there Frances Mornay pitched over, but Dorgan was ready for it, and lifted her in his big arms. They passed out of my sight into the house.

Then I gave some orders. I told the Mexicans to get out of the way and clear out from the patio. I told Wong to go back to his kitchen and cook up some of the strongest black coffee he knew how to brew. When he had it ready, he could come back to Palliser's room. There was no reason why they should have obeyed me, but the fellow who seizes authority in a crisis generally is obeyed.

As they scattered away, I turned into the room once more and closed the door. Shirley was where you would have expected a weak-nerved man to be—actually hanging over the dead face of Palliser. Horrors are irresistible to people who are afraid of them.

I looked down—and there was Rags between my feet. All this time he had been with me, of course, but I hadn't noticed him in the patio, or racing up the stairs, or breaking into the room of the dead man. Now I saw him for the first time, with his ugly little head cocked to one side and his bright eyes gleaming. I can't express what a comfort he was— like the rise of the sun, you might say. He took away half of the horror at a stroke.

Without turning, Shirley said: "Great God . . . Jones! There's something in his mouth."

I went to look and saw what I hadn't noticed in

my first glance—perhaps because the lamps were not turned up so high at that time—a little bright gleam of something behind the parted lips of the captain. I reached in and took out a silver coin—it lay wet and cold in my fingers, and, as I stared down at it, I knew that it had the pattern of the silver coin that had been thrown through the window and onto the floor of the room.

Although he hadn't been able to touch the thing, Shirley was now leaning over my shoulder, and he said with a snarl of wonder and disgust mixed: "That's a Spanish silver coin, isn't it?"

"How do I know?" I asked.

"Well, see the crest."

I wasn't familiar with the crest of a Spanish coin. I laid it on the edge of the table, and Shirley brought the lamp close beside it.

"It's a piece of eight," he said, "and confound me if this don't bother me a good deal. A piece of eight . . . in the mouth of a dead man! What can it mean, Jones?"

I stared at him helplessly, while through my mind drifted the various things that I knew. The flinging of the coin now had an immediate and sudden relation to the death of Palliser, it appeared, and, if that were the case, perhaps the guilt would be lifted from the shoulders where it lay now apparently.

"Shirley, Shirley," I groaned to him. "I wish to God that I had the brains for this sort of work, because I think that I know more about this dirty business than any man in the world."

"Do you?" said Shirley coldly, and his eyes narrowed at me.

"Maybe you think I know too much, eh?" I said.

At that, he gave me a faint, twisted smile, and said: "No, I'm not such a fool. For a moment . . . but, after all, you couldn't have been on the outside breaking down the door, and on the inside doing the murder . . . all at the same moment."

"Thanks," I said as dry as could be.

Then I stopped him as he went toward the dead body. My idea was that we should not disturb a thing in the room until some wiser head than mine should arrive on the spot. I had read and heard enough of such matters to know that it is best for all to be as it was found, for then the mastermind, if there is one, may put one and one together and get on the path of a million.

I doubted very much where any mastermind would be able to work out this job, while I had a certain wisp of hair and a certain sapphire in my vest pocket, but at least they should have a chance. In the meantime, I wanted a fair chance to find any other token of Ruth Derrick that might have been left behind in the room.

He had to agree that it was best to leave everything untouched, but he was terribly excited. Yet there was a great deal of man about him. I noticed that when he lit a cigarette, he did not have trembling fingers, and, when he smoked, he was exceedingly careful to put the ashes into a saucer, so as not to let anything fall on the floor.

We talked over what we should do. It was obvious that someone ought to remain here in the room of the dead man. If the place was deserted, the murderer might return to remove important clues. But it was also highly important that we should send for a representative from the sheriff's office.

The journey, which had required a week for us to make with our clumsy, slow wagons, could be made in a single day, perhaps, by a hard rider with a pair of extra mustangs along for mounts. Perhaps it seemed logical that I should go for that help, but it seemed just as good to entrust the commission to one of the Mexicans.

I shouted from the window for José, and pretty soon he came running from the direction of the stable. He called up to me, and he listened to what I said, and nodded. Then he ran back toward the barn.

I told Shirley, after this, that we might as well make it watch and watch about until the sheriff sent someone to us: "If there is any sheriff to send anyone."

"What do you mean by that?" asked Shirley.

"Shevlin is probably dead on the trail," I said.

"The devil!" he exclaimed. "What makes you think that? Because Rourke went after him, do you mean?"

I looked straight at Shirley and tried to read his face. Then I said: "Do you mean to say that you didn't know that Cattrin is back here?"

He jumped up from his chair, but then he sat down suddenly. "Great God!" Shirley gasped. "Cattrin back? And Shevlin dead, do you mean?"

I was about to answer that was the only answer I could make to the riddle when there was a firm, decided knock at the door of the room. I called out: "Who's there?"

"A friend," said an unfamiliar voice.

"Come in, friend," I said, "but come slowly!"

The door was pushed wide, and in the entrance I saw a man standing with what looked like a Moorish turban of white wrapped around his head. The form came in more to the light, and I saw that it was an awkwardly twisted bandage, and the face beneath the bandage was that of Sheriff Jack Shevlin!

# Chapter 26

Shirley went up to the sheriff with both of his hands stretched out, like a blindfolded man. He actually caught hold of Shevlin and said to him: "There's no dream about this . . . you're here, Sheriff Shevlin, and you're not done in."

"I'm here, it seems like," said Shevlin. "And I'm here a bit late, it looks like."

He glanced down at the dead body of the captain as I might have glanced at the dead body of a horse. I've known a lot of fine men in police work, and I've known a lot of fine doctors, too, but I've got to say that they make my flesh crawl a little—the careless way that they take human blood.

Shirley turned to me with what was almost a smile on his lean, handsome face. He looked like a drawing out of a magazine—one of the collar ads, I mean, or the young fellow on the front cover that's supposed to take the eye of the girl readers.

"It's having a wish, and the wish coming true," he said. He turned back to the sheriff. "We thought for a moment that Rourke might have overtaken you."

As quick as the point of a cat's paw, the sheriff said: "What made you think that?"

"Why . . . er . . . ," began Shirley, and he looked at me, as if to beg me not to say what I knew. But what was Cattrin to me?

"I saw Cattrin in this house this evening," I said.

"He came back, did he?" remarked the sheriff, as casually as you please.

"And because he got loose . . . you see, we knew that Rourke was apt to. . . ." Shirley paused again.

I didn't see why he had to bring in Rourke so persistently. It looked like a fool's blunder. If he wanted to cover up the mention of Cattrin's name, he could easily have left Rourke out of it. But that wasn't necessary, because Shevlin said: "I've met Mister Rourke, and I've found that he's just as fast and as straight with a gun as I suspected beforehand." He smiled and nodded at me, as though to recall what he had said about there being a gunfighter with our party, from his observations along the trail.

This made me feel none too good. I begged him to tell me what happened, and Shevlin told it the easiest way.

"He's a fair man," said the sheriff. "He didn't shoot from behind. He just rode out of the trees and sang out to me . . . and I pulled my gun as I turned. That was all. I wasn't as fast, and I wasn't as straight . . . that time. . . ."

He left a little upward tilt in his voice, like he was asking a question, and you could see that he wouldn't mind meeting Rourke again. As a matter of fact, all of the real gunfighters are like that. No matter what they say about simply doing their job, and hating trouble, they battle for the sake of the battle and very little else. This fellow Shevlin, with the blood still drying on his wound, and the pain of it making his eyes squint, wanted to have another try at Rourke, who just had downed him.

That was all he would say about it. You could gather that the bullet had glanced off of his head and flipped him out of the saddle, stunned, and that Rourke had taken Cattrin and ridden off with him. There was a little more to the story than that, as I was to learn later on.

At any rate, Shevlin stopped talking about Cattrin and Rourke at that point, and he went on to nod at Palliser. He wanted to know his name, and, when he heard it and his profession, he asked me if Palliser was the man who had spent some time on the China Sea, and I admitted that he was. After that, Shevlin said that we had better spend the night on this work. He asked Shirley to go to bed and be ready to stand the next watch with him in the small hours of the morning. Shirley seemed glad to go, only pausing a moment at the door and hoping that he would be able to work out the solution with us.

When he was gone, the sheriff said to me: "Is he right?"

"How?" I asked.

"Is this a mystery?"

"Why, of course!"

"You mean that there's no sign leading to the murderer?"

"No," I said firmly. I was firm, because I was turning my back on telling the truth that pointed toward Ruth Derrick. I suggested that we had better put the corpse on the bed, but the sheriff wouldn't hear of that.

First of all, he wanted to hear what I had to say. I told him. I began with the moment I was sitting in the patio, and how I had seen Cattrin's face behind me in the window, and how the ghost had walked, and then the murder, and how I battered in the door.

He wanted to know why I had been sitting there that late, and all alone, and that led me up to the story of the departure that I had planned with the captain, and the way in which events had led to that in turn. This brought me to the throwing of the silver coin through the window, and after that, with quick, short questions, he took me along to the point where I was looking out the window of the hotel, waiting for Rourke to wake up, and saw Rags for the first time in the yard of the hotel. In fact, he got out of me, very boiled down and short, everything that I knew about everything and everybody, except what I held back about Ruth Derrick. I had to. Whatever I did, I couldn't help remembering that she and me had been partners.

The sheriff was a great listener. He sat without moving, his hands in his lap, and kept his eyes fixed steadily upon mine. Like a boxer, you would say, who looks you in the eye in order to see what your hands are doing. I was a good deal interested in the way he tackled things. I knew from his work on the trail that he was expert, but there was nothing mysterious in what he said. He just went from point to point.

As I talked alone to Shevlin, I must say I lost a good deal of the confidence I had had in him. Talking about the open trail, he had seemed a mighty formidable sort of a man. Talking here in a room beside the body of a dead man, he seemed weaker. City police, after all, have more experience in being detectives.

When I got through, which was quicker than you would imagine, he said to me: "Who do you think would have done this?"

I said: "I don't know. Most likely some Mexican woman."

"A woman?" he said.

"Well, naturally. I saw the one that walked across the top of the wall there."

"Are you sure that was a woman?" he said.

"Why, yes."

"Will you tell me why, partner?"

"Because . . . why, she was wearing a woman's long nightdress, and I could see her long hair, too."

"Well?" he said.

"A crazy woman, I should say."

"Why crazy?" he asked.

"Because who but a crazy woman would walk in a nightdress at that time of night across the top of that wall?"

"Let me see that wall again," he said.

He went out onto the platform at the head of the stairs and threw the light of a lamp across the top of the wall. He spent a few minutes there and then he came back into the room, looking thoughtful.

"Well?" I asked.

"Either a crazy person," he said, "or else someone who could walk a tightrope. Because that wall, in places, is as narrow as a rope, almost, and a damned sight more rough and irregular."

I agreed with that. I had been watching the top of the wall at the same time that he had squinted along it, and it looked like the edge of a dull saw.

He put the lamp down, then he picked it up and went over to look at the bed and the body of the captain.

"It might not have been a woman," he said.

"It must have been. Think of the dress and the long hair."

"Anybody can buy a nightdress," he stated. "And anybody can buy a wig."

I felt like a fool. It was strange how that remark knocked part of my idea sky-west, and yet I could have laughed to see how this man with his cleverness was taking his thoughts away from the true line of Ruth Derrick. I didn't argue the point with him.

He picked up one of Palliser's arms and rolled up the sleeves of his coat and his shirt—of course he was dressed to leave the place and not in pajamas. Then Shevlin said to me: "I don't know who struck the first blow, but I think that a man struck the second one."

I blinked. "How can you guess at that?"

"Look at that arm," said Shevlin.

I looked. It was a thick arm, with a great knot of muscles below the elbow.

"Look here," said the sheriff. "The first blow was struck while he was lying in bed. Here's the stain of the blood that ran out from his throat. You see where it soaked through the sheet and left a dark spot on the mattress? But then he grappled with the person that struck the blow, and he grappled with those arms. He couldn't use his legs, you said?"

"No."

"Then his arms were probably as strong as the arms of a young man. Look at them. He grappled with those big hands. Would a woman have been able to stand the pressure of those fingers?"

It was a new idea to me. I looked and moistened my dry lips. I was beginning to hope against hope.

"That first blow wouldn't have killed him at once.

He would have lived half an hour ... an hour, maybe longer. But the second finished him the instant it was sent home. Look there ... look at the width of the mouth of that wound over the heart. See the bruised flesh around it. A man's arm sent that blow home, I should say, Jones."

I closed my eyes. I was seeing Ruth Derrick on her way to freedom, and the brains of the sheriff taking her there.

# Chapter 27

A good deal of the distrust I had been feeling for the abilities of the sheriff now cleared away. It seemed to me he was slugging away in a manner that would perhaps free poor Ruth Derrick almost entirely, no matter what appearances were against her. For that reason, I decided I would show the sheriff the letter Palliser had given to me. I was certain that the truth would appear in that letter, and I held my breath as I said to Shevlin: "Sheriff, I have a letter in my pocket that Palliser gave to me before he was killed. He was afraid something like this might happen, and he wrote out something that he said I was to open in case he died before I was able to get him away from the house. Here it is . . ." I reached into an inside coat pocket where I was reasonably sure I had placed the letter.

It was not there. I thrust my other hand, in haste, into the opposite pocket, and there, as in the first, my fingers touched on nothing. I sat gazing at Shevlin, and for the first time I saw his color change. A slight pink began to glow in his brown cheeks, and he snapped at me: "You're a grown man, Jones!

God knows you ought to keep the hands of strangers out of your inside coat pockets."

"That's not possible," I told him. "Nobody could have reached into one of these pockets and taken the thing out. It couldn't be done. Why, man, look at them for yourself."

The sheriff was willing enough. They were deep pockets. My clothes are made for comfort and use, not for looks, and there's nothing that I hate worse than shallow pockets. Any one of those pockets of mine would hold a Colt, for instance, and the lining is specially put in with strong cloth that won't wear through and drop out something.

Shevlin paid attention to all of these details, and he was so detached as he went on with his examination that he even remarked that it was a grand idea, and that, after this, he would have the pockets of his own clothes remade in the same fashion. That took some of the sting of his contempt away, but still I felt a good deal like a fool.

He asked me particularly what I had done after leaving Palliser. He and I agreed that it must have been at the supper table that I lost the envelope. I was sure that I must have lost the envelope while leaning over to pick up a napkin, say, although I couldn't remember having done that.

Shevlin right away made the experiment. He put a flat-sheathed, heavy knife in the pocket. Then he had me button up the coat the way that I wore it— which was with the two lower buttons fastened. When I leaned over to either side, the upper button of the coat drew the cloth tightly around me, and the pocket was strongly bound. The heavy knife and its smooth sheath did not slip a fraction of an inch, and it was plain as could be that an envelope could not have fallen out.

I began to get red and hot in my turn. I felt like a fool, because it seemed clear that my pocket had been picked.

"Who sat beside you at the table?" asked Shevlin.

"Ruth Derrick . . . ," I said, and tried to shut my teeth on the name too late. There it was, openly stated, and a cold chill settled in the small of my back and stayed there.

"Ruth Derrick was sitting alongside of you," said Shevlin, and yawned a little.

I thanked God devoutly that he had not noticed the way I had shut up.

"Perhaps she picked your pocket?" he said.

I laughed. "Hell, man," I said, "I would as soon suspect Saint Peter."

"Would you?" Shevlin asked in a gentle way. "Look here . . . how long have you known this girl?"

"Sheriff," I said, "there are times when you get to know people awfully quick."

"Of course there are," he answered. "But that's the sort of thing that it's hard to prove to a jury."

"Great heavens, man," I said, "what possible motive would she have had for such a crime?"

"We'll get to motives later on." Then he added: "Who else came near you at the table?"

"No one," I answered very gloomily.

"How did the food get onto the table? Did you carry it there yourself?"

"No, of course not. José, the Mexican. . . ."

"He waited on the table?"

"Yes."

"Suppose that José got it, then?"

"Sheriff," I said, "I got a lot of respect for you, but I gotta say that there ain't a man living that could lean over my shoulder and take a fat envelope out of a deep inside coat pocket without me seeing . . . or without some of the other folks at the table seeing."

"How do you know that they would have told you if they *did* see?"

"Are you going to make Shirley and Ruth Derrick both guilty?" I asked, getting angry at the impossibility of it.

"They's a mighty good rule in the law," said the sheriff, "that says that nobody is to be considered guilty until he's proven guilty. But for a gent like me, that has to run down crimes to the ground, there's only one way to start, and that's to figger that everybody is maybe guilty . . . until they've been proved innocent."

I glared at him. I could only say: "You can go your own way, Sheriff. You know a lot more about this business than I ever shall. But I gotta say that when you start in suspecting a girl like Ruth Derrick . . . why . . . of murder . . . of murder like this. . . ."

"You like her, eh?" said the sheriff.

"Why . . . she's just a fine, decent girl," I said.

"Sure," said the sheriff. "Did you ever tell her so?"

I gagged.

"Why not let her know?" he asked. "It might make a difference."

"I started to," I admitted.

"What stopped you?"

"She said that I was talking nonsense, if you have to know."

The sheriff grinned. "That'd stop most men," he agreed. "But about picking of pockets. I was on the trail of a pickpocket, once, and that fellow laid for me in a crowd and picked out of my trousers' watch pocket the fine gold watch that my father had given to me. It made me pretty sick. Well, I was a younger gent, in those days. I wasn't much older than you, and it didn't look possible, seeing that that watch was on a big heavy fob, and that it fitted tight in that pocket."

That shut me up a little.

"It might have been either José or the girl," Shevlin suggested.

"Meaning that only one of those two could have killed Palliser?" I fairly shouted.

The sheriff sighed, like a man talking to a child.

"I'm talkin' about the pickin' of a pocket, and not about the murder of a man, just now," he said. "But let's get down to suspicions. Pretty near everybody comes under that heading, in this here house."

"Everybody?" I gaped at him.

"Why not?"

"Me?"

"Well, you was outside of the room when the killing took place. How do I know that you didn't plan the whole thing, and that you smashed at the door and pretended to be keen to get in . . . but all the time you simply were workin' with the thugs that slaughtered Palliser, here, like a pig."

I turned from hot to cold, and the sheriff went on in his quiet voice: "That would get me over one of the worst parts of this here job . . . which is that after Palliser was murdered, the murderers disappeared. That's easy taken care of if you were in on the job. You just lowered him or her or them out of the window on a rope, and then you chucked the rope down to them . . . and there you are!"

The way he talked about it made the thing so clear that I almost thought that I *had* done the dirty job.

"All right," I said, standing up, "there ain't much use in a probable killer wastin' your time and talk now, Sheriff."

Suddenly he grinned at me, and it was amazing

the way that his face could brighten up and turn human when he wanted to make it.

"Don't be a jackass," said Shevlin. "Sit down, will you?"

"You got that question out ag'in' me," I said, "and I wouldn't feel any way comfortable with an idea like that floating around in your head while we sat here."

He nodded up at me, and said: "I know what you mean. But I'll tell you what, Jones. A man can't get on even as a sheriff unless he takes a few chances, now and then, and the chance that I take on you is that you're square, and that I can trust you. You and me are going to try to work out this case together."

I have to say that nothing in my life flattered me any more than that. But I said: "Thanks, Shevlin, I take that mighty friendly. But at the same time, I've got to tell you that I haven't any head for this sort of work. I don't like it, and I don't know anything about it."

"That's all right," he assured me. "I dunno that smart brains help a great deal. I'm not one of those book detectives, but I try to take one idea at a time and examine it. Suppose that you and me just chuck ideas and questions at one another and see which of 'em are no good, and which of 'em split the plate for the time being?"

I agreed to that, naturally. I was surprised and pleased to think that a man like the sheriff would want to let me in on the ground floor. I had a guilty pleasure, too—because now, if things began ever to point toward Ruth Derrick, I could ward them off from her and give them a turn in a different direction. It turned my heart to a stone to think of the sheriff even considering her.

I asked the sheriff if he didn't want to examine the

room carefully first of all, but he said that the room was willing to wait, and so was he. He said it was better to work our brains first, and our eyes second. So we sat down to talk.

# Chapter 28

I won't take up everything in detail the way that he talked it over, but I'll try to give you enough to show you how he went at a thing, cold-blooded and exact, and missing no tricks.

He said: "We'll start with the women. Because you thought that it was a woman that walked across the top of that wall."

"Sure," I said, "but you pointed out that any man could have been wearing a nightgown and a long wig."

"That's right," he said, "but there's something in the brain of a man that sees the difference between a man and a woman. The fact that you seen a woman walking there maybe meant that it *was* a woman. Nothing to the contrary come into your mind."

I admitted that was right, but I began to sweat. I was bringing the game too close to Ruth to suit me in the very beginning. I said that I couldn't understand why anybody but a crazy woman would ever want to play the part of the ghost and walk across there, plain to be seen.

The sheriff went after that idea like this. He said: "The ghost wanted to kill Palliser."

"Yes."

"Then it had to get to Palliser's room."

"That's right."

"How could it get there?"

"By the stairs, or by climbing up the rear wall the way the gent from the gray horse did, or by going across the wall."

"Anyone seen climbing up that rear wall would be spotted, if you saw him or maybe if the Mexicans did."

"Then why didn't the murderer wait until the time when I was in bed?"

"Because probably the killer knew that you were planning to make a getaway with Palliser that same night. They knew, and their hands were forced."

I hadn't thought of that, and I admitted it.

"If the murderer went up the steps, he'd have to come into the patio, close to you, and you'd have a better look and a better shot at him . . . or her. If he went across the wall dressed up like the ghost, there was a pretty good chance that you would get nervous and miss, even if you did start shooting. And that was what happened."

I said: "I could have swore that I'd put two bullets straight through that thing in white."

"I've seen a time" said Shevlin, "when I could've swore that I'd put half a dozen bullets straight into the body of a bear at point-blank range. But when I got him, I found only one slug that had happened to wander to the right place."

I had nothing to say to that. I knew that the same thing happens all the time in the hills.

"Well, then," said Shevlin, "we've got down to the idea of why the ghost wanted to walk across that ridge of wall. It was mostly on account of you and the Mexicans."

"All right," I said, "we'll say that is proved."

"We'll begin by sayin' that the chances are that a woman was inside those white clothes, and we'll start with the most important woman . . . Miss Mornay. . . ."

"Sheriff," I interrupted, "have you ever seen her?"

"No."

"Then you better wait."

"Because she's got a pretty face, eh?"

"Why," I explained, "there's a light in her . . . there's a light of goodness in her, and beauty. You never seen such a woman."

"All right," Shevlin said, "but in a murder case everybody is no more than a name . . . with chances for and chances against. What kind of a motive would she have for doing this murder?"

"She would rather have cut her own throat."

"Maybe. But I don't see that yet. She was the niece, eh?"

"Yes, she was."

"What did she have to gain? Was she down to get any of old Palliser's money?"

"Everything was coming to her," I said.

"Ah . . . ," Shevlin mused, nodding his head very significantly.

"All right," I said. "She killed her old Uncle Ned, then. Stabbed him in the throat and then in the chest as he begun to maul her and fight for his life. What next?"

"You throw that idea out," said the sheriff, "but look at it in this way. A woman in white walks across the top of a wall and comes to the room of Palliser and murders him. And the woman who's to gain the most by it is this Frances Mornay. Maybe she's a

saint. I dunno. You see that the idea is pretty interesting, anyway."

"To you," I said, feeling a little disgusted.

"What really have you ag'in' it?" he said.

"Wouldn't it take a regular mountain climber or a
tightrope expert to walk across the top of that wall?"

"Yes," he said.

"Wouldn't it take a woman without no nerves?"

"Yes, it certainly would."

"Well, this Frances Mornay has been half dead,
lately. She's as nervous as a poplar leaf in a wind!"

"However," said Shevlin, "it was a pretty fine
murder for her, wasn't it? If it brought all of the captain's coin into her hands, I mean?"

I shrugged my shoulders, and Shevlin, too,
dropped that subject and went on to others. I've
given this in detail so that you can see what his
method was like, turning over every stone in his
mind, and sort of fighting me on each name to make
sure that every person in the house was guilty.

He took off on Ruth Derrick next as a matter of
course. I didn't say any more in praise of her, because I felt that I would be pretty shaky on that subject. He made out that Ruth Derrick was a strong,
vigorous girl, which she was—that she had good
nerves, as she'd shown by the way she could use a
rifle, hunting—that she was familiar with big
knives, because I myself had taught her how to quar-
ter and skin a deer.

I put in here: "She's able to shoot like a man, with
a rifle or with a revolver. Wouldn't she have finished
off Palliser with a gun? Is a young girl apt to do a
murder with a knife?"

"Partner," said Shevlin, "in this sort of work you
don't pay no attention to what folks are apt to do,
but what it's possible for them to do. When you

come right down to it, no murder is probable . . . but still, a lot of 'em happen." He went on to find a motive for her crime, and here he stuck a little, as I had been stuck before him.

At last he said: "There *is* a motive, although it don't appear to be a very bang-up good one. Frances Mornay is her friend. She's mighty fond of Frances, ain't she?"

"Yes."

"So she makes up her mind that she'll cut the problem short for her and force her to leave this here house, where so much bad luck always has hung around for the Mornays. She might have a little other motive, too. Suppose that Frances cuts in for a lot of money from Palliser, then ain't she pretty sure to remember her pal, Ruth Derrick? Sure, and with a fine, fat legacy."

I had listened to about as much of this yarning as I could stand, and now I said to him: "Shevlin, ain't there any men in this house?"

There were and he admitted it. He had never intended to leave them out, and now he went for them, one by one, in a way that made me sweat to hear. There was something kind of devilish in the logical way that he tackled them. He left out not a single soul in all that place; I've already shown you how he threw the tar brush at me, and then rubbed me clean of suspicion for a minute or two. But still I felt that I was under his sharp eye, no matter who else he might be discussing.

Starting at the bottom: Wong was a Chinaman. Palliser had been on the China Seas. Well, then Wong was a man who had been wronged by the captain, perhaps in trading. And he had come across the world to get even with him. Knife work was right in line with Chinaman's talents, too.

Dorgan was a sailor. He wore a lot of tattooing. He might have met up with Palliser, too, and have an old grudge.

There was the man on the gray horse, who had been able to say enough to make Palliser groan and cry out like a small boy being flogged. We would have to wait to find out more about that man.

The Mexicans next. They were brigands, no doubt, ready to murder Palliser for the sake of the money in his sea chest. And José, picking my pocket of the letter. . . .

"Why should he want that letter? How would he know what was in that letter?"

"It wasn't there at noon. He found it there at night, and he got to wondering, so he helped himself to a look."

"That's easy to say."

"I'm not hanging folks on this sort of testimony, but I'm *trying* to hang them."

He went on from the Mexicans, only stopping for a minute to point out that they were just the people to work with the knife, and the next person that he came up against was Cattrin.

Somehow, he didn't think that Cattrin would have walked across that wall. But Cattrin might have climbed up the rear wall of the room, after seeing that I was safe in the patio. In the room, he might have helped after the first blood had been struck by somebody else.

There was Rourke, too. Admitting that Rourke was a fellow who was straight enough, ordinarily, he already had showed that he was pretty insane with love for Frances Mornay. He'd shot down a sheriff, and why shouldn't he murder Palliser?

"Because he loves fair play," I said.

"Women are poison, son," said the sheriff. "Sometimes I wonder where they get the constitutions to stand themselves. She might've turned Rourke's brain into a fever."

There remained only one other person, and that was Shirley, and against him Shevlin made out a case, too, although I didn't see how he was going to do that, at first. But he rested his case against Shirley chiefly upon the motive of cash. Shirley was engaged to Frances Mornay. If Palliser died, Frances got the coin. That meant that Shirley would get it through her. So there you were. Shirley could have done the thing, and had a motive for it.

"Then everybody in the whole damn' place is guilty!" I cried at Shevlin.

"Everybody and nobody," said Shevlin. "Maybe it's somebody whose face we've never seen. You didn't see who threw the silver piece through the window."

# Chapter 29

Now that Shevlin had finished up with his accounting of the motives—which seemed to paint one member of the house as black as another, he started what I should have done the first of all—an examination of the room.

Once this began, however, I had no complaints to make. I mean to say this examination was a great deal more careful than I should ever had dreamed of making it. For an example, he took the distance from the door to the bed and from the bed to the windows, and he lowered a long piece of steel tape and with it he measured the distance from the windows to the ground. Then he went over the floor itself with a strong magnifying glass, although I pointed out that such a glass, by the light of the morning sun, would show him more in five minutes than he could see in hours by using the light of the lamps in the room, for there were only two of these, and both were mere single burners.

When I made suggestions like these, however, Shevlin would stop his work and listen with a good deal of attention, but he always cut me off with some simple remark—about time being better than sharp eyes, etc., until you would have thought that he actually expected guilt to grow and ripen like a crop of wheat.

I grew more and more impatient; I was almost glad when Shirley came in, rubbing his eyes and yawning, and suggested that it was time for him to take my place and go on watch. Then I wished them both luck and left Palliser's room, only stopping in the patio to look at the stars and wonder vaguely that they should be so different from the face they had showed in the earlier part of the evening. I have noticed before that the stars never seem to move if you watch them steadily; it's when you take your eyes away that they may be seen to gallop across the sky. They had galloped in this interim.

But what struck me as strangest of all was that the whisper of the fountain and the showering of its spray went on in exactly the same fashion that I had heard before, the stars seemed brighter, and the whole world was given over to night more completely. When I looked around the patio, I could not help centering my attention a good deal on the blank window out of which I had seen Cattrin looking earlier in the evening. It had a personality, while the rest of the windows that stared down on the patio seemed empty and unmeaning, but out of that one I still could imagine that the contorted face of Cattrin was looking.

There was a good and an easy way of satisfying my doubts. I caught hold of the lower sill of the window and heaved myself straightway into the room. Inside, I dropped on the floor and remained motionless for a moment, as much frightened as though I had put myself under the muzzles of half a dozen hostile guns. While I remained there, it occurred to me that, if there were anyone in the room, it would

not be hard to distinguish the top of my head bobbing up and down against the stars beyond the window, so I changed my place, crawling gradually
around the room until I reached the first door. I
closed this, found the key, and cautiously locked it.
Now I had the satisfaction of knowing that I was
alone in this room and I was fairly well satisfied that
I was alone in the chamber, so eventually I forced
myself to light a match.

I was right, and there was not a soul in the place.
There was very little in this room, other than a small
homemade table in the center of a rag rug and an
old wardrobe in the corner, looking as it must have
been hauled around the Horn by some clipper, and
then dragged by oxen out here to this corner of the
mountains. But there was something richer than furniture in that room for me. On the floor there was a
coating of the thickest dust, and in the rich, thick
dust I could see the tracing that I had made when I
went upon my hands and knees around the border. I
also could see other sign that I had *not* made.

In the first place, there was the distinct marking of
a man's shoe, short and broad-toed, that crossed the
floor from the doorway, and then paced up and
down before the window. I could have sworn that
while that man walked up and down, I was sitting in
the courtyard just under the window. By the grace of
God, he hadn't seen me, for, of course, I could swear
that the man in the room had been Cattrin.

There was something else that exercised me a
good deal more than the trace of these shoes and
that was the mark of a smaller size that could only
have belonged to a child—or a woman! I looked at
these sign in the dust with a sort of despair. I could
remember that Frances Mornay wore pointed toes
and high, foolish heels that made her look taller

than Ruth Derrick, although in reality she lacked an inch or so of that height. But the shoes of Ruth herself were a different matter. They were extremely sensible. They had round toes and a flat, broad heel. So much so that you could hardly have told them from the shoes of a cowpuncher, except the cowpunchers were so foolishly vain that they would pinch and crush their feet to make them look smaller. But, for all of their pinching and for all of their crowding, there was one dimension that they could not force to look smaller, and this was the distance from the heel to the end of the big toe. There was not enough of that distance here to allow for the foot of any grown man that I ever saw. It was the mark of the shoe of Ruth, I was certain.

Straightaway I went across that floor with a handkerchief and made a smear of every one of those marks, while I burned my fingertips holding lighted matches for the job. When I had finished that, I didn't think of anything more important to be done. I was only anxious to get out of the room and to my bed, and it was only by the sheerest chance that I struck a lump under the corner of the rag rug.

I would not have stopped to see what it was, if it had been closer to the center of the rug, but since it was close to the edge, my conscience, what there was of it, forced me to have a look. I flipped back the corner of the rug, lighted a match, and there I saw a long knife that would have done for the skinning of any bear, but with a blade a little straighter than would actually be handled for that sort of work. The blade looked a little filmy and blue. When I touched it with the tip of my finger, it appeared sticky; I held another match close to the handle, and then I saw that the hilt was covered with more of a dark fluid that had half dried. I knew what that fluid was. It was blood, and any fool could have guessed that it came out of the heart of Palliser.

I looked at this knife, and then I remembered the short footprints that I had just wiped out from the dust on the floor, and a sicker man never walked the face of the earth than I was. But still, when I looked back at the sign, it seemed to me to disprove itself, for I couldn't imagine a hand like that of Ruth Derrick handling a knife of that size. I tried to tell myself, over and over, that this was not the exact same knife that I had given her, having bought it myself before the trip and carried it along as a second.

The proof was stamped in the butt, the sign of the maker, and I dreaded more than poison to pick up the knife and see there the initial that would mean that my guess was right. Well, that hard time came to a point. I took out my handkerchief and picked up the knife, and, turning it up, point down, I saw by the light of a match that what I was afraid of was true—the initials were stamped deeply into the butt. I grew a little sick after that. I kept the knife and the handkerchief still in my hand, and I went to the window and kneeled there, hanging my head over the sill. Slowly the cool freshness of the open air breathed on my face and restored me a little, but again and again the shudder came over me.

Finally I slipped through the window and down into the patio. I regretted with all my might that I ever had climbed up through the window and found what I had found. But now there was nothing for it but to take the knife along with me. There were such things as fingerprints. They seemed worse than dragons to me, just then, because I could remember back to stories that I had heard in which a clever detective comes along and by means of a bit of cigarette ash and a fingerprint, he traces a criminal from London to Cape Town.

Frankly I was afraid that I held the death warrant of Ruth Derrick in my hand, and I carried that death warrant to the central fountain and was about to drop it in when it occurred to me that the very first place that any smart police officer would look would be in the fountain itself, and therefore I'd better not tamper with it. There was a bottom to every well and to every fountain, of course, and perhaps even if the finger marks were washed off, there would be a quality in the blood itself that would hang the guilt on the girl.

So, instead of doing that, I wrapped the knife more carefully in my handkerchief, and then I carried it back to my bedroom and crouched there in the dark, as guilty as any damned anarchist with a murdering bomb. For I felt that I had the bomb that would destroy Ruth Derrick!

Well, in spite of all of this misery and excitement of mine, just as I had gone to sleep the night before in spite of handicaps, so I went to sleep this night, and, although I was miserable enough to have all my dreams colored by my own wretchedness, still I was not waked up by what I felt. What did rouse me, just as on the morning before, was the brightness of the morning sun that shot through my window. I looked across to it as peaceful as a child, until I saw the ragged great gap in the pane.

Then I could remember back to what had happened to that window. I turned my head and I saw the two indentations marked upon the inner wall, where the bullets had landed. These bullet marks were not three inches apart; by that I could tell how narrowly death had missed me. A little less luck and both of those slugs would have gone through my brain. Then my mind jumped forward from that point, and I rehearsed everything that had happened the night before.

# Chapter 30

At that moment, Rags jumped from the floor onto my bed and yipped, and there was a knock at the door. I sang out, instinctively gathering up a Colt as I did so—and then in walked Shirley, looking pretty down.

He had been up all the night, he said, listening to the talk of the sheriff. He said: "God in heaven, Jones, nobody in the world is free from guilt, according to that devil of a man! He even touched . . . but no matter for that." He snapped his fingers and leaned back in his chair with a frown on his face. The closer you looked at Shirley, the nobler he appeared. I had taken him at first for a sort of sulky pretty boy, who would take the fancy of a girl, but the longer I knew him, the more seriously I had to take him.

I said: "Did he take a look at Frances Mornay, for instance?"

Shirley started violently in his chair, but he'd been so worked up before this, apparently, that his color didn't change. "How did you guess that?" he said.

"Why, because he talked the same way to me. He put the tar brush on everybody . . . including you!"

"And on you!" Shirley exclaimed. "I've never heard of such a thing."

We looked at each other, and then both of us began to laugh a little.

"He does his thinking aloud," I suggested.

"Yes . . . perhaps that's it."

But there was something else on the mind of Shirley, as I could tell by his absent look. I waited for it to come out, and turned the talk for an instant on the broken panes of my window. I couldn't help remarking that whoever had done that job should have waited until I was sound asleep, and then have fired through by daylight.

"Yes," said Shirley, "so that there would be daylight for the hunt to be carried on."

There was a good deal in that, too, and I thought more of the brains of Shirley than I had before.

Suddenly he broke out: "What do you think of this, Jones?" He put into my hand a ring that had a battered look. It was a golden band, and the gold had been scratched and bent out of shape a little, and the setting was partly filled with what looked like blue glass.

"I don't know what to think of it," I confessed. Which was a fact, because it didn't connect with anything in my mind.

He said very slowly: "I think that's a sapphire . . . or the last of a sapphire, in there."

The words went drifting through me like fire—and again they went into my mind and left it burning. Sapphire.

He went on: "You know that Ruth Derrick had a sapphire ring. And . . . and I picked this up from the floor of Palliser's room." He jumped up from his chair and went pacing up and down while I looked at that ring with a very sick face and a very sick heart. I remember that at the bottom of the sapphire that I had found in the same place, there had been a bright flaw, as if the stone had been cracked across. I could remember the shape of the stone so clearly that it was plain that it had come out of this setting.

In the meantime, Shirley went on talking. He said in a rapid, muffled way: "I don't know what to do. God knows that I don't want to hurt Ruth. I haven't any right to bring this sort of news to you, Jones, but I haven't been blind, and I could see that you and she are great friends. Friends? Why, I thought that everybody in the world ought to be the friend of Ruth Derrick." He laughed a little, and, stopping short, he snapped his fingers in a nervous way that seemed to be taking hold on him.

I couldn't make any remark. I tried to say something to show that I couldn't believe she had anything to do with this affair, but I didn't have to talk, because Shirley was so filled with emotion that he went right on in good style, and filled up the pause well enough.

He said: "When I found the ring lying on the floor and picked it up. . . ."

I broke in: "How under heaven could you have found it on the floor? The sheriff went all over the whole place."

"No doubt he did. And he has the eyes of an owl . . . the devil! But the ring must have hit the wall and rolled back with a good deal of force. It was lodged just under the edge of the rug . . . half lost in the fuzz, do you see? And, after all, the sheriff only had lamplight to work by."

"And what did you have?" I asked.

"Luck!" he announced. "Bad luck or good luck, as you please to call it. I was fumbling and pretending to help him search, but, as a matter of fact, I was too tired and sleepy to be any good . . . when my fingers struck this lump at the edge of the rug. I picked it out and exclaimed. The sheriff said . . . 'What is that?' So I was about to show it to him, when I saw the glint of the blue in this setting . . . and I remembered Ruth's sapphire ring . . . and, my God, how my heart failed me! I called out to him that I'd run a splinter of stone under my fingernail, and he muttered an oath and paid no more attention."

Shirley went back toward the door and threw himself into a chair. He said nothing, but I never have seen a more miserable face.

"I don't know," I finally confessed. "I haven't the slightest idea what to say or to do."

"But could she have done it? *Could* she have done it?" said Shirley.

"You've known her longer than I have," I reminded him. I was too miserable to say anything positive.

"That's true," said Shirley. "But I'll tell you, Jones, as long as I've known her and as well, I've never heard of her or seen her in anything that wasn't straightforward and fine and clean. She's a fine girl, and she's a lady."

"I believe that she is," I said. "And so she couldn't have anything to do with this."

"She couldn't. She couldn't have a hand in it," said Shirley rapidly, to himself. He jumped up from his chair and began to pace the floor again. "Besides, what would her motive be?" he asked.

I quoted the sheriff. "To help Frances Mornay."

Shirley stopped and threw a hand in front of his face. "I thought of that," he said so low that I barely could hear him.

He jerked out a handkerchief and began to mop his forehead. Then he stuffed the handkerchief nervously back into his front coat pocket. I never have seen a man more nervously upset. Finally he started out at me by saying: "Jones, no matter what the truth may be . . . to me, Ruth Derrick can't have done anything wrong."

I stretched out my hand. "By God, Shirley," I told him, "you're all right!"

He shook my hand with a good deal of warmth, but his hand was as chilly as stone.

"We're together on that?" he said.

"Until hell freezes over," I confirmed.

"That's good, that's good," muttered Shirley. "By God, Jones, that man Shevlin has almost broken down my morale. I'm half of a mind to say that everybody in the world is a crook . . . capable of murder . . . after listening to him all the night. Great God, what an outlook on life! What a lot of poison to carry about in one's mind. Ruth Derrick. Why, I know her like a sister. Exactly."

I liked Shirley better and better. And I've noticed this: That when you begin to like a man very little, and when you gradually come to see more in him, he will finally stand out in a brighter light than ever will a chap who you meet and take a flare to at once.

He snatched the ring away from me and stared at it again, saying: "I've tried to make out that it's a different shape of setting from the one that Ruth wears. Eh?"

I shook my head.

"You remember it?"

"I don't have to remember the shape of it," I said. I took my coat from the chair beside the bed, and from the vest pocket I lifted out the sapphire. It fitted easily into the setting; the little gold grillwork reached up and snagged it into place, except on one side where it had been bent outward.

Shirley threw up his hand with a groan.

"Is that it, man? Did *you* find that there?"

I looked at him without saying a word. Words didn't mean very much, just then; we stared at one another.

Shirley said: "Jones, I suppose there's not much doubt, after this. If she's to be saved from the prying mind of that devil of a sheriff, we'll have to work with a good deal of care."

I nodded.

"Can you keep those things safely?" he asked.

"I'll throw them into the cañon," I said.

"Into the cañon? Well, what could be a better idea than that?" said Shirley.

We paused in our talk.

Shirley slipped to the door, opened it, and looked out. Then he came back and leaned against the wall, looking sick and white, his head thrown back with fatigue, and his eyes half closed.

"I don't see the way out, as yet," said Shirley.

Nor did I.

The guilt of the girl had to be covered, but how were we to shut away the cleverness of the sheriff from her?

"I've half a mind to . . . to do for him!" broke out Shirley, his jaw setting and his nostrils expanding.

It gave me a shock; the man looked fierce enough for anything.

"Steady, old fellow," I prodded gently. "He's an honest man, you know."

"Yes, yes, yes," gasped Shirley. "I think I'm getting dizzy."

"You'd better go to sleep," I suggested.

He nodded at me, fumbled at the door, hesitated, and then jerked it open and was gone.

I could hear him going down the hall, rapidly, but stumbling like a man dead beat.

# Chapter 31

If the sheriff was keeping his watch all by himself in the room of Palliser, it was high time for me to go up there and relieve him or, at least, to sit with him. So I got up, shaved, took a sponge bath, and began to feel that perhaps everything wasn't lost. It's very odd that a shave always makes a man's heart lighter.

I had just finished that when I heard a tap at the door, and, when I opened it, I found Frances Mornay. She was dressed in something blue, as light and thin as a mist, and Mimi was coiled up in her arms like a tuft of golden flame, watching me with her curious, violet eyes. She hated all men, that cat, and I hated her more than a cat should be hated. But, after all, it's not easy to like them. I didn't have eyes for the cat very long, since Frances Mornay slipped into the room and closed the door behind her. She leaned against it, looking frightened, guilty, and wonderfully beautiful so that it seemed more than strange to me that anyone under a king or a duke, at least, had ever been able to get her attention. Shirley by himself had seemed a very fine sort of a fellow, but, in the light of his fiancée, he looked kind of shabby.

She said to me: "Is it safe to talk here?"

I told her it was perfectly safe and asked her to sit down. She didn't seem to hear the invitation, but said to me: "Have you had any word from Dennis Rourke?"

I told her that I had not, but that I expected to before very long.

"You . . . you think that he'll come back?" she stammered at me. "Ah, and then he'll run straight into the arms of that dreadful sheriff, and I. . . ." She sank down suddenly in a chair and looked at me helplessly as though her strength had run out. "And then they'll be sure to fight again . . . and the second time there's sure to be a. . . ." She stopped. Her eyes filled with tears. "I didn't know," she went on, "what would happen. I only knew that I was afraid for poor. . . ."

"Cattrin?" I couldn't help snapping. "I wouldn't worry so much about that fellow, if I were you!"

She was like a child, opening her eyes at me. "Do you think he's a bad man?" she asked in a ghostly whisper.

"I know that he is," I said.

That made her mute and staring; you would say that something had been stolen away from her, and I could guess that it was all her faith in Cattrin. Why should such a skunk have meant anything to her? Why, because of old associations, I suppose. A woman will get used to a bad man the same way that a dog will.

She broke out at last, rapidly: "I know that I must do something for Dennis Rourke because he thought he was helping me when he went to save my friend. How *can* I help? I've tried to think, and this is all I could find to do. I have some money with me. It isn't a great deal, but, if you could find him, there would be enough to get you both safely away from that dreadful man, Shevlin. Here it is, John. You'll take it, won't you? Oh, it isn't a price or a reward, but just a means of getting you away . . . because, otherwise, that little dusty man will follow until he's come to Dennis Rourke again and then . . . I should have on my soul . . . a murder."

Now, having said this in a trembling voice, she gathered the golden cat closer to her with one hand and with the other held out a bundle of bills. I saw 100 printed in the corner of half a dozen of them and I knew she must be offering me a couple of thousand. Well, it was a temptation. To get hold of Rourke and slide out of that place with him, with enough coin to take us around the world, was as good as anything I could wish for. But I saw that I couldn't do that. I was committed to stick and see this thing through at the house of Mornay. If the girl had been able to see things from a man's point of view, of course, she never would have made the offer, and I explained this to her as quietly and simply as I could. And when she asked me about Rourke, I lied to her, and told her I was sure to see him as soon as he came near the house, and then I could keep him out of mischief.

She seemed a lot happier, after this, and went off with Mimi looking at me over her shoulder.

Then I went to Wong and got a cup of coffee. Wong was not very happy. He looked nervous and restless, and, while I was drinking the coffee, he kept walking around the room, pretending to be busy with one thing after another, until I got a pretty firm thought in mind that Wong was simply trying to keep from meeting my eye.

I noted that to tell the sheriff, and went on up to Palliser's room, where I found that Shevlin was working with a microscope—a little pocket microscope and what looked to me like mere dust on the glass slides.

When he saw me, he nodded and smiled a little, and started to put away his apparatus, wiping the dust carefully into one of those manila envelopes of his. I asked him if he didn't want a few hours sleep, but he seemed surprised when I put the question. He assured me that he never had felt better in his life and I had to believe him.

He looked as though he had had the soundest sort of a sleep. His eye was as bright and active as the eye of a man who had just made a million and expects to strike it rich again in no time at all. He looked about the room then, like a housewife who has put everything in order after breakfast, say. He even went over to where poor Palliser was stretched under a white sheet and raised a corner of it to look at the dead face.

Then he said briskly: "Suppose that we step out for a walk, Jones?"

I was willing to get out of that place. As we went down the stairs I couldn't help saying to him: "Look here, Shevlin, you like this business. You're happy at it."

He glanced aside at me, and then he laughed with pure pleasure, so that I got the creeps.

"It's my business," he said. I snorted, and pretended that it was a sneeze. But he went on: "Ask a 'puncher if he likes the range?"

"Sure a 'puncher does," I said. "But what has that got to do with it?"

"He has to boil in summer and freeze all the winter," said the sheriff. "Isn't that a pretty rough job?

Mine isn't much worse. A dead man ain't a lot colder than a blizzard, to my way of thinking."

I didn't say any more, because I could see that he wouldn't understand, no more than you can expect to make a horse understand words. He was a pretty fine fellow, but his idea of poker was a murder with five cards wild. You can't talk to a man that likes that sort of a thing.

He said that he wanted to have a look at my room through the window, so down we went and looked through, and then he began to examine the path and asked me if I had found any tracks there that looked suspicious. I pointed out that the path was covered with big gravel that wouldn't take a good impression and, besides that, a lot of people walked up and down it every day.

He agreed with that, but still he smelled around, so to speak, on his hands and knees. Then he went out with me into the woods, with Rags bouncing ahead of us. He wasn't disappointed about not finding anything, apparently, at my window. Whether he made a find or not, he never showed his emotion, but put each thing behind him.

At last I said: "How does it make you feel, Shevlin?"

"The woods?" he said. "Why, they make me feel fine. The smell of the leaf mold and the smell of the pine needles, things dead and things living, y'understand, Jones?"

I didn't, exactly, and I told him so.

"It's all working. That's what I like about it," said Shevlin. "The leaves workin' over your head."

"In the wind?" I said.

"In the sunlight," he answered. "Drawin' out the stuff that the trees need ... every leaf doin' work that a whole blacksmith shop never could manage.

And under your heels the roots grippin' deeper, hunting water, sopping it up ... big roots like your leg ... little roots a damn' sight finer than ferns ... fine as dust ... hunting water, eating the rotten leaf mold ... making good trees like these here ... sound trees, y'understand, Jones?"

"I sort of begin to," I told him.

He went on in the quiet voice of a man who is talking to himself more than to his companion: "Why, life is like that ... rotten dead things underneath and good clean strong men and women showing up on top. You take a man himself. He's got the two ends. You foller me, partner?"

I said I didn't, which was true. It would've sounded kind of crazy, except that this gent from the desert was talking it.

Shevlin went on: "I mean that every man and woman has got the leaves ... living in the sun and making something out of nothing and looking at the sky and the mountains, and enjoying life. But, also, every man and woman is fixed in something dark and miserable as mud. That's why I like my game. It's the only game. You see?"

"Because you see the rot in folks?" I asked him, getting mad.

"Because I see both ends. Look at the fools that go to a show." Here he laughed and made a gesture, as though he was picking handfuls of gold out of the air.

"What they got? A made-up yarn. No truth in it. Nothing really strange. They don't see any more than the wrinkles in the skin. But look at me ... here. I see ten faces on every man in the house. I see them looking in all kinds of directions. I work down into the roots where they're the darkest, or up in the tops ... in the leaves. I tell you what, Jones, you get a good lot of crime out of the sun, in the middle of the sky, as you might say."

This I didn't follow, and I said so, but he didn't care to explain. That man actually was too happy. You'd say that he'd got a legacy from somebody that he'd never heard of. So happy that he talked like this, kind of crazy, the way that a young boy talks that don't know hardly what he says.

# Chapter 32

Rags ran a squirrel up a tree, and then he found that he could scratch his way up in a furrow of the trunk, and the first thing I knew, he was twenty feet over my head, looking at the squirrel that had turned into a gray streak and was disappearing in the tree, too, scattering yells as he went, the scaredest squirrel you ever heard of.

Shevlin approved of that, and stood by for a long time. He wouldn't let me help Rags down from the tree because, he said, that any fool could get into trouble but that it took a wise man to get out. "What do you call a genius?" Shevlin explained. "Why, a man that takes chances and makes his way home every time. But the tenth time he comes home loaded down with loot."

This fellow Shevlin couldn't help talking that morning. He run over with words, the way that hot beer runs over when it's uncorked. I could see that he was frothing with excitement. Well, he would tell me as much as he pleased, and that ended it.

We watched Rags. He never yipped or asked for help except to look at me for a minute, and, when he saw that I was standing back, he wagged his tail as much as to say that if this job was left all to him, he was willing to tackle it. He squinted down the channel in the trunk up which he had climbed. Going up, it must have looked like a pretty good ladder, but going down, head first, was like what a hundred-yard devil's slide would have been to me. However, he had the nerve and down he came, bracing his feet, but sliding faster and faster in spite of himself. A dozen feet from the end he was knocked off balance and came down in a spinning wheel. He hit the ground with a *thump*, and, when he got up, he staggered around and around in a circle.

I felt sick and mean and wanted to pick him up, but the sheriff dragged me away, saying: "Don't show him no sympathy, because that turns a man or a dog into a baby. That's a dog, partner. That's a real dog. That's one that I could use."

"He can trail like a bloodhound," I said.

"Can he?" Shevlin asked. "Lemme see." He pulled one of his eternal envelopes out, took a handkerchief from it, and let Rags take a smell. Then he pointed to a spot on the ground, and, in a minute, Rags was scuttering through the leaves ahead of us as happy as could be.

That was a finisher for me. I saw all at once that while I thought we were out for just a walk, the sheriff had been following a trail, all of that time. I asked him if he really could see anything, because the ground looked pretty empty to me. At that, he pushed away from the surface some of the needles and showed me a little depression in the damp of the ground. It was the footmark of a man, right enough. I asked Shevlin how in thunder he could see such marks when the thickness of the leaves covered them up.

"It ain't hard," said the sheriff. "But all kinds of

prints look difficult, if you don't know how to read. Every trail is printed mostly in foreign language. You only get a word here and there that you can understand, and the rest is guessing at the drift."

"Will you tell me whose footprints you're following?"

"Him that killed Palliser, maybe," Shevlin said.

He said it so off-hand that it was a minute before I could understand what he had meant, then I gave a jump and started looking around me.

"The man that did the murder?" I said.

"The man that shot the two bullets through your window, anyway," said the sheriff.

"And you've followed his trail all this way?"

"I have."

"You *did* find a sign of him near the window?"

"Sure. Right under it. How would you stand to shoot through a window? Out on the gravel? No, but as close up as you could get, because you're looking through glass that blinds you unless you get right on top of it. Even then, it puts waves across your eyes, which is why those shots missed you. Now, you'd put your left foot forward, wouldn't you, in a place like that? And hold the gun with your right hand? Anyway, that was what he did."

"Sheriff," I said, "if you can bring me up to the hound, I'll be in debt to you as long as I live."

"The pleasure is all mine, Jones," he said.

"You've got no idea who it could be?"

"Well," he said, "if I was you, I'd keep my eyes on Dorgan."

"Dorgan?"

"Yes."

"He committed the murder?"

"He tried to murder you, didn't he?"

"What does that mean?"

"I dunno. Don't ask me questions right now. It spoils a man's thinking to have to boil his thoughts down into words too quick. But that was a handkerchief of Dorgan's that I gave the dog to smell. You seen how he put that scent together with this trail?"

"I don't want to bother you," I told the sheriff, "but why should Dorgan want to bump me off?"

Shevlin stopped a minute and looked at the treetops.

"You missed anything, lately?"

"No."

"You're sure?"

"Haven't missed a thing."

"That's strange," said Shevlin.

"Why should it be? And what has that got to do with Dorgan?"

"You're sure that you ain't missed a solitary thing, Jones?"

He scowled at me, and I thought back and shook my head again.

I said: "The other evening, I thought I missed a boot, but I found it, all right. I'd simply shied it into a corner."

"Yeah?" drawled Shevlin. "Well, that's all right, then." He went on, walking slowly and nodding to himself.

"And what has that got to do with Dorgan?" I asked.

"Dorgan?" said the sheriff, coming halfway out of his thoughts. He put a hand on my arm and said: "Dorgan. I've told you . . . you watch him. If he's around, have your guns ready. He'd murder you as soon as he'd take a breath. He's done murder before."

I cursed a little to let off steam, and then I told him I hoped that we'd meet Dorgan soon. I don't want to be made out a fighting man, but this idea of Dorgan hounding me upset me a little, and I wanted to get at him quick. Dorgan! I saw his rough make again. That fellow was capable of anything. I could tell that, once the sheriff had pointed it out to me. Like recognizing a story when you hear the tail end of it.

We came on Rags again, at a run of water, completely beat, and Shevlin said that it was no good to go any farther, because Dorgan could have gone down that stream and pulled himself out of the water by any one of the branches of 500 trees. That was true, and we couldn't spend forever trying to make this out.

"Now we'll walk for fun," said Shevlin. "Afterward, we'll come in and bag Dorgan."

I wanted to go back to the place right then, for fear that Dorgan would be lighting out to get clear, but the sheriff said that he wouldn't do that, because, if he did, he naturally would pull the suspicion of having done the murder right onto his shoulders. That seemed fair enough, and yet I was still worried as we walked on.

We put a good couple of miles behind us, never trying to stay to any trail or path, and Shevlin all that time as cheerful as a man could be. He never talked to me, but he looked always around him, at the trees, at the ground, at the squirrels, and stopped and laughed when a rabbit jumped up in a clearing and turned itself into a streak of dust.

We got down into a hollow where the trees grew so close together that we had to take a good deal of care to find the right path, and, in the middle of this, Shevlin stopped short and gripped my shoulder.

"Look there," he said.

I looked in the direction he had pointed and asked him what it could be.

"I never seen brush of that size growing where the trees stood so close," Shevlin said.

It hadn't struck me as anything. But Shevlin walked up and looked at the big shrubs that crowded in between the trunks of the evergreens, and then it appeared to me maybe a little odd that enough sun had sifted through to bring up the heads of those bushes so high. The sheriff looked at it and jabbed at it with a stick that he had picked up to walk with.

"Damnation!" he broke out after a while. "It ain't a fact."

"There it is, though," I said. "You can see where they've curved themselves around the trunks of the trees, too."

"You talk like a fool," Shevlin announced, all acid.

I didn't take offense, because it's foolish to get mad at what a man says when he's thinking, just as it's foolish to get sore at a horse that kicks you when you've come up to him on the offside.

Shevlin walked up and down and squinted at the tops of the trees, and then at the trunks. He got down on his hands and knees and grubbed up some of the earth in his hands. "Ah," he said, "it's rich enough, pretty near. And there's a strong midday sun, Jones, ain't there?"

"Sure. Like fire," I answered.

"Damn it!" said Shevlin, and he began shaking his head once more and grumbling. Finally he walked up to the biggest of those shrubs, took a good grip on a couple of the branches, and gave a strong jerk. He almost fell on his head, when that big bush gave way at once. The reason was clear, because it hadn't any roots. It had been chopped off level with the ground and brought here. Shevlin had been dead right. Looking through the gap that the removal of this bush made, we could peer into a dim circle, and in the middle of that circle was the fine gray mare that I had seen before in the woods.

# Chapter 33

Rags started to go inside, but the sheriff kicked him away. The gray whinnied a little, but Shevlin carefully put back the bush to close the entrance, and then spent a good deal of time to arrange the branches exactly as he had seen them before. I couldn't make this out, but I was tired of asking questions. It was pleasure enough to see that man's brainwork, even if you didn't know what direction it was taking him in. When he had the bush arranged to suit him, he scouted about through the trees and finally he found what he wanted. I could see it myself—the print of a man's shoe as plain as day. He gave Rags that for a scent, and Rags went after it and ate up the trail, so that I had to keep whistling softly to draw him a bit back to us.

That trail wound a little, but on the whole it kept steadily on toward the house. It was a half hour, and we'd covered a mile, going back, when we heard Rags barking loudly ahead of us. When we came up with him, he was scratching at the side of a heap of leaves and dead brush at the bank of the creek, where the high waters had piled this stuff. I called Rags. He ran to me and went back again.

"Leave him alone," said Shevlin. "He ain't trying to dig out a mouse."

He dragged the top brush away as he spoke, and with it came the upper layer of the leaves, and then we both could look down into the face of that man I had seen twice before—the man of the gray horse. He looked as though he were asleep, although it was strange to see the litter of dead leaves on his face, but his eyes were closed. He smiled a little in his sleep, and his hands were folded across his breast. His face was covered with the thick growth of beard that had made his features disappear in shadow the night that I saw him in poor Palliser's room.

The body was locked in rigor mortis, but Shevlin, without a word, went on to examine it a little. He turned back the collar of the coat to begin with, and managed to slip his hand inside the coat. He brought out a wallet—empty of everything except three fifty-dollar bills and some smaller greenbacks. He went through the other pockets, and took out a knife, a chain purse with some silver in it, and a piece of chamois with a spool of silk thread in it, and a needle stuck into the thread. After that, he pried up the arms from the breast a tiny bit and showed me a spot of blood around a small hole. This stranger of the gray horse had been shot through the heart. I began to feel pretty clammy, but Shevlin continued in his businesslike way to heap the leaves back over the corpse and lay the brush on top exactly as he had found it. Then he went off to the side and lighted a cigarette and sat down on a fallen log. He leaned his head against a tree and closed his eyes, saying: "It's hard, Jones. It's mighty hard."

But he wasn't unhappy, no matter how puzzled. I had a hundred questions on the tip of my tongue, but I managed to keep them all back except one: "Why should he have been killed, Shevlin?"

The sheriff shrugged his shoulders. "He knew too much, I guess."

That was all. Like opening a door a crack, and then slamming it in my face. Knew too much about what? Who thought he knew too much? Who fired the shot?

When Shevlin opened his eyes, he started up at once, and scouted around until he found the trail that he wanted. Rags took us down it once more while I walked on needles, half expecting another dead man before us at any time. But there was nothing more. Only, a hundred yards from the edge of the trees beyond which stood the old Mornay house, Shevlin stopped at a little burned patch in the grass and leaned over it. It was not a foot across and looked as though someone had dropped a match here and stamped out the fire as soon as the flames began to spurt in the dry grass. I never would have paused over it, but the sheriff gave it a good deal of time.

Over a little curved wisp of ash—like the ash of a twig that had gone up in flame—he bent down and looked like a man praying. Then he took out a bit of paper and drew some lines with a great deal of care. When he stood up, his face was perfectly calm, and, for the first time that morning, he looked a little tired.

"Is it a blank trail, after all?" I suggested to him.

"You know, Jones," he said, "that every riddle looks simple when you get the right answer." He walked on, very slowly, and finally he halted, leaning against a tree. "Maybe you'd better go on by yourself," he said. "Back to the house, I mean."

I would have given a lot to have stayed with him, because even though, most of the time, I didn't understand what he was about, it's not every man who can take you out for a walk and show you inside of an hour and a half a concealed horse and a dead man heaped over with brush and leaves.

I had to fire one question at him before I left, and I said: "What makes the most difference, Shevlin? The horse, or the dead man, or the bit of ash?"

"What?" he asked, staring out of his thoughts. "Oh, the smudge in the grass, of course." He added through his teeth: "The devil!"

That, you might say, scared me out of the woods and sent me into the open again, and I walked down toward the old house wondering at it, because to see it, you never would have connected it with murder. It looked simply big and livable—the sort of a place that when a woman sees it, she wants right off to start remodeling, and says how cheap it would be to build a wall here and make a living room there, with a fine big fireplace where you can burn whole logs that you cut in your own woods. But yonder in the west wing, in the upper room was Palliser lying dead!

I walked around that end of the house, not that there was anything I expected to see, but because I didn't want to go in and take up the watch beside the dead man once more—which would be my place and my job, I took for granted. But as I went around the end of the buildings, I saw big Dorgan in the corral, saddling a mule.

Now the sheriff had as much as said that I was to keep my hands off of him. That is, I was only to watch him until Shevlin himself was around. Then we were to bag him together, but, when I saw Dorgan, I got hot and couldn't hold it. I mean to say, I thought of the big fellow standing outside of my window and taking that pair of shots at me, and the idea rankled in me worse than a knife in a wound.

I slipped around among the stone walls of the old corrals until I was ten steps from Dorgan, and then I saw that he was working fast and hard to get that saddling done. He didn't seem to have much luck, because the mule that he was working on was mean and restless. It kept backing around and wouldn't let him pull up the cinches, but still kept sidling off the way a mule will, and, now and then, taking a bite at his shoulder. Dorgan cursed, but he cursed beneath his breath. His hand was unsteady, too, and suddenly I knew that Dorgan had a shadow in the back of his brain, and that he was a mighty scared man. Somehow, I could guess why—he suspected that the sheriff had walked a piece down his trail. Perhaps it was Dorgan that had finished off the rider of the gray horse, too.

I waited until he had the cinches up, and he was about to jam his foot in the stirrup. Then I sang out: "Dorgan!"

The big fellow dropped away from the mule with a sort of a groan, but even if he were staggered, he was a fast man and a two-handed man, and he turned on me with a pair of guns in his hands. But there was no use in that. I had the drop on him complete, and I was looking at him right down the barrel of a long, blue-nosed Colt. I suppose the mouth of that gun must have looked a yard across to Dorgan.

I told him to drop his guns, and he did it, one by one. He found his tongue, then, and asked me why in hell I had jumped him like that. I only smiled, and

I had the mighty big pleasure of seeing him turn green. Still, he asked me what I wanted, and I said: "I want your liver to see the color of it, Dorgan."

"What have I done to you?" Dorgan asked, his face streaming with sweat. He knew what I'd say, but he wanted to hear it.

"You sneaking night killer!" I hissed.

Although he must have been expecting it, his jaw sagged as though I'd landed a hard right on the point of his chin. I made him turn around and push his hands over his head, and then I fanned him and got nothing more than his hunting knife. Then he put his hands behind him, according to orders, and, with a bit of the twine that I'd always found handy to have about, I lashed his wrists together. Twine beats rope fifty ways. It's snugger, it takes less time, and it's stronger than any hemp twist.

Footfalls came scattering over the pebbles about this time, but, since I had Dorgan where I wanted him, I could afford to look back, and there was the sheriff coming full tilt. He was cursing, too, the worst I ever have heard a man curse, and the curses were all aimed at me.

When he came up, he called me a jackass and a wooden head, to begin with, and then he got serious and called me other things that don't go well in print.

But I felt that maybe I had done wrong, and I didn't answer back.

"Go on, then," Shevlin said. "Get him out of the way. Get him up to his room as fast as you can."

Dorgan lived in the shed beside the barn. The Mexicans that worked in the stable had one end of the shed, and Dorgan had the other.

Shevlin said: "Walk straight ahead, Dorgan. You ain't a dead man yet."

And, with a touch of his knife, he cut the twine and set Dorgan's hands free. Mind you, those were hands as big as the sheriff's and mine put together, but I didn't dare to question what Shevlin did.

"Walk up beside him!" Shevlin snapped at me. "Walk along like friends. Talk about something . . . I hope to God that he ain't been seen with his hands tied, or else everything may go smash."

# Chapter 34

When we got up to the stone shed, beside the barn, we went into the room where big Dorgan had been living, and there we saw that the bird had been ready to fly. He had a pack made up, and the sheriff told me to go through the pack while he went through the clothes of Dorgan. I was as careful as could be in undoing and searching the pack, but I found nothing very worthwhile, except some sailor's gear. However, when I saw how the sheriff was going through Dorgan's clothes, I began my search over again.

For Shevlin had made the big teamster strip, and then he examined every pocket and every thick fold of the cloth, and he passed what looked to me like short, very thin hairpins through the material. Afterward he threw the clothes at Dorgan, and that giant dressed himself. He had not said a word since we started toward the shack with him, and he maintained his silence now. But he was worried and sullen. I never saw an unhappier look on the face of a man.

While Dorgan dressed, Shevlin told me that this

would never do, but that we had to find something more exact about this man, and that this was the smallest haul that he had ever heard of getting from a sailor. "Because most of them are fools," said the sheriff, "and they carry about themselves enough stuff to identify a regiment."

We began searching again. Shevlin said that perhaps Dorgan had left a lot of stuff in his chest, but, when we jerked open the lid, we found that the chest was as empty as could be. Then Shevlin pulled open a back door of the shack, and the first thing we saw was a smoldering little heap. The smoke had a foul odor of burning woolen rags. We kicked that fire apart and bits of paper showed up as bright red edges as the air fanned it.

The sheriff was gloomy in turn coming back. He looked at big Dorgan sitting with folded arms and head hanging down in a corner of the room, and he said to me: "That fellow's still afraid that we'll find something."

Dorgan jerked up his head. "You lie!" he shouted.

Then he bit his lip as the sheriff grinned. It was a pretty easy trap to have caught an experienced and mature man like Dorgan, but you never can tell when the simplest stroke will undo the most complicated sort of a brain. Dorgan, red and sweating, squirmed his shoulders deeper into the corner and damned us under his breath, while Shevlin stood smiling in the center of the room, as if already he had found what he wanted. Then he told me to start work on the sailor's box. He would begin to sound the walls of the room.

He started around them, tapping on the stones carefully and yet rapidly, while I took the hint and worked in the same way on the box. I didn't have the slightest idea that I would find anything; I never had used that method before and didn't know what to expect. But I couldn't help noticing that the bottom of the sea chest seemed very thick, and in a corner, presently, it sounded differently beneath the rapping of my knuckles. With my knife I cut through the surface of the soft wood, as easily as though it were cheese, and exposed a shallow tray inset in the bottom of the trunk. In that tray there was a flat layer of tarnished silver coins. One glance at them showed me that they were about the same as the strange coin that had dropped on the floor of the captain's room—or that had been found in the mouth of Palliser when he lay dead.

I gasped as I called the sheriff, and that moment Dorgan came out of his chair in a silent despair and rushed me. I don't think that I ever could have gotten around in time. I had my gun ready and was swinging to fire, but I think that the big, reaching fist of Dorgan would have landed on my head first. However, the sheriff hopped in behind, as nimble as a cat, and rapped Dorgan over the head with what seemed his open hand—the heavy sound of the blow showed that it was something else. Dorgan went down in a heap.

I took care of bringing him around. Shevlin had slapped him with a slung shot, fastened around his wrist with an elastic band, so that whenever he wanted to use it, he had only to flip it down into his fingers. It had not seriously hurt Dorgan, only making a slight cut in his scalp that brought hardly any blood. I simply opened the sailor's shirt, and he jerked upright on the floor, then pulled himself slowly to his feet. He was still dizzy enough to be glad to slump into a chair.

The sheriff, in the meantime, had spread out on

the bed's blanket everything that he found. There were four of those silver coins, and there was an envelope out of which he took a fold of yellow paper and read out to me a word or two.

"Aboard the *Tamerlane*, eh, Dorgan?" said the sheriff.

"Oh, damn your gizzards," said Dorgan. "But everything that you think will be wrong. Now go ahead and make a pair of fools of yourselves."

"It don't make much difference to you what the law finds out about you," said Shevlin, "because if the hangman don't finish you off, Jones will."

"Him?" said Dorgan. "Ah, I'd eat three pair like him." He lifted his upper lid at me, like a snarling dog.

Rags didn't like the look of him and came between us and backed up against my leg, growling at the big teamster.

Then Shevlin got on with his reading aloud, just saying to me first: "I hoped for something like this out of Dorgan. I told you beforehand that sailors mostly are fools enough to keep all their luggage with them . . . even the kind that will hang them."

This is what he read:

*Aboard the* Tamerlane

*Dear Charlie,*

*If you're surprised that you get a letter from me on the* Tamerlane, *that'll be because you haven't heard yet what happened to the* Wanderer. *The last I seen of her, she was sinking by the head a hundred mile from the* Hughli. *She had her fun before she went down, and this was the how of it. Coming down the China Sea, before Anjers, we run afoul of a junk in a fog. We thought the yellow fools were going to board us. They thought the same thing and went into the water like so many rats, and the last we seen of them, they were crowded into their boat and dropping astern as fast as they could row her.*

*It looked to the skipper like this was a present to us, and he told the boys that we could pick her clean. The crew spilled through that ship like ants through a sugar sack, and the skipper, he took me to look at the captain's cabin, so's to see that everything was squarely divided that he should find there. But the first thing that we cracked open was a little chest filled with silver. We didn't know how much, then. It turned out later to have $2,500 worth of silver in that chest.*

*The skipper give me the wink, and I winked at him. They were funny-looking coins; how the Chinks ever got them, I dunno. But, anyways, we said no more, and I fetched that chest aboard and put it into the captain's cabin and said not a word. I knew that the old skinflint would give me a third of it, at least, and that was more than I'd ever rate if it was split up among the whole crew.*

*After that, I had things easy, with the skipper making a pet out of me until the boys in the forecastle began to snarl a little. But about this time we were up in the Indian Ocean, and there we ran into our special slice of hell.*

*It was more than we could eat. It blew thirty-six hours, snapped our masts off, started a bigger leak than the pumps could handle, and stowed me in a corner with a leg busted bad below the right hip.*

*In the first lull, they decided to leave the ship—she was canting far to the side—and by the eternal God, Charlie, they run off without me! They* wouldn't have me on their hands in a time like that. And the only half-white one was the sails, that brung me a jug of water and some ham, and dragged me into the captain's cabin.

There I lay for near a week, water gone, the heat worst than you could think, waiting for the hulk to go down. But she wouldn't sink! The cargo must've shifted over the leaks. She wallowed lower and lower, however, and the waves were beginning to lap at the door and slosh through under it, when I heard the sound of warlocks and then voices on deck. I let out a yell, and yells answered me, and then in come the skipper of the Tamerlane.

Even low as I was, I passed him the wink, and he managed a minute alone with me, so I told him about the chest of silver, and he winked back.

I was carried aboard the Tamerlane and found a bunch of good shipmates, and particular the chips. I'm to give him this letter and a little package. If I don't live to reach the land, the chips is to mail them both to you.

You wonder why I should never expect to see the land? Well, I dunno. I got no great lot of trouble with the broken leg, just now, but the fact is that they's a terrible disease on board of this here ship, and the name of it is Palliser. He's our skipper.

He might be the death of me. It would wipe out my claim to any part of that damned money, which I wish I'd never seen. However, I'm hoping. But if ever your eyes light on this here letter, that hope will be gone, and I'll be sleeping in canvas at the bottom of the sea, unless the sharks swaller me on the way down! In the package you'll find the Dago silver. I've sent it along to help you to trace the rest of the coin, and if ever you can give Palliser as *much hell as he deserves, you'll be more of a brother to me than you ever was in the past.*

> *Luck and good weather to you.*
> *Jim*

The sheriff finished this, which under the circumstances was the most interesting letter that I ever sat through the reading of, and then he folded it and put it back into its envelope and passed it into his pocket.

"Now, Jones," he said, "d'you think that this here letter will hang Dorgan as the dirty murderer that split the heart of Palliser, and then dropped the coin in his mouth?"

# Chapter 35

We took Dorgan down to the house. The sheriff was a lot easier now, because he said that he knew what he wanted to know, and that it was very unlikely that the Mexicans, or Wong, would make an attempt to turn our prisoner loose. Certainly there was not a hand raised while we marched Dorgan down to the patio of the house and took him inside. We kept him ahead of us, and before we went inside the ruined gate, the sheriff picked up a length of old baling wire, rusted but still with a strong enough core.

He used this to manacle the hands of Dorgan behind his back. That teamster was purple with anger and white with fear; he was streaked and spotted with those colors. Like some people when they're excited, he repeated one phrase over and over again.

"All this while the real crook is getting farther away from you. You god damned fools!"

When we go into the patio, we found Frances Mornay playing with the golden cat. Shirley was off in a corner, watching. Of course, they jumped up and swarmed over to us when they saw us marching Dorgan ahead of us. The golden cat, at the sight of Rags, climbed up onto the shoulder of its lady and balanced there, silently making faces at the pup. And Rags danced and shivered with joy at the thought of chasing that biddy.

Dorgan sang out: "Miss Mornay! He's going to tell you a yarn about me, but I want you to know that it's a lie! Every word of it, mostly. I. . ."

Shevlin was a gentle-acting sort of a man, but he could have his rough moments, and he showed one now. He tapped the chest of Dorgan—a chest like one side of a big round barrel—and said to him: "You'd better choke off and be quiet. I'll do the talkin' for you, old son."

Frances Mornay came running up to Dorgan, holding her cat steady with one hand and loving it against the side of her face. Then she stood before Dorgan, looking small enough for the wind to pick up, and beautiful enough for the wind to want to. She said to the sheriff: "But this is my friend, Dorgan! He can't have done anything wrong. Why . . . I know all about him. We've talked about everything, haven't we?" At this, she laughed a little, uncertainly.

Big Dorgan took on a good deal when she was so close to him, looking at him with a child's fondness for a big man. He worked his hands behind him and his chest worked, too. Then he said: "Aye, aye, miss, and everything that I told you was true. Even though I didn't tell you my whole life."

"It is all an unhappy mistake," said Frances Mornay. "I know that. And I know that the sheriff will set you free."

Shirley came over beside her. He nodded and smiled down at her, but he had sense enough not to interfere directly with the sheriff. He merely acted like a man who wants to have something proved.

Shevlin read the letter to them, and the point of it was too direct for even a girl like Frances Mornay to miss. She backed up a little and looked as though Dorgan had turned into a ghost. Shirley told her that she had better go into the house, and she obeyed without a word, only turning at the arch to look back at us—wonderful graceful and wonderful pale— then she turned and fairly ran on into the house.

"You see how people take that letter?" said Shevlin.

"I see how you've made her take it," Dorgan responded. "But she's only a girl. What does she know? She ain't a jury. . . ." He bit his lip as he said that, because he must have thought what a lot harder deal any twelve men would give him. He glowered at us all, and was silent.

Shirley said in a matter-of-fact way: "You think that this man is a perfect scoundrel? That he really came all the way from the East to trail Palliser . . . that he found him and murdered him in cold blood, and then that he put into his mouth one of the silver coins . . . almost as the Parthians did to Crassus."

"I dunno what the Parthians did to Crassus," said the sheriff.

Nor did I.

"Crassus was a little on the side of avarice. When the Parthians got him, they poured melted gold down his throat. Well, this fellow put the silver coin into the mouth of old Palliser."

"Ha!" said the sheriff. "Then that accounts for the coin that Jones found in the mouth of Palliser."

"Damn you!" bellowed Dorgan. "There ain't a line of truth in what you're sayin'!"

"I reckon that there's enough to hang you to a pretty high tree," Shevlin said. "We'll wait and see about that. If this theory is right. . . ."

"I'm gonna say one thing," said Dorgan. "Will you tell me how I ever got across that wall in a white skirt or even in trousers?"

I looked at the hulk of Dorgan, and I had to say: "Sheriff, that's too big for what I saw on the top of that wall."

"Of course it is," agreed the sheriff at once. "I don't doubt that, though it's a pretty cool man that can figger out the height of a walking ghost that he sees on the top of a wall. But suppose that he didn't go that way. I've already told you that I think that two people had hands in that murder."

"Ha!" cried Shirley. "How on earth did you think that out?"

"Why, by the wounds on the breast of Palliser and in his throat . . . different hand and different knives made 'em, I'm sure."

"That's damned extraordinary," said Shirley. "I never would have thought that. Really different?"

"They are."

"A cut is a cut and blood is blood, I would have said," Shirley remarked quietly to me. "But Shevlin understands those things wonderfully well."

He seemed filled with admiration, but I had heard the idea before.

"As for Dorgan getting into the room," said the sheriff, "of course, he could climb up the wall on the west."

"Me? It ain't possible for any man," Dorgan insisted.

"Jones has done it, for one," said Shevlin.

Dorgan started to answer, but he finally closed his mouth and said through his teeth: "You're ag'in' me. I ain't going to say another word." And he kept his promise. Not another syllable could be pried out of him.

"But," Shirley said in his thoughtful way, "it seems to me that there's one very major point . . . how did they get out of the room of the captain?"

"That's a point," agreed the sheriff. "But I've sounded the walls of that room, and I don't hear a hollow place. What I figger is that my partner Jones, here, was not counting time any too well. And there was longer wasted in breaking into that room than he thought. After all, what time would it have needed to throw a line out of the window and climb down it? Aye, or even for two active people to get down the surface of the wall itself, using the cracks between the rocks for finger- and toeholds?"

He looked at me, and I tried to think back. Well, it seemed to me that there really hadn't been time between the end of that crazy laughter I heard and the time when I looked out from the window for anybody to have got away. If they had used a rope, yes, possibly they might have managed. But there would have been a rope left hanging from the window. And if they tried to climb down, it was not such an easy job—ten times harder than climbing up, you understand, because it would be such a lot harder to look for holds of any kind. It would be hard enough to find two people to do that sort of a job together and as fast as they would have had to slide down that wall in order to get shut of it before I looked down at them.

But, still, a good many strange things are done, here and there, and the minute that you say a thing is impossible, you read in the paper the next week how it was done. I simply shut up and said nothing, except to point out: "It would take a circus performer to cakewalk across the top of that wall. Let alone shinnying down the wall outside the captain's window."

"Here's a sailor for one," said the sheriff, jerking his thumb at Dorgan, and Dorgan's face wrinkled, but he wouldn't speak.

We talked for a while about where we could keep Dorgan secure before we started back for the town. It was arranged that Palliser should be buried at dawn of the next day, and that then the whole lot of us would light out and make a forced march for the town. He would send one of the Mexicans ahead on a good horse to get to town and bring in our news.

They talked of other things, then. There didn't seem to be any importance about their conversation, at first, and it wasn't until it took a sudden turn that it began to have a lot of meaning. The result was that I don't remember very well how the subject began, but I think that it was the sheriff talking about how well Frances Mornay was standing up under the shock of the murder. Shirley's idea was that it would hit her hard later on, and that she was apt to have a nervous breakdown. Just now she was fighting hard to keep her head up. They switched from that onto the fact that the captain hadn't spent much time with his niece because he was always off at sea and she was raised on land.

I can remember exactly what happened in the talk from that time forward.

The sheriff said: "Ruth Derrick's an old friend?"

"She's been with Frances for years. They saved her from a life as a bareback queen, or some such thing."

The sheriff showed a good deal of interest, and Shirley explained that Ruth had lost her parents when she was very young, and that an aunt or a cousin, or someone, took her on with a traveling circus. The girl was picking up all kinds of stunts. She was riding horseback and doing trapeze and such things, when the mother of Frances picked her up.

Shirley was not very sure about the story of that, but he had an idea that there was an accident, the circus moved on, and Ruth Derrick was left behind. Then the mother of Frances got hold of her and had taken her into the family. Shirley said that could be proved by asking Frances, of course.

But the sheriff shook his head. He got up and walked up and down and up and down. Then he snarled at Dorgan to walk ahead of him. He and I took Dorgan into a room that suited Shevlin.

It was like a dungeon, and it was cold and dank even on that bright summer day. There was one small window that it would have broken a cat's heart to crawl through, and there was nothing but bare floor to sit on or sleep on. When Dorgan saw the place, he gave Shevlin one fierce look—but that was enough. Then we went out and the sheriff locked the door.

I remarked that perhaps Dorgan would be just as safe if he were to throw in a straw mattress to him, but the sheriff shrugged his shoulders. He said that for a murdering devil like Dorgan, he had less respect than he had for a pig, and like a pig he would treat Dorgan.

That surprised me. It was by all odds the worst side of the sheriff's character that I had ever seen.

Then he went back into the patio with me, after he had seen that the door of the cellar locked properly.

In the patio, Shirley was back in his chair, reading his book again, and he seemed surprised and only mildly interested when Shevlin came up to him again. He only said: "I haven't congratulated you, Sheriff, on the fine work you've done here. This is the sort of thing that ought to get into print."

Shevlin said: "I don't want congratulations. I want

to know how old Ruth Derrick was when she left that circus."

"She was around ten or eleven, I believe."

"Did she do any tight-wire work?" asked Shevlin.

"I think she did, a little," Shirley answered.

Then he jumped from his chair. I jumped, too, and looked at the thin, ragged top of the wall along which the "ghost" had walked that night of the murder.

# Chapter 36

The sheriff didn't speak again and he didn't have to. I turned to Shirley, hoping that he would have something to say, but one look at his sick face showed me that he was seeing the same picture that I saw. He was dumb with it.

Then Shevlin went into the house, and I knew why he had gone.

He came out again in about ten minutes, and he said that Ruth Derrick could not be found. None of the servants had seen her.

At that, my last thread of faith snapped. I said gloomily: "She's cut and run, Sheriff, when she had a glimpse of us bringing in Dorgan. She saw her partner gone."

"Partner to a rough sailor and teamster like Dorgan?" cried Shirley. "Sheriff, I can't sit by and hear such nonsense!"

"You'll have to, though," said the sheriff.

"Great God," Shirley cried, striking his lean hands together, "what could have been the purpose . . . what motive could have induced . . . ?"

"She has a soft berth with you and Frances Mornay," Shevlin explained. "She saw that Palliser might live on for years, making everybody miserable. Besides, she was afraid that something would happen to Frances in this house where things have happened to other Mornays. It was that streak of superstition in her that made her determined to play the ghost herself. She made an agreement with Dorgan. How they broached it, I don't know. But when two people want the same thing, it's easy enough for them to find ways of talking about it."

There was no doubt about that. We had proved that Dorgan wanted the death of Palliser for a hundred percent revenge for the death of his brother. Now the hand was pointing so straight at Ruth Derrick that suddenly I groaned out: "Shevlin, I thought she was the best and the squarest that ever stepped. But you've proved that she's not, and you've proved it all by yourself. Now I can tell you the fact myself. Here's the proofs that will hang her. I found them in the room when I went in. I found them before another soul was there." I took them from my pocket and placed them before Shevlin—the wisp of red hair and the broken sapphire.

The sheriff pinched his lips together as he took them.

I said: "That hair I found in the hand of Palliser . . . I found this stone on the floor. It's the hair of Ruth . . . and that was out of her ring. God help her!"

I ran out of that patio as though there was a whip hanging over me, and I got Pinto and rode the heart out of him across the hills. Rags went with me, and the three of us kept on going until I was pretty nearly lost, and had to lay a careful course to return to the house of Mornay again. And when I came over the edge of the hill in the dusk of the day, I shook my fist at that house and cursed it with my whole heart.

They would have Ruth Derrick, by this time. There was not much chance that they would hang her, though. No, the juries in the West are always merciful to women; besides, the majority of the crime would be loaded onto the shoulders of Dorgan. She would simply drag out a dozen years behind the bars and come out as I had seen other women come from prison—hard as steel and brittle as glass!

That house had become the most hateful thing in the world. I had to force myself to gather up the reins ready to start on again when Rags whined, and I looked around into the face of Dennis Rourke.

It looked like a head hanging there among the branches of the tree. Then the wind stirred the boughs, and I could see the man and the horse better. Rourke was grinning at me in a pretty cheerful way, and to see the smile on his face made me angry.

I said to him: "You poor sap, why do you sit there and split your face? What have you done to be proud of?"

"I was laughin' at the fool look you wore, kid," said Rourke.

I almost forgot my troubles, Ruth Derrick and all, while I looked at Rourke's smile.

"What do you live on out here, Denny?" I asked. "Excitement, or fern roots? Come around and I'll chuck a heel of a loaf of a stale biscuit over the wall to you."

"Thanks," Rourke said. "That's spoken like a real bunkie. But I live on news, Johnny. It keeps me fat."

That made me blink again. Suddenly I said to him: "Denny, come out and tell me the truth . . . you wanted to help Frances Mornay, and so you sashayed up the back wall and slipped through the window and knifed. . . ." I stopped. While I talked, I realized more and more that, no matter what crazy idea got into his head, Rourke wasn't the sort of a fellow to run a knife into an old man like Palliser. He couldn't go crazy enough to do that. Not even the face of Frances Mornay was pretty enough to make him so wild.

"Go on," Rourke coaxed.

"You ain't bad enough to interest me," I told Denny.

"I'm not bad, I'm just playful," said Rourke. "How is the sheriff?"

"He was a mite upset by that bullet of yours. You can thank God that you didn't kill him."

"I did," said Rourke. "I thanked God twice. Once for dropping the sheriff without putting out his lights, and once for enabling me to set loose my playmate, Cattrin."

"I had a guess that your friend and you must've got pretty chummy," I stated.

"Him and me? Like two sisters," said Rourke. "I been hangin' around waitin' for another look at his pretty face."

"I've only seen him once, and that time he looked like he'd just swallowed a rusty nail," I told Rourke.

"He'll swallow more than that when I meet up with him again," Rourke said. "That boy is a bad one, Johnny, and, if I was you, I'd wear padded gloves in handling him. Otherwise, he'll put a brand on you."

"Thanks," I said, "but, when I meet him again, I'm going to handle him with my feet like a dog-gone juggler, Denny. What news have you been picking up around here?"

"Most what I get when I follow you and the sheriff," he admitted.

"Follow us?"

"Sure. To where hosses are cached away, and dead gents are laid out under the leaves. That was a mighty jolly little show that you and him staged this morning. What's on for this evening?"

"Is that the last that you know?" I asked.

"The morning paper was the last that I read."

I said: "Ruth Derrick and Dorgan are the ones who murdered Palliser."

"Who found that out?" asked Rourke.

"The sheriff. That gent is a devil. He can find out anything."

"He can do even more," Rourke said. "If he was able to find out that, he can tell you anything. He's a dog-gone mind-reader and a prophet rolled into one mouth."

"Are you kidding me a little?" I asked.

"I'm trying to feed you some sense by hand," Rourke stated, "but you don't seem able to take nourishment that strong."

"What sense?" I asked. "What do you mean, Denny?"

"Aw," he said, "I dunno. I'd simply say that they ain't hung Ruth Derrick and Dorgan yet."

"That's bright and useful," I told him. "Is that all that you have to say? Is that all that you know, Denny? Man, man, do you know anything more, anything real?"

"I know enough to eat three times a day and sleep seven hours," said Rourke, "and that's about enough book learning to suit me."

"You damn' knuckle head!" I yelled at him. "I've got a mind to soak you, Rourke!"

"You keep your eyes open and look around, because maybe you'll see something worthwhile," Rourke said.

"Denny," I pleaded, "if you know anything, for God's sake, will you tell me . . . ?"

"The girl is in your head, eh?" said Rourke. "The Derrick girl, I mean."

"She is!" I confessed. "I've seen it proved that she's a murderess. But I can't help being stirred up about her still. Denny, if you even know enough to explain. . . ."

"You keep right along at the right hand of your little sheriff," said Rourke, "and you'll graduate at the head of your class."

He pulled his horse around, waved his gloved hand at me, and went off, and I didn't follow. I felt too beaten and miserable and confused to make any sort of an effort, but I went on down to the stable and jerked the saddle and bridle off Pinto. José found me at work, and he began to talk with two eyes and two hands, the way a Mexican will. He told me that Ruth Derrick was gone, and that the sheriff had found her out trail.

# Chapter 37

That put the crown on everything. I went down to the house as fast as I could and came in for supper in the patio with my hair on end and my head aching.

It was just as José had told me. The sheriff said that he had spent three hours cutting for sign, and he had found the out trail of Ruth Derrick, cutting across the hills. He hadn't followed, because he knew that she would be brought in whenever we got to town and sent out a telegram giving her description.

Shevlin didn't pull me to one side and tell me all of this. He chattered it out at the table, in front of Frances Mornay. I never heard of such lack of sense in any man.

Up to that evening, I had figured Shevlin as a level-headed, mighty decent, and intelligent fellow, but now I changed my mind, I can tell you. It's too bad that when a man is successful he has to puff. He can't let his success stand by itself, but he has to put a margin around it and write in his own comments.

He wants to have everybody point and stare and say: There goes the man who. . . .

I've seen more flat-headed millionaires talk that way than ever there was buffalo in the old days, making roaring on the prairies. I'd rather hear a bronco bawl or a cow mourning all night for her calf than to listen for five minutes to one of those double-joined jackasses called "self-made men."

But Shevlin, for all the brains and the sense that he had showed before, now talked like one of the worst boasters. While he was praising himself, he couldn't dwell on things he'd done in the past, but he had to dwell particularly on his work that day, and most of all about how he had made out that Ruth Derrick had left the house and gone down the hollow.

And there was Frances Mornay, listening to this talk about her friend and growing sicker and sicker. Finally she excused herself and got up, and the sheriff, he stood up like a fool, too, and said that she wasn't eating enough. And that perhaps the cat ought to have a bite, at least, before it went.

We had broiled trout, and mighty good ones, and the sheriff broke off a bit and gave it to the cat on the handle of a spoon. It's a sight to see any cat swallow fish, and the golden beauty was no exception. Then she pulled in her head and looked dreamily at the sheriff, so that you couldn't tell whether she was praising him or thinking of eating him next.

Frances Mornay stood through this nonsense, and then she said good night to us all, prettily, and went off, carrying the cat.

When she was gone, Shevlin said: "That girl don't look none too well, Shirley, and she's clean off of her feed."

Shirley was too disgusted to say anything. He looked across at me, and I chimed in.

I said: "Shevlin, do you think that the brand of talk you've been turning up this evening is the kind that would freshen her appetite any?"

"I dunno what you mean," he responded.

"You wouldn't," I said. "I mean a while back you didn't know your drift any more than a calf in a November blizzard up Montana way. My God, Shevlin, what made you carry on in this way?"

"I dunno what you mean," said the sheriff. "How have I been carryin' on? I've been showing the way the business is done. That's all. Is there anything wrong with that?"

I pointed a forefinger at him. "Suppose that you had a brother that a doctor had done a fine operation on . . . but your brother died. Well, would you appreciate what the doctor said, if he started a long yarning about what a smart operation he had made?"

"I wasn't talking about an operation," Shevlin stated.

I gaped at him. Everyone has noticed that the smart fellows, who are so able to talk about themselves, are always able, at the same time, to work up a blind point from which they can't see a thing. Still, I was amazed at Shevlin because always, before this evening, it had seemed to me that his *heart* was right, of that I am quite sure. But there never was any more clear proof of wrong-heartedness than he was showing now, or had showed during that meal. He couldn't understand what I was driving at, because the fool didn't see that he'd been tearing the heart of Frances Mornay to bits.

"Ah, well," put in Shirley, who always was reserved and in control of himself, "we'll soon be through. We'll start back tomorrow, Sheriff, I suppose?"

"At daybreak. I'm having the grave dug tonight," Shevlin commented. "We'll drop the old fellow into his grave, and then away we start. We ought to make better time going back . . . the grades will all be in our favor."

You can understand from this specimen the way he had been talking all during supper; only it was worse when he told how he had parted some leaves and spotted the place where the heel of Ruth's shoe had made an imprint, and his reasons for looking in just that place, and why it was that he suspected that the ground would be soft enough to take an imprint even through the layer of leaves. And how he had come to the top of a hill, among the trees, and seen the course that she must have looked at ahead of her—through woods and wilderness, with the blue mountains far off and the white streaks on their summits. Of course, that made Frances Mornay sad. She stuck to the table as long as she could, with her head down and her shoulders quivering a little from time to time. But at last she had been driven away.

Even after she was gone and we could use our tongue freely on the sheriff, we were not able to show him that he had been a combination of brute and jackass. There's nothing worse than a fool, unless it is not to be able to make him see his folly.

Shevlin was carrying on in this cheerful little talk about the dead man and the grave, when a window slammed up, and we heard the voice of Frances Mornay ringing clear and sharp across the patio: "Hugh! Oh, Hugh! Mimi is sick . . . she's writhing and screaming . . . she's sick!"

We could hear the voice of the cat yip and howl at that moment.

Shirley got up. The sheriff got up, too, and I had to admit that he was a queer mixture of good and bad heart when he said that he knew something about veterinary treatment, and that he would do what he could.

That left me alone at the table, and, in spite of myself, I could not sit still. I had to get up and walk, and, wherever I walked, I couldn't be easy unless I had in the corner of my eye the window out of which Cattrin had looked at me and the wall along which the figure in white had walked. The patio seemed to be getting bigger and emptier and colder all the time. The whispering of the fountain began to frame words behind my back—if only I could understand them.

I was losing my nerve and I knew it. I could thank God that we were pulling out from this place in the early morning, but I dreaded a good deal worse than ten years in prison the night that lay between me and the dawn of the next day. Perhaps that is a sign that I have a streak of prophet in me, although that is a kind of pay dirt that don't sell very well on any market.

I had to look back to Rourke, too, and somehow the sassy way in which he had talked made me feel a good deal better—I mean to say, it made me feel as though perhaps the sheriff could be wrong. Not that I banked much on Rourke's way of talk. He always used that high-handed way when he didn't know what else to do.

About this time, back came Shirley and the sheriff, and it turned out that the sheriff had cured the cat's stomach ache by using some kind of ginger on it. The cat was now sleeping sound, and Frances Mornay felt a lot better.

By this time, Shevlin was well oiled up for blowing about himself. He turned loose on how he happened to be such a good doctor, and told how he had learned something from the Comanches about horses, and something from the Mexicans about cows and other animals.

Shirley said good night in the middle of this, and I did the same, but the sheriff threw a shot of cold misery into me when he said, in the most matter-of-fact way that you could imagine, that he supposed that I wouldn't mind sitting watch in Palliser's room that night. It simply drained the heart out of me, and I looked at him and groaned out that I was pretty well beat.

"You had *some* sleep, however," said the sheriff, "and I didn't have a wink, you know."

"There's Shirley, then," I pointed out.

The sheriff looked at me in an odd manner, and then he said: "What's the matter? Are you nervous, old-timer?"

You would think that pride would keep me from saying it, but it didn't.

"Nervous?" I said. "Nerves ain't the way to express it. I've got a tangle of chills all the way from the top of my head down, and I'm plumb icy around the heart."

He nodded while he watched me. Then he came closer and took my arm and led me down the patio, and he said: "Jones, you're gonna sit up with the captain's body tonight."

"For God's sake come there and sit with me, then," I pleaded.

He considered, and then he shook his head. "I have to be some other place," he said. "Besides, two would be no good. One will look more like a bait."

"A bait?" I echoed. "Thanks, old son. I've been in a trap before and I don't like the fall of the jaws when they close down on you."

"You'll do this job, I reckon," said the sheriff. Then he added to me: "This is the night that tells the story. I may be right, and I may be wrong. I don't know. But God forgive me if I've slipped up. The harm will be done before the morning."

"To me?" I asked.

He didn't answer, but, as we had come to the foot of the stairs that led to the room where Palliser lay, he waved his hand to me. I couldn't resist, but like a poor 'puncher that always has taken orders, I turned around and went up the steps.

# Chapter 38

Mostly a fellow will have enough spirit to get himself through jobs that require action. The working of the muscles is a big help to a man, of course. When you're in the saddle, you can swing along into the face of anything, but to sit in the room of a dead man, a murdered man, that takes the starch out of your backbone and turns you into a jellyfish. At least, I turned into one, and sat there getting colder and colder, and something rising in my throat, harder and harder to swallow.

Anybody with any sense is fairly sure to set his thoughts in order, in a time like that, and think his way back to a grip of things. For instance when you're a youngster, you can argue yourself out of being afraid of the dark by telling yourself what the room is like in the sun, and reassuring yourself that it's just the same in the dark as it is in the light. But now it didn't work. I tried to tell myself all sorts of things—that the sheriff had only been playing a part at the table—that in reality he didn't think his game was finished—and that this night would tell a new story, perhaps. But in the wind-up I always came back to the fact that this was a trap, and that I was the bait in it.

I went over to the window, and looked out at the lines of the mountains, very dim, mostly, and hard to tell which was mountain and which was cloud, until your eyes got used to the starlight. Just about the time that I was enjoying the spread of the mountains, I reminded myself that the glow of the lamp in the room behind me made me a pretty good target for any friendly fellow that was wandering around with a rifle in his hand. I stepped back about half the length of the room in one stride, and then I sat down and saw that it was nine-thirty. I had thought rings around every subject in the world, rehearsed my childhood fights, and tried to tell myself funny stories, but it was all no good, because I had waded through the lot in about forty minutes. The night was just beginning!

I mopped off the sweat which that idea raised on me, and then I decided to be a man, as they say—which usually means to eat your heart out with your pride. About the time that I had got myself strung up in good shape and was ready to punch a tiger on the nose, I saw the dead man move. I mean to say the sheet trembled over his face, as it would have trembled if he had breathed on it from underneath. Although I knew that there was nothing in this idea, I couldn't help seeing everything in steady progression. That is to say, I could see him breathe, and see a little purplish color come in to the white face, and the lips grow less hard, and the eyes open a crack, and the dead smile disappear from the lips and turn into a scowl, and the forehead begin to gather in a frown, and—at about this point, I wanted to scratch my way into the wall.

I felt that if ever I came really near that door, nothing could keep me from being pulled through it, like a leaf in a strong draught, and, once I got outside, I would run so fast that a jackrabbit compared with me would look like a galloping turtle. I could feel all the nerves of speed hitching my legs to my back bones, and all the muscles of speed in my legs began to move and slip and harden. I felt as though I could jump the length of that room from a standing start.

Being all unpeaceful like that, I took to walking, but the trouble with the walking was that there was always something behind me. If I turned one way, I could see a silhouette of a man with burning eyes sidle into the frame of the window at my back. When I turned about, the silhouette of the man turned into the shadow of a mountain pasted against the western sky, and the burning eyes were a pair of stars that rubbed shoulders. That was comforting, but now, from the other end, I could see the dead man move, stir, and sit up stealthily in the bed. No matter how often I argued with myself out of these notions, they kept coming back on me, and every time they came back harder and crisper. The more familiar you get with a nightmare, the more it freezes all of your blood.

At last, I gave up. I closed those windows, and I pulled the curtains across them. I didn't like to do it. It was shutting the outside fear away, but it was locking in the inside fear, and me with it. Nobody would be climbing through the windows, but the cold fear of hell would begin to steam up out of the floor of the room. I locked the door, too. Then I looked to my guns, and I practiced a little, making quick turns and working with the heavy Colts until I was breathing hard. But, all the same, I couldn't get the numbness out of my wrists or the weakness out of my elbows.

I tried another business then. Over on a shelf beside the bed, the captain had a few books, and I looked them over. They were the sort of books that you would expect to find, dating back to the wooden hulls and the fine flat sails of the clippers. There was Harbird's *Glossary of Navigation*—and God knows if any duller book ever was printed, or a more useful one for sailors. There was *Two Years Before the Mast.* Coming down to present days, there was Lubbock's *China Clippers*, which used to race from the Minghome to London with the first tea of the season.

I tried that book, and it was good reading, with a lot of facts and figures that go pretty good to a fellow who has been trained to keep percentage figures in his head from the baseball reports. I read about the opium clippers, and the junks, and then up to the flowering of the perfect sailing craft in the *Sir Lancelot*, and *The Thermopylae*, and the *Cutty Sark*. It was grand reading, and it snaked me through three hours, nearly.

Then something sighed in the room, and, all at once, I didn't give a damn about whether the *Cutty Sark* or *The Thermopylae* was the fastest ship. I looked up, with prickles in my skin, and saw all the curtains trembling before the windows. A breeze was blowing up, and I wished that breeze off to the China Sea, where the skippers used to pray so much for air on the way down to Anjers. I told myself that the sigh was the effect of the wind, but the telling didn't do much good. I heard the sigh again, directly behind me. No—the sound was a quick indrawn breath, such as a man takes before a violent effort—like driving a knife into your back, say.

My head spun around like an owl's, but there was nothing behind me. However, I now chucked pride away. I went over to the farthest corner. I wedged my chair in where I had solid wall on two sides of me, and I pulled out a Colt and laid the muzzle on my knee. Then I pretended to read, but it was a pretty sick job. And in the midst of this, I heard something like a light scratching at my door.

"The wind," I said.

Immediately afterward came the same sound repeated. But this time the wind was no explanation. I made myself get out of the chair, and, with the gun stretched before me as though I were fumbling along in the dark, I went along the side of the wall to the door. By the eternal God, I heard something breathe at the crack of the door. Hysteria will take the place of courage. I slipped the key in the lock and jerked the door open.

Right at my feet was Rags, his eyes twinkling with phosphorescence, like a cat's. He came in with me. I locked the door again, with shaking hands, and wondered why I was such a jackass as to have forgotten Rags up to this time. It was almost like having another human being in the room with me. It was better really, because the senses of Rags would not jump the track and lead him off on any false trails. What his ears told him would be true, and what his nose told him, also.

I was so much reassured, that I pulled my chair farther from the wall and sat down with Rags on my knee, a good light beside me, and actually got through a paragraph and knew what I had read. But as I finished that bit, I felt Rags stiffening on my knee, and I saw that he was sitting up rigid, with his ears pricked, and his head turned straight toward the bed where the dead man lay. I don't really know what passed through my head then. But when I saw the trembling of the sheet again, I got up and crossed the room and jerked down the edge of the sheet with a quick gesture. No living man lay there, but, even so, I touched the clammy cheek, and then *backed* across to my chair.

Rags was not contented to come back to me, however. He kept halting and looking back at the bed, and I had to damn him in a whisper to make him come to me. Whispering, mind you, for fear lest someone should hear me. Then I sat down and squinted my eyes shut and took a hard grip on myself. I told myself ten times in half a second that everything was all right, and that nothing could happen, and that a dead man, after all, was simply so many pounds of nothingness. Then, as I reached something better than hysteria, I saw Rags had started for the bed in the corner of the room.

Mind you, there is nothing in the world easier to make out than the manner and the gait of any hunting creature. You can tell it in a cat, or in a child, because there is an inimitable something that goes with all things that stalk. Now, in the middle of that night, Rags was stalking the bed in the corner and the dead man that lay upon it. Sweat ran suddenly out on my face; sweat drenched my body. I felt my lips grin back and freeze with mortal terror, while that parcel of dog slipped across the floor, lifting one paw after the other, and putting it down as though he were walking a tightrope.

A few feet from the bed, he stopped, with one foot poised in the empty air, and at that moment I heard a cry like the moan of a man in delirium, high-pitched and weird and far away. And yet I knew that sound was in the room in which I sat.

# Chapter 39

I got out of my chair and followed Rags—not that I wanted to find the thing that had made the cry, but because I was afraid to be too far from that cocksure little dog.

We were almost beside the bed, when Rags stuck his head beneath the edge of the bedstead and sniffed, and exactly then I heard the cry a second time, but lower, so that it seemed to come wavering up from the floor. It gave me enough courage, after all, to get the lamp and put it on the floor so that I could look under the bedframe, but there was nothing on the floor. Yet yonder stood Rags, scratching cautiously at the floor, as though he wanted to dig his way through, and yet as though he was afraid to make a noise.

The bed was on large casters, so that it was easy to roll it to one side. I started to study the stones of that flooring like the page of a book, moving here and there, and perfectly sure that the floor itself must have some meaning, when a stone gave under my weight, and immediately afterward a section dropped noiselessly and left me standing giddy and sick on the edge of a three-foot hole.

Rags dropped instantly down into that pit. I heard a scratching and gasping, and then, holding the lamp in both hands to steady the shaking, I was able to see that the little devil had by the throat the golden cat, Mimi. I climbed down at once and dragged Rags away, but Mimi was done for; those needle teeth of Rags had got at her lifeblood, and there was a great wet smear of crimson on her throat. She only kicked once, and then lay still.

The flame in the lamp cowered and almost went out, for there was a strange draft blowing down through the hole in which I stood, and I could tell the reason as soon as I had cherished the light and made it burn again. I found that I was standing on a small platform and beneath me a circular stairs, very narrow, went straight down. When I canted my ear, I could make out distinctly the sound of water running, and knew that beneath me was the passage by which the stream tunneled under the house.

I climbed back to the room above, determined to call the sheriff, but then I hesitated. Now that the ghostly voice had turned out to be the *meowing* of a cat, my nerves were wonderfully steady. The mystery had been snatched away. There was no doubt, now, how Dorgan and Ruth Derrick had managed to get out of the room so quickly—they had simply gone down through the trap. All that remained unknown was why the girl had chosen to march across the top of the wall that night. If there was such a perfect exit as this from Palliser's room, of course it made an equally good entrance. It seemed utter madness for her to have taken the other route, and I searched back earnestly to try to remember signs of freakishness in her, but her eyes looked into my memory as matter of fact and clear as anything I ever had known.

At any rate, I felt so much better, and the weight of the Colt in my right hand seemed so honest and friendly, that I got back into the mouth of the stairs. There I thought that I had made a new discovery. The air had a very damp, cool feeling such as it only could have in coming off the surface of moving water, and this was obviously no secret stairs. It was not very small, and it ran around and around a small well. I tried to throw a light from the lamp down that gap, but always there was a draft that made the flame leap and almost die. Rags was already a few steps down and looking back at me, so I decided to follow him, for just then he looked like good luck to me. Besides, I think what was uppermost in my mind was to prove to myself that I was a man, after all, and not a nervous fool.

I started down the steps, and, the farther I got, the more convinced I was that I was right. This actually was simply a well for drawing up water from the stream below, and the room that the captain had occupied had once been the tank where the supply was kept. Since this wing of the house stood on the highest ground, it would be easy for the water to be piped around to the rest of the place. No doubt the last Mornay to try to live here had had the idea. He had built the stairs and all, but probably something had induced him to change his mind. Windows had been broken through the sides of the "tank" and it became simply another room of the house.

When I got to the bottom, I saw that I was right. There was a circular opening, and past this the water rushed at my feet. To the side was an arched way that followed the course of the water and gave it a channel beneath the building. I turned into this, and, in ten steps, I came to a wide space that looked as though the water had hollowed it out in the old days. It would have overflowed it now, except that the stream was kept in its channel by low stone walls on each side. It was impossible to follow the course of the water any farther, and there was something better to follow immediately before me. That was a narrow, arched entrance that went up a stairs where Rags was already before me. I climbed after him, the lamp in one hand and the gun in the other. At the top of the flight was a door that gave as soon as I pushed against it.

I stepped into a more open space. That was all I could tell for the instant, because the flame of the lamp squatted and almost died in the rush of air. I thought I made out a dainty sweetness. Then I saw a distorted face beside me and half the world crashed on top of my head. I went down. There was one little tag of consciousness remaining, and that was a sense that the lamp was caught from my hand as its grip relaxed, and that Rags had begun to bark at the top of his lungs.

When I came to, I was lying in blackness that was lit up by red lightning flashes. Then my eyes cleared all in a moment. I was lying on a carpet in the middle of a room and over me leaned Cattrin!

He had me done for. My hands were lashed behind my back. My feet were fastened, and even my knees were lashed together and my legs held stiff by a stick that was passed between them. My jaws ached with the gag that had been worked in between my teeth.

Cattrin was pleased. There was no doubt of that. His face was the face of an angry devil, just as I had seen it look that evening in the patio. It had meant murder then. I had no doubt that he had *done* murder. He and Dorgan and Ruth Derrick, then, as a trio.

"There's no brains inside that head of his," said Cattrin. "Nothing but India rubber. Look! He's come to already!"

As he said this, I heard a faint whispering in the air, and Frances Mornay appeared at the side of Cattrin and looked down at me.

She was exactly as ever—as beautiful to see, as delicate, but the baby softness was gone from her face. I closed my eyes; all the blood flowed from my brain.

I heard Cattrin say: "The shock you give the fool is worse than the whang that Shirley landed on his head. You've smashed a golden ideal for him today, honey!"

Then I heard the laughter of Frances Mornay, softly sweet, with a touch of huskiness in the sound of it that made it different from other voices, as fine old velvet is different from other fabrics to the touch.

The dizziness left me, and I looked up at her again. She had leaned a little to watch me. Now she actually dropped on one knee. "I thought you had cracked his head to bits," she said, looking aside.

The lean, sad face of Shirley came into my range of eye.

"I wish I had," said Shirley. "It would have been better for everyone."

"Better for him, poor dear, of course," said Frances Mornay. She put her hand on my head. "Dear me," she said, "but what a *dreadful* bump!"

I remembered how she had poured her sweet sympathy on Dorgan.

She stood up again. "I'm sorry, Johnny," she said. "We didn't want to take you. We thought you were really much too stupid to find your way into trouble."

"He was," said Cattrin, "but the dog found it for him, I'll lay my money."

"You'd better hurry to catch that beast of a dog, dear," Frances Mornay said to Shirley. "I have a queer feeling about it. I hated it the moment I laid eyes on it."

"And the man who owned it?" Cattrin asked, grinning down at me.

"Dear Johnny," said the girl. "Yes. At first. I didn't know that he would turn out so harmless. Because you haven't given us much trouble, Johnny, you know," she said, smiling brightly at me. "Only once when you fired at me on the wall. And then your shots went wild. Oh, very wild. You were a little nervous, poor boy."

She nodded at me and caressed me with her eyes. Out of the bottom of my soul a loathing for her rose in me, such as you feel for unclean or unnatural things. And all at once I could see why it was that she had been able to fool everyone so completely. The reason was simply that she was so far from ordinary womanhood that normal people couldn't place her.

Usually you hate the fellow you've wronged. You have to tighten your mental muscles, so to speak. But she was different. She could kneel beside me and have pity on the lump on my cracked head while she was getting ready to murder me, or have me murdered!

She insisted to Shirley: "I wish that you'd get the little beast of a Rags. I won't feel easy until you do.

Suppose that he barks again, and the sheriff hears him. . . ."

"The sheriff?" sneered Cattrin. "He's off running down some more of Ruth's footprints, of course . . . finding them pointing out. . . ."

"Well," said Frances Mornay, "the poor dear really *is* heading out, and I suppose there isn't much chance that she'll come back, either! *Will* you go and get that dog?"

"I will, I will," said Shirley. "We'll have to move this lump first."

# Chapter 40

Shirley took my head and Cattrin my feet, and they carried me like a log back down the steps by which I had climbed to the girl's room.

"You'd better stay behind," said Shirley. "If the fool of a sheriff *does* have an idea. . . ."

"If he comes while I'm gone," said Frances Mornay, "what difference does it make? I've simply been out walking. I'm so dreadfully nervous since the disappearance of Ruth that I can't sleep, you know." She laughed again, and the sweet sound rankled up and down my blood.

"I tell you again," Shirley reiterated, "that you ought to be back in that room. Don't be a stubborn little devil."

"And don't browbeat me, darling," purred Frances Mornay. "I'll do as I think best, and I think it best, just now, to go down and say good-bye to dear little Ruth. Poor Ruth. If any of you knew how I'll miss her."

Shirley exclaimed something beneath his breath that I didn't understand, but Frances apparently did, for she said in her gentle way: "Does that shock you, you great big, strong hero, you?"

"We can talk afterward," Shirley stated. "I don't want to talk now. We have something to do, Frances."

"Ah, yes, dear. We have *two* things to do, and I suppose that poor little Frances will have to do it." Once more she laughed, and the horrible loathing went through me.

They brought me from the stairs into that wider space that I had noticed before, and there I was put down, with my back propped against the wall.

"Put a light down here between them so that they can see one another," Frances Mornay suggested. "The poor darlings. Let it be his own lamp. Have it with you, dear?"

This to Cattrin—that soft tongue of hers caressed everyone in turn. The lighted lamp was put down on the floor, and I saw Ruth Derrick just opposite me, tied as securely as I, and gagged. I saw her start. I saw agony in her eyes. And then I remembered the train of guilt that I had traced to her, and the absolute conviction of the idiot sheriff—and I began to despair of something more than my life.

"Will you get that beast of a dog?" Frances Mornay snapped.

"*You've* made enough blunders in this business," Shirley reminded her. "Don't begin with commands now!"

She lifted her head. "You'd better go, Hugh dear. You really had."

Shirley took off, and that lovely fiend laughed softly and sweetly.

"Blunders, you see," she said, "because, after all, there was no necessity of my using the wall and being a ghost. If only my dear Hugh had talked out and told me everything. But he was keeping a little secret from me . . . the little secret of this safe passage to poor Uncle Ned's room. He was going to surprise me with the good news . . . and he kept his information until it was too late."

The smile left her face for half an instant, and I saw the faintest glint in her eyes and a tremor of her nostrils. Even that faint shadow in her face meant murder, and I knew it very well, as though suddenly I had had the whole secret of her nature read out to me.

"But what a time," she said, "to talk of my affairs. You've such a short time together, you two. Poor, dear Ruth! Poor darling. Oh, if you knew how often I'll think of you. While all the rest of the world writes 'murderess' after your name, I'll know the truth, and, because I have the secret, won't I keep it all the more sacredly my own? Won't I, poor darling?"

She had actually moved to Ruth and reached out a hand, and Ruth Derrick flinched and closed her eyes.

"So sorry that you're nervous," Frances Mornay cooed. "But now you two ought to rouse yourselves. You've such a little time left. You can't talk. You've only your eyes. Do you know, Johnny, that this poor, simple child didn't understand the sheep's eyes that you've been throwing at her for so long? And all the while she was keeping me awake at night, sitting on the edge of my bed in the darkness and whispering to me about wonderful John Jones. She doesn't mind your scar. She doesn't mind your broken nose. It shows what a life you've lived and what a bold fellow you've been."

Frances Mornay laughed again, and I stared at Ruth, and she stared at me.

"And then you showed one touch of cleverness,

Johnny," said Frances Mornay. "Circe couldn't turn you into a pig. You looked at Ruth, and she was the flower of moly that kept your head clear, although now and then you grew just a little dizzy when you were talking to poor, unhappy Frances Mornay. Is that true?"

"Great God!" said Cattrin. "Let them die in peace, Frances. You've knifed them enough."

She touched his arm. "I haven't, my dear," she said. "Not yet. You don't know the hours of misery that I've spent with this honest, blundering fool on my mind. Oh, a clever fellow like Shevlin, I never minded. But this sort of a creature . . . you can never tell when his pawing will break through into places where he shouldn't be. As he has tonight . . . as he has tonight . . . and God have mercy on him! For the hours you've kept me awake, worrying, I freely forgive you . . . tonight, Johnny." She turned: "Cattrin!"

"Well?" Cattrin stepped forward.

"Why doesn't Hugh come back?" Frances Mornay questioned.

"Why? Because he's gone to catch the dog . . . and he'll have to close the trap into Palliser's room, as well. That may take a little time."

She closed her eyes. "It wouldn't take this long," she murmured.

Cattrin had turned pale in an instant. "In the name of God what are you saying?" he said.

She whispered: "I'm afraid. I'm afraid. Why hasn't he . . . ?"

Into the middle of that whispering sentence came a sighing breath of wind.

Cattrin leaped as though he had seen a leveled gun. "The door of your room is opened," he said.

"It's Shevlin," she said. "He's found the way. Do

you hear? You have your guns. Give me one."

Cattrin breathed: "God, God, God."

Something scampered in the passage, and little Rags came for me and swarmed over me, kissing my face and hands with his joy, wagging his tail out of sight.

I thought that Frances Mornay would send a bullet through him, by the look she gave the little dog, but her attention was called forward to the black archway from her room. She had barely faced it again when I heard the voice of Rourke speak out of the passageway leading down from the room of Palliser.

"It's no good, Cattrin! You're rounded up and ready for branding now, with both the gates watched!"

Cattrin whirled about with a screech that still rings in my ears and was met with a bullet that split his forehead and sent him stumbling to the floor. In spite of that, Frances Mornay was not done, but ran forward and tried to dodge past Rourke. As he caught her in one arm, I saw a knife flash in her hand in a thin, bright arc, but Rourke gripped her by the wrist. So, holding her helpless, he drew her in, bent over her, and kissed her mouth, and then he threw her away from him, and she went down the passage like the wind.

Shevlin was shouting as he plunged down the steps: "Don't let her up, Rourke! She's the main devil! Stop her, man!"

When Rourke did not move to do that but, on the contrary, turned her loose, Shevlin tried to pass him, but Rourke caught at him. They whirled around in a brief struggle, but suddenly Shevlin gave in.

"Shirley?" he asked.

"He's with his sidekick," Rourke responded.

"They will be crowdin' the gate of hell at about the same minute, I reckon. Let Frances go, Shevlin," he added. "She ain't worth any care . . . except to me . . . except to me."

He groaned those last words, and the sheriff nodded slowly.

"Besides," Shevlin said, "there's only one flaw in her makeup. She's not meant for fast travel over rough country. She's a jungle cat, Denny. We'll soon have her in hand on this range."

The sheriff, who had made almost no errors in this strange affair, was as good as his word. If he had not been, I suppose that by letting her get away, Rourke would have allowed more poison to get into the world than ten Cattrins and Shirleys would have been.

Rourke turned toward me and, taking a hard grip on himself right away, said to Shevlin: "Look at Johnny. Damn me if he ain't perishable stuff, like glass. Look at the way they got him wrapped for delivery."

Then he set me loose. The sheriff freed Ruth. All three of us worked to get Ruth up the stairs and into the room of Frances Mornay, and out of it again as fast as possible. We had sense enough not to let her open her eyes in that room. She had fainted when she saw that she was safe. You take a right kind of a girl and it's always that way. She'll see the pinch through, but she goes to pieces afterward, pretty often.

I stayed with her, with my coat rolled under her knees to make the blood flow into her brain. Shevlin and Rourke went on to Palliser's room to make sure about Shirley, and there they found a pretty bad picture.

Rourke's clubbed Colt had only stunned Shirley,

instead of braining him as Rourke thought it had done. He had come to and tried to get out the door, and, just as he was fumbling at the lock, Frances Mornay had come up from below.

She had seen by one glance that, in his condition, he never could get away, and, for fear lest he should talk too much, the little beauty had slipped her knife into him and left it in him while she had gone on. But even that hadn't killed Shirley. He was still alive when Shevlin and Rourke got to him. He'd been born for the hangman's hands, after all.

# Chapter 41

The sheriff went out of the cellar passage like a terrier, and, although Rourke must have known that Shevlin was after Frances Mornay, he made no effort to interfere. I was calling to him, and he came back and helped me to carry Ruth Derrick up the stairs. Cattrin was past help. We left him lying on his face, and got Ruth up to the patio. We preferred it to her own room, because the night was warm and there was more air stirring in the court. We folded a blanket on the pavement for her, but she was hardly settled on it when she stirred and sat up with a cry. Then she was on her feet and looking around her, desperately, as though she wanted to run away.

We talked to her at the same time, telling her that it was all right, and that we were her friends—but she looked around, wildly and blankly. I thought that she was upset in the mind for good and all, but finally it was Rourke that she recognized and clung to. In response Rourke put his arm around her and stroked her head as though she had been a child.

He got her settled into a chair, while I kicked José

and the rest of the Mexicans out of the patio. They had come swarming in, and it did me a lot of good to boot them out and damn them thoroughly. I took a look out through the gate, but there was no sight or sound of Shevlin.

When I got back to Ruth, she gave me a pale smile. She was mighty nervous, and every now and then she would throw a look at one of the black mouths of the windows or up to the ragged edge of wall to the north of us. However, she grew steadier every minute, making a big effort. I rubbed her ankles and Rourke her wrists, because the devils had tied her so tight that the blood had stopped circulating.

"You'd better talk," Rourke advised Ruth.

"No," I said. "Forget it. Rub it out of your mind."

"It would be easier to rub out a toothache," said Rourke. "No, let her talk it out if she feels like it."

"I want to talk. I want to get rid of it. Someone else has to know," Ruth said, and the trembling grew less in her voice as she spoke.

"Then start back at the beginning. That's the easiest way," Rourke recommended. "That'll bring you up to tonight better."

I was a good deal surprised to hear Rourke talk like this. He was showing more horse sense than I'd ever seen him show before, except on the back of a horse.

She said: "I don't want to try to tell everything. I couldn't. It would take days. Only, of course, I have to tell you how Frances's mother took me out of the circus."

"You *were* in the circus, Ruth?"

"Yes. I was raised for it. My mother didn't know anything else. I used to work pretty hard. I did bareback and trapeze work a lot . . . but mostly tight-wire walking. Nothing but that, the last year."

I looked up at the thin edge of the wall, and in spite of myself another shadowy doubt came back over me.

"Missus Mornay took me out of that and gave me a sort of a home. We were wandering from hotel to hotel, but she was glad to have me as a companion for Frances, and it was heaven to me. I was taught with Frances. We were like sisters, I thought, until Missus Mornay died. And then there was a difference."

She stopped talking and stared before her, anxiously. She twisted her hands together, while Rourke said softly: "You don't say anything you don't want to say. Only talk what comes easiest."

I was proud of Rourke. He was showing sense. Little Rags popped up on my knee and sat there, wagging his tail and cocking his head at Ruth. At that, she broke into a laugh, and then cried, and then she was a lot better and nearly her old self.

She said: "I'll tell it straight out, the way everything seemed to me. Missus Mornay had left me a good deal of money . . . though most of it went to Frances, of course. But inside of a few months I could see that Frances was spending over her head. She loved beautiful clothes and everything that was fine . . . because she was so lovely herself that it was only natural. . . ."

Ruth looked at me as if for sympathy with that idea, but I must have seemed pretty hard. Frances Mornay looked a long ways from lovely in my eyes.

Ruth went on: "Finally she had to come to me for money. Of course, I gave it to her. I began to see less and less of her. Finally there were only telegrams for more money. I gave her the last I had, and I had started to work as a clerk in a store when she came to me again. She had made some money in speculations, she said. Friends had given her good tips. She was wonderfully dressed and had some beautiful jewels. Although she didn't pay back the money she had borrowed, she gave me a fine sapphire ring. Shirley was with her. Cattrin came later. I liked Shirley, but I was always suspicious of Cattrin.

"But what worried me most was a gradual change in Frances. She had always been rather quick and gay. Now she had another manner. She acted as though she were just a little childish, particularly when men were around her. When we were alone, often it was quite another story. I even spoke to her about it, but she said that everything was a stage, and a woman's job was to learn what part she could play and then get it by heart.

"She said other things like that from time to time. I could see that I bored her and I wondered why she was so nice to me or, at least, why she was trying to be nice. Then one day she told me that her uncle, Captain Palliser, was coming to see her.

"She wanted me to be with her. And she wanted to meet him in my room. Mind you, I had a little back room that I had taken when I had to go to work as a clerk. Frances came there in the simplest clothes, almost shabby. And she made me promise that I'd let her uncle feel that this was the way she always lived. She got a job in the same store with me, and that was the setting of the stage when the captain arrived.

"He seemed very interested in Frances . . . partly because she was pretty and partly because she was poor. The second time he talked with us, he said that he was going to fit us out with new top-hamper and rig us new throughout. He said we were like a couple of barges, but we had clipper lines and he was going to make us sail the seas.

"I liked him. I think he liked me. He was always a little uneasy with Frances. He never seemed very sure of her, do you see? And her friends didn't please him. He used Cattrin as an errand boy, and he never liked Shirley, although Hugh discarded his fine clothes before he met Captain Palliser. However, the captain got on very well with me. I didn't mind his swearing when he swore at other things, but, when he swore at me, I used to have a quarrel with him. He said that I was the only person in Europe that made him feel at home. He said that I made him feel as though he were only a mate again, or even before the mast.

"Frances saw this. In the meantime, she was pretending to be rather an invalid. Because sympathy opened purses, she used to say, better than a knife. And then the captain had the idea of going West to the old Mornay house, the only remaining part of the estate . . . and it remained so simply because no one would buy it. Frances had the plans to the old Mornay house, and one day she gave them to Shirley. He came rushing back to see her that night. He was greatly excited. He said that he had an idea that would make them rich. I went out of the room to leave them alone, and I'm afraid that was the moment when the plan began to be made for the . . . the murder of the captain. It seems simple enough to realize that . . . looking backward.

"When the plan was made to come here, Frances begged me to come with her. She said that I was worth my weight in gold for keeping the captain in good humor, and so I finally went along. I was a good deal worried, but I hardly knew by what. The first definite thing was when I heard Frances once say to Shirley, after we got to this house . . . 'You'll have to get rid of Jones. He's the only one who can't be hypnotized.'

"That frightened me. I went to you that day, John, and begged you to leave. Thank God that you didn't." She broke down for a moment. But she was not the stuff to weaken, and she got control of herself and went on. "When Cattrin was accused of murder and taken away, I was so frightened that I was sick. It was not Cattrin that I cared about, but I knew that he and Shirley were very old associates. And there's that proverb about birds of a feather. I went to Frances and told her what was in my mind and begged her to look into Shirley's record. She thanked me and said that she would, and she looked at me very thoughtfully. . . ."

"My God!" Rourke gasped.

But Ruth shrugged her shoulders and went resolutely ahead. "She was in her room, seeming sick with a headache, her eyes closed and her face really white. Her hands were clenched at her sides, and I thought it was from the pain, but I know now that it must have been because she was thinking her way through to the end.

"I sat beside her bed and rubbed her head and was sorry that I had talked as I had when I heard a soft sighing of the air, as though a door had been opened. I looked up with a gasp and saw that a section of the wall was swinging open. Against the darkness inside, I saw the face of Cattrin, the murderer, and like a murderer he looked at that moment. He usually looked rather soft and pink. But now his face was puckered. . . ."

"I know," I said.

"My voice was frozen in my throat. I couldn't

move. Before I had a chance, Frances threw herself at me like a wildcat and locked her arm around my throat, so that I couldn't make a sound. She helped Cattrin to tie me hand and foot. And then she helped him again to take me down to the place where you found me. She sat down beside me for a moment and smoothed my forehead. 'Poor little Ruth,' she said. 'If you only could have been a nice little blind girl for one more day. . . .'

"Cattrin said that they ought to get rid of me that moment. But Frances smiled at me in a way that seemed suddenly horrible to me. She said that it would be better to let me rest there and think, because I always had been such a good, thoughtful girl. And then they both left me . . . in the dark. . . ." Ruth's voice choked away. She stared wildly before her.

"And so here we are with Johnny and Rags and the rest," Rourke commented. Ruth slumped back in her chair and smiled at him. She looked rather sick and weak, but I could see that Rourke was right and that the worst was over when we heard a voice from the patio gate saying: "One of you place a chair for the lady, please."

We looked around, and there was Shevlin bringing in Frances Mornay!

# Chapter 42

Shevlin hadn't secured Frances Mornay's hands. He simply walked half a step behind her, and the two of them sauntered in as though they had been out for a walk together.

Ruth jumped up, shaking, but Frances Mornay nodded and smiled at her.

"Poor darling," Frances said. "What a wreck you look! And how glad I am that I wouldn't let Cattrin have his way. Resting and thinking was better, after all, wasn't it?" That silken sweet devil was as calm as you please, and she sat down with us, smiling and easy.

Rourke leaned forward with an elbow on his knee and stared straight at her until she laughed and held up a hand.

"You've recovered, Denny, I see," she said. "But you had a fine time while it lasted, didn't you?"

It wasn't very long before we were all more interested in her than ever before. When you go through a zoo, the lions and the tigers and the elephants are fine to look at, but after a while you go by a cage that seems empty. Then you see a deeper pool of black in a corner, and out of the pool come eyes like agates, and finally you can make out the panther. The rest of the zoo looks pretty amateurish, compared to that. That was the way we all felt, watching Frances.

I lost a good deal of the malice I felt toward her, too. No one blames the panther for snaking natives out of their huts at night. Rather, you admire it. I think that we all admired Frances, too. Now that we really saw her, we could tell that she was no more like other women than prussic acid is like the peach pits it comes from. Same fragrance, say, but the effect is a good deal different.

"How is Shirley?" asked the sheriff almost at once.

When I had kicked the Mexicans out of the patio, I had told them to look in Palliser's room. Now José and a couple more of the rascals came down the steps, carrying Shirley. He had luck. The Colt should have brained him, and the knife of Frances Mornay should have split his heart. But the gun only had stunned him, and the knife had slithered along his ribs. He'd lost some blood and was weak, and a little dizzy, but there was nothing seriously wrong with him. When they got him to the patio level, he said he could walk, and they brought him forward, their teeth showing white and their eyes glittering, they were so proud of what they had done.

How could Frances greet him? That old companion she had tried to murder? She actually waved to him, and, as we settled him into a chair, she said: "This is jolly! This is like old times . . . we're only lacking two."

Cattrin and Palliser she meant, of course. Shirley looked at her with his upper lip lifting a little. The rest of us might be admiring her, as we would have

admired a devil, but, after all, we had not felt her
teeth so sharply. Shirley looked as though he would
like to cut her throat, and I think he would have
done it, if he could have reached her.

She said cheerfully: "There's no use being so dark
about it, Hugh, my dear. I thought that you might
talk a little . . . and it's better to die by the hand of an
old friend than with the hangman's rope."

"As you will," Shirley said coldly.

"Don't be rude," Frances said. "We have our
chance to hear what the sheriff has to say, and it
ought to be interesting. Where were we wrong,
Sheriff?" She couched her chin in her hand, and
then she leaned forward with her eyes wide open,
like a child about to hear a pretty story.

Shevlin grinned at her. "Once upon a time . . . ,"
he began.

"Isn't he a darling!" Frances Mornay exclaimed to
herself and to us all.

Shevlin sat up and said briskly: "It's time some of
us went to bed."

"Shirley, can you stand it?" I asked.

"I can," he said. "You might as well know. The
case is too cold against us to pretend."

There *was* a streak of manliness in him.

"It hung on two things, in the first place," said the
sheriff. "I learned one the night of Palliser's death
and the other the next morning."

"And let us wander around . . . to play our little
harmless games?" Frances Mornay muttered. She
looked at Ruth with her violet eyes as cold as stones.

"I knew enough to convince me, but not enough
to convince a jury," Shevlin admitted. "Especially
about a pretty girl. Excuse me."

"Ah, yes," Frances said. "Those chivalrous Western juries . . . God bless them." The husky sweetness

of her laughter floated across the patio. It was a little too much. I stared at her, but she saw nothing but the sheriff. "What were the two things?" she asked.

"Shirley should have been satisfied with leaving the ring and the strand of Ruth's hair," said the sheriff. "But even that he might've done better. A man like Palliser, if he'd caught that good a hold, would nearly have jerked her head off. There was about twenty or thirty hairs in that bunch, ma'am."

"And what of that?" Frances asked almost sharply. "I picked them out of Ruth's combings . . . excuse me, darling"—she glanced at Ruth—"and I made sure they were all of the same length."

"Sure you did," Shevlin continued. "But hair that combs out ain't the same as hair that pulls out . . . the roots are different. A microscope will show you that. Besides . . . try to pull out five hairs at one time. Then try twenty. It'll bring blood, I'd say!"

"I overdid it, then." Frances nodded. "Most interesting, isn't it, Hugh?"

Shirley looked at her with a silent snarl.

"And then?" she asked brightly.

"I hadn't the hair to work on. Jones took care of that." He grinned at me. "But when Shirley came back into the room, he called the attention of Jones to the coin in the mouth of Palliser. The idea was that if the clues didn't point to Miss Derrick, they would surely point at Dorgan." He paused, studying Frances Mornay for a second, then asked: "You knew about Dorgan, eh?"

"We'd been through everything he had," Frances said. "I did that myself. We knew why he was here . . . he and Wong."

"Wong?" said the sheriff.

"He had a father who sailed with Uncle Ned and had a hand almost crushed in with a marlin spike.

Dear Uncle Ned. He had such a heavy hand. Wong came with Dorgan. They were going to split the profits . . . one to Wong and two to Dorgan. But do go on about the coin. What was wrong with it? Not Shirley's fingerprints . . . or anything like that?"

"No, but when Jones took that coin from Palliser's mouth, he told me it was wet and cold in his hand. Now a few minutes had passed since the murder, and Palliser still was warm. If the killer had put the coin there, it should have been hot to the touch."

"Ah, ah," Frances said, "what a lovely, neat mind you have, Sheriff. I never should have thought of that."

"It meant that Shirley himself had put the coin there," Shevlin went on, "and then he called Jones's attention to it. And this meant only one thing . . . Shirley wanted to cover the tracks of the murderer, or, perhaps, he was the murderer himself."

Shirley muttered to himself, then opened his coat and adjusted the bandage that José had strapped around him.

"In the morning," continued Shevlin, "I looked at the narrowness of the wall. I saw a projecting stone, four or five feet up on the side of the wall of the room. There was a little marking on that stone. The surface had been newly rubbed away, and a line left. And Jones, like a good, careful fellow in telling me his story the night before, had told me about finding a little bit of fine wire."

"Your work this time!" Shirley hissed savagely at Frances.

"My work," she agreed. "I thought it was so clever, too. But go on."

"It wasn't hard to work out," said the sheriff. "I dusted off the surface of that stone. I saw that the marks were thin as knife cuts. When I examined the dust under my pocket microscope, it wasn't hard to see the little bright bits of steel. I knew that a wire had been wrapped around there. Then I took the first chance to get around the patio and go up to the other end of that wall. There I found just the same marking on a stone. I then knew that when the 'ghost' had walked across that wall top, she really had a railing under her hand . . . that film of wire, you see, to steady her."

"Beautiful!" exclaimed Frances Mornay. "Were you sure it was a she? Could you trust the eyes of clever John Jones?" Her look at me was a knife thrust.

"You gotta trust the instinct of a man when he sees a woman," Shevlin assured her. "If that ghost had been a man, nine chances out of ten, Jones would have said it was a big woman, or a woman stepping with a long stride, or something like that. But he didn't say any of those things. That made me think it was you or Ruth Derrick."

"And you settled on me?"

"Because Shirley was your friend. And because finally I learned that Ruth had been in the circus and could walk a tightrope there."

"But wouldn't that have qualified her for the wall walking?"

"She was in the circus until she was ten or eleven. The tricks she learned there must still be with her. If she could walk a tightrope for wages back then, she could walk now for the sake of a murder. She wouldn't have needed the steel wire to help her. So that ruled her out."

"And still you didn't have evidence enough?"

"I wanted to arrest you when I made up my mind to that," said the sheriff, "but then Ruth Derrick disappeared. I'd hoped that when I arrested Dorgan,

I'd put your minds at ease so that I could go on gathering evidence, but, when Ruth disappeared, I was afraid to stir, for fear that she would get a knife in her throat from one of you."

"Ah, that was a ticklish position for you," Frances commiserated.

"I pray God," Shevlin stated very soberly, "that I never go through another evening like that last one."

"And yet," Frances postulated, "if Shirley had acted like a man of sense, there never would have been a chance to find the killer of poor Uncle Ned. Tell your pretty story, Hughie."

"I'll talk no more," Shirley snapped, "and, unless you're a fool, you'll keep still, also."

"Tush, dear," Frances said, "you forget that Ruth and clever John Jones both heard us talk together . . . when we thought they wouldn't be apt to repeat anything. You'll be interested, Sheriff, and you ought to have a chance to know. You mustn't think that I was such a fool, after all. But I was forced . . . a bit. Shirley had the plans of the house, and on the plans he spotted the secret passage from one room to the other. That minute he made up his mind to get Uncle Ned there, finish him off, and get back through the water tunnel to my room. Mystery, do you see? But he wouldn't tell me. He was keeping the thing up his sleeve and pretending to have lost the plans. I never had looked at the moldy old things, do you see? And after we came here, still he held back."

"Even after he picked Jones's pocket and read the captain's letter calling attention to your past, ma'am?" Shevlin asked.

"Did you know that?" Frances Mornay said, astonished. "Did *you* read the letter?"

"No, but I knew that Palliser had seen a detective of Dutton and Green's agency . . . the man who rode the gray horse, Johnny. I knew him before. He'd even worked with me."

Light jumped across my brain. "And when he went to see the captain that night . . . ?" I began.

"Sure." The sheriff smiled. "He brought in a full report on Frances Mornay and the report showed that the suspicions of Palliser were right. You got to the window in time to have Palliser hear the worst about her. That was why he yelled out. Because he was in pain . . . because he knew about you then, Miss Mornay."

For once she seemed impressed. "I wonder," she said slowly, "if he really was fond of me? Because then I might have used a different line."

"But after you knew the detective's work . . . after Cattrin had found him and left him dead in the woods . . . ," Shevlin explained.

"By God," broke in Shirley, "you know everything."

"Footprints." The sheriff smiled again. "I say, after that, you felt that there was no time to lose, eh?"

"None," the girl confirmed. "And that was where we slipped. Where *he* slipped." She looked fiercely at Shirley. "I told him we would have to do something. He only laughed and said that, before morning, he would put everything right. Then he left my room. Ah . . . the fool! I thought it was mere bluff of his. I finished thinking and determined to do the trick. And . . . so I tried."

"If you had waited . . . ," Shirley stated.

"Don't talk to me," she snapped at him, furious for the first time, openly.

"I'd gone back to her room, with my mind made up to let her into the secret of the passage, at last,"

Shirley said, "and, as I got in, I found the room empty, with the Victrola singing. . . ."

"And the repeater on it?" asked Shevlin.

"Did you *know* that or guess it?" Frances asked sharply.

"I found a bit of ash-burned celluloid in the grass of the woods," Shevlin explained. "I measured the section of the curve of the ash . . . it fitted with the idea of the little trick that makes a Victrola repeat a record."

Frances settled back in her chair with a gesture of surrender, as much as to say that she could not compete against such keenness. I remembered how the needle had scratched at the end of the record as the "ghost" walked the wall, and then how "The Meditation" had begun again.

"I wondered at the empty room," Shirley said. "I was upset. Cattrin was back, demanding that we make a quick move. You, Sheriff, had scared him to death, the cowardly devil. Then I happened to look out the window and I saw the 'ghost' almost across the wall. I knew that Frances had taken the job entirely into her own hands, and. . . ." He finished with a gesture.

Shevlin picked up the story: "You opened the secret passage and sprinted down it, found Palliser grappling with Frances Mornay, and gave him the finishing blow, eh? And then your nerves gave way a little . . . you laughed a bit, Shirley. Had a touch of hysterics?"

"It was a damned fearful thing," Shirley said with a shudder.

"But how did you get at us, down below there?" asked Frances of the sheriff.

"I'd found Rourke in the woods and managed to persuade him that I was a better friend than an enemy. He promised to come in and help Jones watch in Palliser's room. When he got there, he had to break open the door, and then he found the opening in the floor and went down through it. In the meantime, I'd gone to your room, Miss Mornay, to see what I could see and listen in a bit if I could. I was in time to hear a fall and voices murmuring. Then a door shut."

"What door could have shut in that room?" she asked.

"I tried the key I'd made to fit that lock, opened the door, and, sure enough, the room was empty . . . but there was a streak of cigarette smoke pointing straight at one corner of the wall. That was enough to show me what I wanted to find out. I'd poisoned your cat for the sake of getting into your room before and seeing what I could see. But that time I found nothing."

"Ah, I almost guessed what you'd done," said Frances Mornay.

"After I found the right door, it was luck that put my finger on the spring that opened it. You know the rest."

"And it was John Jones, after all, who brought everything on," Frances Mornay said, her cold, violet eyes fixed on me. "And what was your clue, Johnny?"

"The cat howled under my floor," I said. "She'd gotten into your passage. . . ."

"Oh, poor Mimi!" Frances cried out.

But there was no interest in her voice for the cat. I could see, then, that the golden cat had been only a part of her makeup.

"Rags spotted the noise," I said. "And Rags showed me where to look on the floor."

"I hated the little rascal from the first minute,"

Frances moaned. "Ah, I'll trust instinct more from this time on."

"It seems to me, Frances," Shirley said with cold politeness, "that, after this, you won't have such a great deal of time on your hands."

At this she merely tilted back her head and laughed. Then she stood up and stretched out her arms gracefully and slowly pirouetted before us. Her head lay back a little, and her dark eyes caressed us, and the light from the lanterns showed them soft violet, and the gold of her hair was gleaming.

"Do you think that they'll kill me?" Frances asked. "Oh, no, my dears."

I stared helplessly at her, and I knew that she was right. No Western jury would hang her . . . that beautiful golden cat.

# Epilogue

She was right, in the end. She was given prison for twenty-five years, I think. Then the sentence was shortened for good behavior—six months of good behavior! After that, she did something in the prison—saved a fellow prisoner in the factory, when the other got tangled in a bit of machinery. At any rate, before I knew it, Frances Mornay had been pardoned and was out and away.

I have told this strange story here and there, at mining camps and whatnot, up to Shirley's confession before he was hanged.

The strangest of all the effects Frances Mornay had was on Shirley. He knew her for what she was. She'd betrayed and knifed him. But in the jail days, waiting for execution, he seemed to soften toward her. The beauty of her changed his mind. Toward the end and through the trial, she had played a smiling part at him.

At any rate, in his confession he told a lot of tremendous lies, bigger than I could daub a sixty-foot rope on. And he managed, somehow, to take all the blame. That was the chief reason the governor had for pardoning her.

But when I've finished telling this in logging camps, or cow camps, or at the mines when the men sit around between shifts, generally one of them will up and ask me how it happens that I'm floating around like a rough, when I've got a wife at home?

But they guess wrong, because Ruth didn't marry me. I'd been friendly to her. And her to me. But at the last, in come Rourke, mighty dramatic, his gun smoking, Cattrin dead at his feet. The way he let the Golden Cat get away seemed to please her, too. Then he was mighty gentle and understanding, when Ruth was coming around. . . .

Well, I dunno how it happened, but I missed out. My busted nose didn't help me any, I suppose. But we're all friends. I don't hold any malice. A gent with a face like mine would be a fool to.

Me and Shevlin go down to Rourke's house every Christmas, and pack along some presents for the twins.

# MAX BRAND®

## MORE TALES OF THE WILD WEST

Filled with beautifully drawn landscapes, high action and unforgettable characters, the six tales in this collection perfectly demonstrate Max Brand's extraordinary talent for master storytelling. In "A Lucky Dog," a four-legged friend is the only redemption for a thief and would-be killer. Both "Inverness" and "Death in Alkali Flat" feature Sleeper, one of Brand's most well-known characters. Also included here is "A First Blooding," a poignant and powerful piece that is the last fiction Brand ever wrote. With these stories and more, Brand brings the Old West alive.

-------------------------------------------------

# Charles E. Friend

# SHANNON'S LAW

Clay Shannon is a straight-shooting, tough-talking deputy sheriff who's been charged with bringing order to rough-and-tumble Whiskey Creek, a mining town where robbery and murder run rampant. But with one lawman already killed, Shannon's job won't be easy. A crooked saloon owner and his hired gun have the townspeople so spooked it's almost impossible to gather any evidence against them. And tracking down clues is even harder while dodging bullets. If justice is to be served, Shannon must make a choice: stay within the law—or make his own.

- - - - - - - - - - - - - - - - - - - - - - - - - - - - - - - -

# CAINE'S TRAIL
# CAMERON JUDD

When Union soldiers slaughtered his family, Simon Caine couldn't just forgive and forget. He reached for his gun. Now it's the U.S. government that won't forget. They want to hang Caine for what he did. But it's not only his past that could get Caine killed. A band of outlaws led by a cutthroat Confederate renegade has kidnapped Caine's nephew. He's proven before that no one can mess with his family and get away with it, and he won't rest until his nephew is home safe. But with the hangman behind him and outlaws in front of him, Caine's caught between a rock and a hard place—and his gun is his only friend!

------------------------------------------------